PRAISE FOR *Heirs & Spares, Book 1 of The Realm Series:*

"With a fresh voice, an intelligent and witty protagonist and vivid historical details, *Heirs & Spares* captured me from the start and never let me go."

– Maureen McQuerry, *Time After Time*

"I slurped down this historical intrigue/romance like a chocolate milkshake. It's both delicious and delightful."

– Kimberlee Conway Ireton, *Cracking Up*

"*Heirs & Spares* is one of those rare books I could have read in one sitting. . ."

– Tamara Leigh, *The Unveiling*

"The sheer joy of this book is the personality effused on every page. . .and we, lucky readers, get a front row seat in the action of a brilliantly imaginative mind. I am so eager to dive into this world again and hang out with Wills and Annelore: they are friends ~ book friends~ the best kind of friends."

– A Fair Substitute for Heaven Book Reviews

"I was engulfed by this story."

– I Hate Cats Book Reviews

"J. L. Spohr brings us to a world where Kings rule, ladies curtsy and true love amongst arranged marriages is an occasional find. A quick page turning adventure through Elizabethan times, my only regret is that it was over too soon. . ."

– Catherine Walker Johnson,
descendant of Queen Katherine Howard

"*Heirs & Spares* is a marvelously researched peek into the 16th Century. . .pitch-perfect with delightful details of the fictional kingdom of Troixden."

– My Readers Block

"Spohr doesn't disappoint. *Heirs & Spares* is a fantastic novel thoroughly researched and full of fully dimensional characters Spohr was obviously in her element."

– Stuck in a Story

"Of all the historical fiction I've read, this one is up there with some of the best. It's not an easy thing to weave history into fiction and keep it lively."

– Rebecca Reads

Enjoy!

God & Ring

Book II of The Realm Series

J. L. Spohr

Plum Street Press

God & King
J. L. Spohr

Printed in the United States of America

Plum Street Press
1037 NE 65th St., #274, Seattle, WA 98115

Prepared for printing by The Editorial Department
7650 E. Broadway, #308, Tucson, Arizona, 85710

For more information about this book visit: www.jlspohr.com

Edition ISBNs
Hardcover: 978-0-9892173-4-7
Trade Paperback: 978-0-9892173-3-0
E-book: 978-0-9892173-5-4

Cover design by Kelly Leslie
Book design by Morgana Gallaway
Author photo by Karly Lee

For Amy, Cari & Stephanie

For therein is the righteousness of God revealed from faith to faith: as it is written, The just shall live by faith.

– Romans 1:17

Chapters

CHAPTER 1

Homecoming

*R*ing William had not been this filthy in years. He floated in his copper bath, eyes closed, head resting against its cool edge, water rippling with each satisfied breath. Gone three full weeks from the comforts of Palace Havenside, he had been camping like a soldier with his retinue of men, seeking assurances of fealty from the Laurelanders in the northeast of his realm. A tentative peace was reached, but how long it would hold kept him brooding.

William breathed in deep and exhaled slow, willing himself peace, if only for a half hour. But solitude was not the luxury of kings. Even then, attendants and councilors scrambled for attention outside his chamber doors, their impatience seeping through the cracks, creeping toward him like vapor. He brushed it away, sinking lower, water sloshing up his chest.

The private door by his bedside groaned on its hinges. A smile tugged the corner of his mouth as he heard the soft rustling of fabric behind him. No peace to be had now.

"I can smell you from here." His voice echoed back at him from the tub's basin. "'Twas a nice try, though."

"And I can smell *you* through twelve feet of stone."

More rustling. He felt a quick drop in temperature as a figure settled itself on the rim of the tub, blocking the fire's heat.

"Never," the voice said, "do that again."

William opened one eye, appraising his queen, perched in royal blue like a peacock, chocolate eyes glinting, soft bosom rising with her breath. Had it doubled in size? He let his eyes roam, finally landing on the smallest of bulges poking from under her bodice. His heir, warm and cooking within her lovely belly.

"Whatever do you mean, my dear?"

Queen Annelore creased her perfect brow. "William, you know exactly what I mean. Leaving me to bumble about the castle alone for nearly a month."

Quick as a porpoise, he thrust up to his knees and seized her face, his mouth attacking hers. She gave a satisfied sigh when he finally sat back, still holding her cheeks.

"Just to behold you as you are right this moment, I would leave again in an instant."

She pursed her lips. "Then I shan't let you out of my sight."

"Well then," he said, moving dripping hands down her arms,

"you'd best join me." He dragged her into the tub on top of him, an "eep" escaping her, skirts bubbling up like boiling laundry.

"What is it you have against my wardrobe?" she said.

"It's only that you wear so much of it." He wiped a droplet of water from the tip of her nose and brought his lips to hers.

She laughed and stroked his cheek.

"Mother of Moses I missed you." It was her turn to kiss him.

"It's only a bit of water, really" he said, looking down at the mass of blue and gold swishing with the tub's tide. "Bernard!"

Her Majesty's meticulous master of the chamber swept in immediately. His eyes widened for a brief beat at the naked king and the fully clothed, fully immersed queen floating in his arms.

"Ah, Bernard, the queen will need clothes and ladies." Bernard opened his mouth to respond, but the king cut him off. "Not now—let's say in, oh, a half-hour's time." Annelore frowned. "No?" She gave his chest a wet thump. "Apparently Her Majesty feels she may not be completely dry by then," he said, hiding a grin. "Better make it a full hour."

"Yes, Majesty." Bernard gave his signature heel-clicking jig and took his leave.

William craned his neck toward the door, spying a wall of courtiers and messengers jostling like pent-up horses, vying to be let in.

"And where's the warmed mead?"

The royal taster pushed his way in, bearing a tray laden with a large kettle and two silver mugs. He placed it by the fire.

"And some victuals please, Peter," William said, "but wait until I call to bring them in." Peter bowed and hurried away. "As for the rest of you," William called, "you may take your leave as well. For the queen and I have much to discuss."

Annelore raised her eyebrows. "Discuss?"

His smile broadened. "For the time being, let's get you out of these wet clothes, my queen."

Annelore looked down at William's damp head lying on her bare belly, watching as it rose and fell with her breath.

"Hello, little prince," he said, tapping her navel.

"The babe hasn't even quickened yet, Wills," she said. "And certainly can't hear you."

"Well, he'd better get on with it." William beamed. "For I expect a son at the top of his game."

Anna laughed, William's head shaking with her. Heavens, it was good to have him home. She'd been keen to help run the palace and court in his absence, but in reality she'd done little more than show off her barely visible pregnant belly and preen for ceremony. The most she'd decided was what color thread to embroider with or what to eat, her only companions gossiping ladies and the ever-so-polite Daniel. It was as if part of her had been shuttered away when William left. It was intolerable.

And yet she could not squelch a pang of concern. Everyone spoke as if the babe were a boy. It was supposedly good luck, as if speaking the words would make it so, but every time a boy was mentioned, especially by the king, she flinched. Would a princess really be a calamity? Seeing William there, deep blue eyes soft, full of hope, her contentedness faltered. A girl could not secure his place on the throne or the country's legitimacy in the world. A girl was only good for marrying into another kingdom. A girl, in short, was barely better than no child at all.

"The babe's barely four months." Anna smoothed a particularly stubborn wave of William's hair. "The quickening will happen soon, or so says Mary."

"Perhaps I shouldn't be so keen." William rose to his knees and slid off the bed. "That's when we must cease coupling, no? When he moves?"

Anna shrugged. "Both Mary and my mother felt the act of love was helpful for a potent pregnancy. Of course, that's not widely held, nor I daresay popular. I doubt the court physicians will allow it."

Having pulled on fresh trunks, William grabbed a leg of guinea fowl, took a bite, and spoke through a full mouth. "Well, if two of the most gifted midwives Troixden has known recommend it, who am I to go against their sage advice?" He smirked, then broke wind.

"Oof." Anna winced and waved a hand under her nose. "If this be your way of wooing me, Majesty, we shall certainly follow the royal doctor's strictures."

"Ha!" He slapped his thigh. "You should feel honored your king is so comfortable in your presence that he allows such displays."

"Ah, so gas be an honor, sire?" She pulled the sheets to her chin, snuggling down into their warmth. "Then I have been inducted into the highest of earthly honors many times over. My nose, however, begs to differ."

He let out a bellow, grabbed the platter, and sat next to her.

"I suppose I've been without the presence of a woman for too long, my dear. You'll have to reform me."

"An impossible task." She leaned in to give him a peck on the arm. He grunted and took another bite of bird. "Come, tell me of the envoy. Did the Laurelanders listen to reason? Did they fall to your feet once they got a good look at you?"

William's face turned down. "They were pleased and honored that I took the news of our heir to them personally. They were also surprised, but gratified, at Norwick's presence. Perhaps hearing of the heir and seeing Robert in the flesh gave them confidence in the royal line."

"I'm sure Robert was quite content to be recognized as the next heir, baby or no."

William looked sidelong at her. "Anna, I know you don't care for him, but he's my cousin and one of my dearest friends. Like it or not, his very existence helps keep the crown on our heads."

She knew full well that the Duke of Norwick would much rather have the crown on his own head, even if her husband refused to acknowledge that.

"They seemed appeased, at least to my face," William said. "But Robert heard more talk of them throwing in with the Lutherans." He looked down at the exposed fowl bone, tendons dangling. "'Tis one thing to threaten a man's pocket, another to threaten his soul."

"They will relent." She touched his thigh. "Many a man's noble cause falls by the wayside in the throes of earthly suffering.

The last thing they want is their lands plundered and their families dead or destitute."

"But if they feel the crown is unstable, they may secede or lead German forces into our lands." He looked at her, sadness in his eyes. "We're a small realm. We couldn't survive that."

She held his hand, caressing it, feeling the bumps and dips, the smattering of hair, his gold ring of office. She never understood why those Protestants were so hell bent on tearing the world apart. Certainly the Holy Church had problems, but when were there not? Devotion to God was what mattered and since God ordained pope and king, that should be the end of it.

"'Tis fine for men to bluster, but they wouldn't be so reckless as to attack their sovereign. King James plunged our country into fractious parts, but there is still Troixden pride, still loyalty."

He took her hands and squeezed them.

"For now, my queen. For now."

CHAPTER 2

The Spanish Plague

obert, Duke of Norwick, watched in barely restrained silence as the men of Council Table glared at his friend Daniel, Duke of Cecile. Daniel had made himself out to be the man with all the answers and his fellow councilors wanted a quick one. Preferably before the king joined them.

"Your Grace," the grand master general said, shifting in his chair, leather squeaking, "as a man who's never seen battle, you're quick to refuse one."

Daniel gave the general a rare sharp look from beneath his white-blond brows. "And for one who has seen so much, sir, you are quick to shed the blood of your countrymen." Rumblings started around the table.

Robert flashed a smile. "Gentlemen, let us not forget ourselves. 'Tis the king who will decide the matter." Robert sat back in his chair and stroked his black goatee.

"But the king," the general said, hands working his own vast, white beard, "listens only to Cecile."

Robert's smile faded as his colleagues rapped the table in agreement with mumbles of "Here, here."

"If that were the case," the king said, striding into the room, making the men startle, "we would have left you all behind instead of dragging you off to the hinterlands." He stopped behind Robert's chair and lay a hand on his shoulder, squeezing. "And yet it was Cecile who stayed at Havenside."

There was scuffling of chairs, bowing, and "Your Majestys" all around as the king settled himself at the head of the table and considered each council member in turn.

"By all means, my lords, continue to besmirch us, for surely we deserve it."

The general reddened. Robert had always thought he looked like a wizard from a fairy tale, fearsome and ridiculous at the same time.

"Majesty," the general said, "'tis just that Cecile is tentative, and in times of danger one needs men of action."

The king looked from the general to Daniel, who scratched his receding hairline and pressed his lips.

"Master General," the king said, "we took all our 'men of action' to Laureland and all of these men—including you—felt that launching an offensive attack would not be in our best interest. And that our Laureland countrymen did not seem disposed to a fight." He drummed his fingers on the table. "Has two days' time changed your mind so drastically?"

The Archbishop of Bartmore yawned with ceremony.

"Do we bore Your Grace?" the king said.

Bartmore shook his head, jowls jiggling. "My apologies, Highness. Age, you see, catches up with one when one least expects it." He gave an oily grin. "But since you ask, Norwick and I have given more thought to the talk of heresy in the north. While 'tis true the landowners seemed to have eased their rhetoric, the general population's penchant for speaking German is disconcerting."

Robert scowled at the man. Why did Bartmore always drag him into these things?

"And that is their heresy?" the king said. "Speaking German?"

Robert turned his laugh into a cough. These papal puppets needed to be taken down a peg, but His Grace was right. Besides, Robert needed him. Might as well stir the pot further and see how the soup tasted.

"Indeed, to speak it is to disrespect the crown," Robert said, with a casual look at William, "and to show their loyalty to another."

"Exactly," Bartmore said. "I have heard they even pray in German. I found and confiscated numerous pamphlets extolling the Lutheran heresy."

The king nodded, all playfulness gone. "We are well aware of their religious leanings, Your Grace. We are not, however, willing to set them ablaze just yet. If we start burning heretics it will be war whether we want one or not."

"And that is my point, Majesty," the general said. "How can you let your people hold you captive by their own heresy?"

"We are held captive by no one," William said, raising his thick brows at the general. "We will decide when, if, and who we fight, based not on hearsay but on facts." The king glanced toward the rotund Duke of Halforn. "And you, dear duke, what have you deduced? You walked amongst the people as well as the lords."

Halforn puffed out his cheeks as he exhaled. "Majesty, I believe the Laurelanders are true to their word. They do not want to shed blood; they merely needed confidence in the new king and court. They are still fearful that the days of your brother, begging Majesty's pardon, will return. But since they've seen you and heard your regard for them—and with an heir on the way—I believe they are satisfied."

"Until the queen has a girl!" The general smashed his fist to the table. The king's face did not change, but his eyes blazed with a ferocity that could turn the table to cinder.

"I daresay," Halforn said quietly, "that Queen Elizabeth of England may have much to say on the topic of female rulers."

Robert snorted and slapped his hand on the table, happy to help break the tension.

"Well said." He turned to William. "And speaking of burning heretics, we see it has not helped her reign."

Bartmore glared at Robert. "You now change your opinion, Norwick? And based on that blasphemous pretender queen?"

"I never said burning people was the course of action." Robert couldn't hide the accusation in his voice, his own mother's burning fresh in his mind as if the ashes were still warm and not scattered by the winds more than twenty years prior. "I merely said that a man's convictions may drive him to stupidity and treason if not put in check."

The king looked to heaven and rotated his square jaw in his hand, making it pop.

"Regardless, gentlemen, we cannot pledge peace with our people one day and turn against them the next without cause. We will wait. And see." The general glowered but most of the men nodded, faces grave. "Now to other matters," the king said. "Your Grace, tell me, are the stables prepared for the Spanish ambassador's hunt next month?"

The Duke of Beaubourg, Queen Annelore's father and master of His Majesty's stables, was eager to speak of his favorite topic.

Robert used the opportunity to shoot a glance at Daniel and wink. Daniel's reputation, for the time being, was restored.

Anna gazed down at her matron of honor and Mary beamed back, holding Anna's blossoming belly in both her hands. Anna's ladies busied themselves with the final preparations of the night, flitting among the shadows cast by candles.

"'Tis four months," Mary said. "Ye look fine, dearie. How do you feel?"

"Tired," Anna said. "I can barely keep my eyes open in mass and privy court."

"That likely means he's growin' right strong." She gave Anna's belly one last pat and moved to pull down the sheets, Anna cringing in her head at Mary's choice of pronoun.

"Though my private audience with Father was a bright spot." She laughed, remembering. "Apparently he'd a letter from Cook about some particularly ornery chickens. With him leaving for Beaubourg today, he's afraid she'll think he rushed home over recalcitrant poultry."

"Ha!" Mary fluffed a pillow. "Cook'll think she's coming up in the world, the duke leavin' council to tame her birds."

"And he says she's already coming up with new pastries for the baby shaped like animals, and he is already seeing about a pony." Anna yawned through her grin and lifted her shift to climb in to bed only to find Margaux suddenly at her side, goblet in hand, hair glowing gold in the low light.

"Majesty," she said, making a curtsy. "Your warming cup."

Margaux had left court months ago, saying she preferred the company of her fourteen-year-old husband Eustace, Earl of Mohrlang, which everyone found hard to believe. Even more surprising, she'd begged to be placed back into service the same day the king and his entourage left court for Laureland. And thanks to her rank, Anna had no choice but to allow her return.

"Thank you, Countess," Anna said, "but where is Lady Jane this evening? Was she not to stay the night?"

Margaux tightened her lips. Something had happened in the short months she'd been gone. Her alabaster face was drawn, her eyes not just cold, but icy.

"Does Your Majesty disapprove of my service?"

"I was simply expecting Lady Jane, Countess," Anna said. "Nothing more."

"Her Ladyship's boy has a cough again," Margaux said, "and she wanted to tend him. I told her I would trade evenings with her."

"How generous of you." Anna gave Margaux a tight smile. "We shall all keep our Lady Jane and her son in our prayers."

"As you wish, Majesty," Margaux said, bowing her head.

Anna dismissed her, then got in to bed, setting the untouched wine on her bedside table. Mary shut the bed curtains with a snap. But even enclosed within her feathered cocoon, Anna could sense Margaux's eyes upon her, boring through the curtains, measuring her. Anna burrowed like a squirrel in its tail and shut her eyes to the cold comfort outside.

Finally the ground was soft and freezes no longer threatened. Anna could plant her herb garden. William insisted she simply tell the gardeners what she wanted and where and they would take care of the rest, but she told him it didn't work that way. She had to feel each plant, know it, urge it to new, fuller life. Needed to tend to them like a mother to a child. Only then would she know when to pick for what purpose. Only then would she feel the garden was truly hers and not one more ornament of the palace.

Other than Mary, Anna was the only one enthused by the project. Even Countess Cariline, who normally took on any job with joyful aplomb, looked befuddled at the prospect of spending the day on her knees, digging in the dirt. Despite all this, Anna led her troop of ladies to the tilled patch next to the cooks' garden.

"Each one of you can have your own section," Anna said, face bright, "and in time, you could learn to make some simple remedies." Margaux smirked at this and whispered something to Brigitte, who covered her mouth and snickered.

"Right." Anna pulled up her skirts and knelt on the cold earth. She grabbed a trowel and started to dig her first hole. "You've got to make it larger than you think so the roots have room." Her ladies frowned down at her. Picking up a rosemary, she held its roots dangling in the hole she had made. "It is important to make sure each plant has sufficient space." She began scooping dirt back in, pressing down with her knuckles.

"But it's so dirty." Brigitte worried her hands. "Won't it make us ill?"

"Dirt? Ill? Bah," Mary said, scuttling out from behind the group and grabbing her own tools. "God made the dirt and a little dirt won't hurt."

"He made the plague too," Margaux muttered.

But even Margaux's sourness didn't dampen Anna's mood at finally being about something she loved, something she was used to, something she was good at. She breathed in the soil's scents of both decay and freshness and soon, all her ladies were playing in the dirt. Even Margaux had a determined air about her.

Anna looked at the bare patch next to her plantings with anticipation. She patted her belly. "And what about for you, little one?" Boy or girl, Anna would make sure her child knew the difference between milkweed and dogbane, thyme and marjoram. She conjured a picture of herself and a bonny brown-haired girl, sitting side by side in the sun, harvesting a bundle of herbs, Anna telling her their Latin names, quizzing her on how long they should dry, a cherubic face beaming up, rosy lips smiling, pudgy hands caked with mud. She planted a golden dwarf rose in her—or his—honor and sat back, satisfied.

She stood, dusted off her hands on her apron, and went to inspect her ladies' work. Countess Cariline's were already snug in perfect rows, her tender sprigs standing at attention, Stefania was content to plant wildflower seeds and witch hazel and Yvette was still digging, lost in her thoughts. Then Anna came to Margaux and Brigitte. Margaux had gathered all the medicinal plants she could find, pennyroyal, mint, anise, smartweed, wort, verbenum.

"Countess Mohrlang," Anna said, "that is quite a collection. Perhaps you would like to borrow a book on these plants and their uses?"

"Thank you, Majesty," Margaux said, "but I have become a student on my own." Her lips formed a tight line.

"As you wish," Anna tucked this information away to ponder later, and moved on to find Brigitte prodding at a hole against the castle wall with a long stick.

"Milady, best to plant farther from the stone," Anna said.

"I thought I saw a worm," Brigitte said, pretty face scrunched with revulsion, "and Mary said they were good for the plants to eat? Or some such?" Brigitte squinted up at Anna, while still needling the ground, disturbing the ancient moss.

"The worms are good for the soil," Anna said, smiling at Brigitte's frown of concentration. The lady itched her hand. "And good soil is good for the plants, so I guess, in a sense—"

"Blagh!" Brigitte startled and dropped the stick, shaking her hand like wet off a cat. "Oh, oh, oh!"

"Let me see that, milady." Anna bent down, reaching for Brigitte's hand. Out of the corner of her eye, she saw the distinctive scuttle of a gnarled brown spider, retreating to its recently disturbed home. She grabbed Brigitte's hand and saw the two red punctures, already starting to swell.

"Mary!" Anna called, voice rising. "Mary, quick!"

Brigitte began to whimper as the bite puffed up more and more. Not only was it poisonous, but Brigitte was having a sensitized reaction. Anna brought the bite to her lips.

"It's a recluse bite," Anna said between sucks and spits. "We must get the venom out if we can."

Brigitte yelped, from fear or pain, Anna couldn't tell. Mary arrived, clutching a peppermint start, the rest of the ladies crowding around.

"Majesty, nay!" Mary fell to her knees, shoving Anna aside with her shoulders.

"There's no time for formalities," Anna said. Mary looked at Brigitte's hand, then crossed herself.

"Send for my kit!" Mary hollered. A page flew through the kitchen doors.

"And you, Majesty, will stay well clear of this poison." She elbowed Anna once more.

"Lady Yvette," Anna said, "get coals from hearth—quick!" She reluctantly turned the bitten hand over to Mary and held Brigitte's other. "Hush, milady. We'll get you back to rights."

"But you said I wouldn't get ill—" She hiccupped a sob and Anna brought the lady to her chest, tucking Brigitte's strawblond head under her chin.

"We won't let you get ill," Anna whispered. "Not under our care."

Margaux, who had strangely disappeared, pushed through the gaggle of ladies, cheeks red with exertion.

"Lady Brigitte!" She flew to Brigitte's side, face all concern. She opened her arms to the lady, beckoning her to leave Anna. "I will make the lady comfortable, Majesty."

"Have your lessons in medicinals gone so far, Countess?"

"She did not wish to come today," Margaux said, "and look at what has become of her."

"Countess," Anna gripped Brigitte tighter, "I will not allow you to—"

Yvette was back, cloth filled with coals. Anna left her test of wills with Margaux for another time and grabbed the coals, crumbling them to ash, spitting, and making a paste. She spread the thick, black substance on Brigitte's bite, pressing the granules into the wound.

"It soaks up the venom," she said, in response to Brigitte's puzzled face.

"Surely, leeches—" Margaux started.

"Countess, enough!" Anna said. "Lend the hand that is needed and asked for, or be gone with you."

All color drained from Margaux's face. She stood, dusted off her hands, stuck her nose in the air, and stomped toward the castle, paying no heed to her cohorts' tender sprigs. Anna watched her disappear around the corner of the castle and, looking to her wake, saw the single bloom of the babe's yellow rose crushed to the ground.

The newly appointed Spanish ambassador arrived a week later to subdued fanfare. It was a delicate balance: one wanted to impress him yet not let him feel overly important. To that end, the throne room was stuffed like a meat pie with dukes, counts, councilmen, ladies—even Brigitte, none the worse for wear—and a few hounds, all flanking the throne in descending order of rank, but no music, no mass, no crowns of state.

The king welcomed the Spaniard, Count Valencia, in the man's native tongue, and the young ambassador gave his steward a look of surprised approval. Valencia looked every bit the conquistador, standing tall and taciturn in his brocade silks, bowing before the royals.

That afternoon, the king and queen entertained Valencia and his entourage in the privy dining room, filled again with courtiers, all waiting to form their opinions of this new face at court. Valencia sat in a place of honor next to the king, his pointed mustache twitching under his long, thin nose. No less than twenty Spaniards wrapped the table like bunting, in matching gold and red puff sleeves. Only the Archbishop of Bartmore stood out, a bruise of purple amid the gold, rising to lead them all in the blessing.

"Holy and blessed Father," he began in Latin, "we give thee thanks for smiling upon the travels of our dear friends so gathered—"

Clang!

All heads turned toward the queen's end of the table, seeking the source of the disturbance. Anna kept her head bowed, hiding her flushing cheeks. She'd been surprised by a queer fluttering sensation near her bladder, like she'd swallowed a live anchovy. She could not help startling, her hand sending flatware banging against her plate.

Bartmore glowered, but William, all the way at other end, peered at her through the dripping flowers and candles, his brows creased.

The archbishop cleared his throat and began again, blessing the meal with such ferocity and length that the soup became cold. The Viscount de Alba, seated to Anna's right, grabbed her hand and squeezed it, smiling at her after all the amens.

She was delighted he had made the journey. He had attended the royal wedding and stayed on at court for a month, during which time she grew quite fond of him and he of her.

"Is there anything the matter, Majesty?" he said.

She smiled weakly. "No, thank you, milord. Just a twitch."

"Ah, methinks you are too young for such curiosities of the body, Highness," he said, picking up a soupspoon.

"'Tis the pregnancy, milord. I have the most unsettling symptoms—all normal, of course, but not quite fit to bring to His Majesty's table."

"Oh-ho, Highness," he said, dribbling a bit of golden broth on his thin white beard, "I thought you and I were past such formalities."

"How I wish you could have been appointed ambassador," she said. He frowned. "Not, of course, that Ambassador Valencia is anything but the picture of decorum—"

"Tut-tut, Majesty," the count said, his easy way returning. "It would have been my wish too. But diplomacy is for younger—"

Anna clutched her belly, her elbow knocking cutlery against her wine, sending it spilling toward the artfully arranged bowls of fruits and nuts. All this as the conversation reached a lull. It seemed the room took a breath, then stewards were upon her, mopping up the mess. Valencia looked as if a mouse had scurried across his meat platter and William dashed to her side, ignoring the questioning brows and grumbles of those he passed.

"My queen?" His face was stern but his eyes were all worry.

"Majesty," she said, attempting a straight face, "'tis nothing— I just startled. Please, enjoy our guests." She gestured to the table. "We shall speak later."

"Nay, Highness," he said, moving closer for some semblance of privacy. "I will know why you grab your stomach so. Are you ill? Do you need rest?"

"Majesty, I do not think it appropriate to discuss in such prestigious company." She flicked her eyes to Valencia, who pretended his utmost to be concentrating on the droning Bartmore.

"Patience isn't a virtue of mine," William whispered as he bent a knee to her. "If you're ill, I'll send them all away—I care not what they think."

She took his hand in hers and pressed it firmly to her belly. He looked at her, confused. She met his eyes.

"Your heir has chosen this moment to make my womb a tumult."

Slowly, comprehension lit his face. "My son quickens?"

She could not help but laugh. "Yes, sire, and mightily to be sure. I thought I might have felt something earlier this week, but this 'twas most definitely a strong appendage."

Leaping to his feet, the king hooted, silencing the room.

"My lords, we have just had the most wonderful news."

"Sire—" Anna said.

"Oh tush, my dear, we're among friends, are we not?" He threw his arms out to embrace the whole room. "Most honored guests, know that you are present at a historical moment—the quickening of the prince!"

Anna blushed scarlet as the men clapped. Surely this was not news to be made public in such a manner, but William was so happy, and her missteps at the table had a satisfactory explanation.

Valencia came to her, bowed, and took her hand, brushing his lips against it, his thin mustache tickling her knuckles.

"Majesty, it is an honor to be present at such an occasion." He rose and bowed his head to the king.

"Perhaps," William said, patting Valencia on the back, "we shall call him William Espania." The Spaniards laughed and clapped as both men returned to their seats.

Anna looked down the table and saw Robert scowling. She almost scowled back, then realized he was staring at someone behind her. She discretely glanced back to find her exotic lady-in-waiting, Yvette, standing behind her, fine black brow arched at Valencia, a satisfied smile on her lips.

Anna had not eaten much of the evening feast and she returned to her chambers feeling the familiar indigestion of pregnancy. Yvette helped her with her last preparations for bed. Anna would not be able to join William again in his chamber until his return from the hunt.

As if on cue, the king entered from his private passageway by the south windows, fully dressed and smiling, apparently sneaking away from entertaining Valencia. He climbed onto the bed next to her, moving his hand under her covers, his cold fingers finding her belly.

"I couldn't let the day pass without another attempt to feel my son." He kissed her languidly. "You seem distant, my dear."

She gazed back at him, cupping a stubbled cheek in her hand. "Just tired. And missing your company."

She would not tell him of the fear that poked at the seams of her days. If the babe were a girl . . . well then, she was a girl. Anna could do nothing about it, but how she wished that extra glimmer would not be in his eyes when he spoke of a son.

"If it were mine to decide, I would lie here all night waiting to feel a feisty kick."

"Your arm might get tired," she said. "It seems the babe only makes an appearance at the most inopportune times."

"A bit like his father then." He laughed and searched her face. "Anna, you really don't seem yourself."

"Don't fuss, Wills." She patted his cheek. "You should return to our guests."

"I should, but I shan't while you're in ill ease."

She traced the outline of his jaw with a slow finger, landing on his lower lip. He took her finger into his mouth, tickling it with his tongue as she studied his face.

"Go," she said, "enjoy the hunt tomorrow. Bring us back a gigantic stag. And once you return, we shall return to each other as we are accustomed. That's what will ease my spirit."

William narrowed his eyes and kissed her, parting her lips, searching for more. Finally, he grunted and rolled off the bed.

"I will hasten to your side triumphant, my dear. And you shan't leave my mind till I return."

"Nor will you leave mine." She watched him go, feeling a part of herself go with him. He hesitated on the threshold, opened his mouth as if to speak, then stopped. Anna pressed the ruby he had gifted her at Twelfth Night to her chest.

"I will keep you ever close to my heart," she said.

"Yes, my love." He took his leave with a sigh of boyish ardor.

Anna settled back in, feeling a dull ache in her lower back similar to her menstrual pains. All that standing and extra weight she was carrying was starting to wear on her small frame. She reached for her Bible only to find Yvette at her side, handing her a rosewater-soaked cloth for her face and neck.

"Majesty, may I speak plainly with you?" Yvette kept her black eyes trained on the perfumed towel as Anna wiped.

Yvette rarely sought her out for private conversations, most of which caused Anna to blush violently. She was a woman of many secrets, though being Robert's lover wasn't one of them—everybody knew or guessed, probably even his long-suffering duchess back in Norwick. In any case, something about Yvette drew Anna into her confidence, despite the lady's close quarter with Robert.

"Now that the babe has quickened," Yvette said, "the king will not be able to take his pleasure with you through the usual means."

"But Mary says—"

"I know what Mary says and it may be true. But know this, Highness. When it comes down to it, the king won't risk his son's life for a bit of pleasure. And neither should you." Yvette flicked her eyes to the others, who were gliding around the chamber extinguishing candles. Anna lowered her voice even further.

"But if it doesn't bring harm—"

"You don't know that." Yvette raised her eyes to meet Anna's. "I'm surprised you would take such a chance, especially in light of the church's strictures on the subject."

Anna rested her head against the carved headboard. Yvette started to close the bed curtains.

"I'm surprised, milady," Anna said, "that you of all people put more store in church law than the wisdom of midwives."

Yvette stopped her progress. "It's not that I have no faith in God. It's that I have no faith in God's men."

Anna looked at her, curious. "But if you counsel me to follow their instructions, surely you must give them some credence?"

"Must I?" Yvette glanced down at her elegant hands. "Highness, I don't like to speak of my time before court, but I do it as a warning. If anything were to happen, if the babe is born blind or deformed—or a girl—they will blame you. And it is these men the king will listen to."

"The king is not put off by superstitions." But she found herself picking at the bedspread, not meeting Yvette's gaze. She'd already heard the whispers about court. If anything went wrong it would be God's judgment against them. Against her. She bit the corner of her lip, bringing a hand to her belly.

"Perhaps." Yvette eyed her. "The point is, you must find a way of keeping another from the king's bed whilst you are unable to couple."

Dear God in heaven. Anna hadn't given a thought to this, amid all her fears surrounding the upcoming birth, the gender, the risk of death ... the baby moved, a hail of kicks raining in her gut.

"The king would not abuse me thus, Lady Yvette," she said tightly.

"'Tis no comment on His Majesty's feelings for you, Highness, but on the quite mechanical needs of the body. I haven't known a nobleman yet who hasn't sought release in the arms of another during such a time."

"Then His Majesty will be the first." He would—wouldn't he?

"That is my wish as well, Highness." Yvette arched a brow. "And that is the reason I wish to give you tutelage in some uncommon ways to keep the king comforted."

"Won't he think me some sort of strumpet?" Anna did not like this conversation at all.

"Better than he bedding the very same."

Anna set her mouth in a grim line. "What did you have in mind?"

The timing could not have been more perfect. The last of the snow had finally melted in the highlands and spring's verdant head was popping up all around as the royal hunting party made its way to the eastern forests in Duven. Gregory, Duke of Duven and chamberman to the king, rode alongside William and Valencia, extolling the views in broken Spanish. William sucked in the crisp air, Duven's prattle becoming a dull buzz as his thoughts turned to Anna.

He could still not believe his luck. She was beautiful, to be sure, but he delighted in the wit that kept him on his toes. And soon an heir. A strapping boy to carry his mantle into the future. William imagined giving his son all the things his own father had not: taking him on salamander scouting missions on the palace grounds, teaching him his first swordplay, sitting him upon his knee at feasts, showing him how to sweeten a lady. Perhaps this kingship business would not be such a bad life after all.

He recalled his queen standing in the castle square that morning, her ladies behind her, blessing him and the men in their hunt. She had kissed him so well and fiercely he had almost forgotten where they were. Her lips strained hard against his, the tip of her tongue seeking, her soft hands pressing the back of his neck. When he finally released her, her chest heaved and she was pink all over. She kept her eyes upon him. Even when she was but a speck of emerald in the distance, he could feel the heat of her stare.

The ambassador interrupted his reverie.

"Majesty," he said in his pinched tone, "my compliments again to your queen and your heir."

William was all smiles. "Yes, my Lord, she is a sight to behold, is she not?"

"Her Majesty exceeds the rumors of her divine beauty and grace." Valencia paused. "Of course, there are other rumors as well."

William frowned at the sinewy man. "And what be those, my Lord?"

Valencia waved his hand. "It is nothing, Majesty. Only idle talk of Her Majesty's . . . how do you say it?" He puzzled. "*Sympathies?* Yes, sympathies."

William clenched his jaw and met Valencia's gaze. "Her Majesty is a tender-hearted woman," he said. "We assume that is what you mean."

"Yes, of course." Valencia gave a slight dip of his head. "And I do not doubt that her tender heart is nourished by her faith in Mother Church." Between that twitching mustache and pointed nose, he looked more and more to William like a rat. And was starting to smell of one.

"The queen is the most devout person I know, my Lord." William's tone was casual, but the steel behind it could not be mistaken.

"King Philip will be delighted to hear of it."

"It seems to me, my Lord," William said, "you are quite. . . how do you say it? *Inquisitive.*"

The Duke of Duven, who could not help overhearing, snorted. Valencia face pinched. "Majesty, I must look after Spanish interests."

"I have no doubt you will not shirk your duty in reporting all your observations," William said. "And now, if you will excuse me."

With barely a nod, William spurred his horse forward with a hearty "He-ya!" leaving the Spanish rodent to his own devices.

Anna strolled through the privy gardens with a retinue of ladies trying to walk off her increasingly aching back. Two minstrels played a gay tune and her favorite spaniels bounded beside her, but she could not shake a sense of foreboding that had come over her that morning and could not name a reason for it, only knowing she would not rest easily until William returned in one whole and handsome piece.

Perhaps it was Yvette's lurid talk the evening prior. Anna imagined the hunting party coming upon a bevy of ladies bathing themselves beside a stream, all more than happy to assist with her husband's "mechanical needs of the body." She saw him lying in their pink arms, stroking his hair and chest.

Damn men and their sport!

She marched off to her herb garden. The child within her gave a flurry of kicks, as if equally incensed by his father's imagined misdeeds.

Seeing Anna grab her stomach, Mary hurried to her side.

"Anna dear, what's the matter? You should be taking it slow, not tramping 'round to wake the dead."

Anna scowled, but seeing Mary's true concern gave her a sheepish grimace.

"Oh, Mary, it's just my wild moods. I can't shake this unsettledness I have at the king's leaving. And only a month after his envoy to Laureland . . ."

"'Tis only two nights, dearie." Mary pouched her lips and patted Anna's arm.

Anna felt a pierce radiate from her pelvic bone to her waist. Mary assured her these pangs were merely growth pains, the womb pushing on the surrounding ligaments as the babe grew, but the sharp pinching still caught her off guard. She breathed deep. *It's all right, little one.*

"Perhaps I will lie down."

She returned to her chambers and shivered as another ligament, this time toward her back, strained. The baby responded with more kicks.

"Save some for your papa, my love." She patted herself and eased into bed, opening her Bible to Ecclesiastes, and propping it on a pillow.

"He'll feel that babe in no time at all," Mary said. "Here, drink this." She handed Anna a fresh goblet of wine. She drank it down, feeling its soothing properties already warming and calming her mind.

"I'll read for a bit. I'm horribly tired and I shall take full advantage of not having to sit court today."

She nestled into her pillows, her back still intermittently throbbing. She groaned and tried to concentrate. *To every thing there is a season, and a time to every purpose under the heaven: A time to be born . . .*

She must have been more tired than she knew, for she dozed off several verses later, with "all is vanity" swimming in her head.

Anna woke screaming.

She had dreamt of those ladies by the stream, laughing and dancing around William, buxom and naked, twining him with colorful scarves. They twirled and twisted, he in a daze as they pulled him inch by inch into the water. Anna ran to the shore calling his name but he could not or would not hear her.

They pulled him in deeper, some turning into otters. They finally plunged his head under the water, holding him down as he thrashed. Anna felt the choking in her own throat, the pain, the thrashing in her own body. She tried to jump in after him but her limbs were stuck, her screams making no sound. William's black horse stamped in front of her, blocking part of her view. One of the women dove under the water, coming up with William's sword and scampered up the creek bed. Anna begged her to help William, but the woman snarled, then cackled as his death throes echoed in Anna's body.

Suddenly the witch transformed into Robert, who took the king's sword and sliced off the strong warhorse's head, ink-black blood drenching her. The horse's death and William's became one, wracking her body to its core.

It was then that she screamed.

"Majesty?" Mary was rubbing her hand. "'Tis just a dream, relax."

Sweat poured down her face, her breathing shallow. She could still feel the pain of William convulsing against his death, could still feel the warm blood spurting onto her body. All she could do was look helplessly at Mary.

Mary brought her hand to Anna's forehead, frowning. She quickly checked the sides of Anna's neck and pressed her head to Anna's heart.

"No fever," she said. She flung back Anna's sheets and stifled a shriek, hand jumping to her mouth. A smell of metal and sweetness . . .

Anna looked down. She was swimming in blood.

"No, no, no, no—" She grabbed at her womb, rocking back and forth. "No, Mary, no, no, no—"

The rest of her ladies had gathered, gaping.

"Carliline, Amelia! To the kitchens—boiling water and lots of it!" Mary ordered. "Stefania, fresh linens and be quick about it! And nary a word to anyone, do ye hear? Not a word, elst I'll have you in chains! Yvette, bar the doors."

Anna rocked, tears streaming down her face, which Mary grabbed between her hands. Not her baby, not his heir . . . the image of the crushed yellow rose came unbidden to her mind.

"My darling girl, ye must help me now. Focus on me, dearie. You've got to help me. We can't lose you both."

Anna gave a cry. Mary stroked her hair, giving her one last tender look.

"We won't lose you both."

Later that evening, Anna woke to a room full of candles, the heat oppressive, her ladies flanking her bed in silent vigil.

"Mary?" Her voice scratched. "It's real, then?"

Mary held her hand tight and nodded.

"Oh, God in heaven," Anna shook again with sobs. "My baby . . ."

"You need to sleep, dearie, get your strength back."

She saw Yvette pass by the foot of the bed, face white and strained. She refused to meet Anna's gaze.

"You can't tell the king." Anna grabbed at Mary's arm. "Please don't. Don't send a message, don't tell him, let's pretend . . . a little while longer . . ." She had failed him, utterly and miserably. She did not know how, but it was her fault, just as Yvette had said. He would never again look at her the same way again . . .

"Shhhhh," Mary said. "The king needn't be told now. As far as I know, no one but the ladies in this room know what happened today and I only let the ladies I trust go and fetch." Anna's shoulders relaxed. "Didn't think a messenger would be a wise way to break the news."

"Thank you." She sighed her relief.

"But we can't go 'round pretending once the king comes home." Anna's face crumpled again and Mary handed her a cup. "'Twill help you sleep, dear."

Anna gulped it down, burning her raw throat as it went. Clenching William's ruby to her chest, she lay back, head spinning, and fell into a dreamless sleep.

CHAPTER 3

Expelled

William woke with the birds at the Duke of Duven's manor. The ravens had interrupted a most pleasant dream—bathing women frolicked with him in the creek bed, all pink and plump in the sun. Not a dream to share with his wife, though it made him eager to return to her arms.

Remembering her state, he frowned. The babe had quickened and he could no longer come to her as he desired. Ah, but that was not such a sacrifice if it meant an heir.

He sighed and rolled over, imagining a bright-eyed little boy tromping through the castle halls. He exhaled, content. And then the picture changed to one of his sister, her curled tresses flopping on her back as she skipped ahead of him, giggles echoing to him, and he suddenly missed her acutely.

He shook his head to clear it. At least the hunt had been a success. They had caught the first of the wild boar for the season and two young stags, but more important he'd learned how tightly Spain was wrapped around the pope. And how tightly Valencia was wrapped around his own aspirations for a bishopric. Valencia and Bartmore would get along swimmingly.

Running his fingers through his hair, William rose and grabbed the dampened face towel offered him by a chamberman as Robert burst into the room.

"Majesty, one more foray before we head back to the castle?"

William eyed the duke while his dressers went about their duties.

"Avoiding something at court, Your Grace?"

Robert smacked his riding gloves into his hand. "Merely hoping to get a bit more information out of our new Spanish friend."

"I've never known you to be so diplomatic." William grinned and popped an olive into his mouth. "But I wish to be home."

"And I've never known you to refuse a hunt." Robert took a swig of William's untouched wine.

"Let us say I've acquired all I desired from this jaunt and am ready to return to my own bed. And my own wife." William took the wine from Robert's hand, Robert holding up his palms in defeat.

"Merely trying to test the Spanish waters." He moved to the leaded window. "Valencia seems quite interested in Her Majesty's reading preferences."

"I shan't stop the queen from reading scripture, cuz, no matter whom it makes squirm."

"Just watching out for our interests, Majesty."

"Which interests, exactly?" William straightened his chain of office.

Robert turned, startled, but chuckled when he saw the mischief in William's face.

"All right, you've caught me," Robert said. "The Spanish ladies accompanying us have indeed caught my eye."

William laughed, holding his arms straight to allow his dressers to continue their work.

"You've always had an eye for the exotic."

"Not all of us are as doggedly constant as you, my liege."

William grunted. "I do still have eyes."

"Speaking of which . . ." Robert began to pace the room. "As the queen is, shall we say, relieved of her duty for a time, is there anyone in particular you would like to look at?"

William rolled his eyes. He did not want to think about this. Not yet, anyway.

"Your Grace, if that were my intention, I wouldn't need your very able help. Though I do appreciate how attentive you are to my person."

Robert bowed low, sweeping his hat on the floor.

"'Tis but my duty as your loyal subject and friend to ply you with the delights due you, Majesty."

Giving one of his explosive guffaws, William led his friend from the room.

"You have always been the best man for distraction, Your Grace. Come, let's be off!" And off they were, not a moment too soon in his opinion. With enough haste he would be in Anna's arms before full dark.

Anna's ladies sat with their heads bowed, speaking in low whispers. They'd lit more candles than Anna could count, but nothing could lighten the pall hanging over the room.

En masse the ladies sprang up, bringing frightened eyes to the queen, then ran to the window. Anna heard hooves and whinnies, deep laughter and shouts—the hunters had returned.

Her desperation mounted. She had not felt so scared, so weary, since her unwanted betrothal.

"He's back." She could feel her hand trembling as she crossed herself for the hundredth time.

"Shhhh, dearie." Mary stroked her the way one soothes a nervous cat.

"He'll put me out. I've failed—"

"You've not failed and he'll do no such thing."

"He's been waiting for an heir—it was the point of the marriage."

"Annelore Matilda Carver, you're talking nonsense. Everyone knows babies don't always come easy. Kings be no different."

But Anna was wrapped, warped in her fear. His anger she could brave, but the anguish and regret? She did not think she could endure that.

William entered his chambers with Robert, Daniel, and Gregory of Duven, to the welcome vision of a bath already prepared. So focused was he on refreshment that he didn't notice Bernard standing by the desk until the man cleared his throat.

"Majesty ..."

"Why hello, Bernard." William's mind raced—what delights had Anna planned for their reunion? "To what do we owe the pleasure of your company? How does the queen fare?"

"I . . ." Bernard's voice trailed off with too long a pause. "The queen is resting, sire."

"Resting?" He began peeling off of his traveling clothes, handing sundry items to a dresser. "Is she unwell?"

"She . . ." Bernard swallowed and looked past William to the top of the hearth. "She is merely resting and you need not hurry—"

"Don't beat about the bush." William hastened to the tub, plunged his hands into the warm, clear water and scrubbed his face.

"Sire, please. Let her rest. Have the feast. Join her after." Bernard's voice hitched up the more he talked.

William looked to his friends. "Do you know of this?"

"How could we, sire?" Robert looked baffled. "But let me investigate. Refresh yourself and I shall be back in moments. I'm sure it's simply the exhaustion of pregnancy."

William relaxed a fraction. That was it. Surely. Nothing to worry about. She rested quite a bit these days. Then why did Bernard look as though he were about to lose his head to an axe?

"Yes. Hurry."

Robert was off. William listened to his steps echo down the long hall to the queen's doors.

"Highness," Daniel said, "if it were anything ill, we'd have been sent word."

William paced his bearskin rug, the bristled fur setting itself at alarming angles. He paused when he heard Robert's raised voice echo down the hall. They were refusing to let him in.

"Enough!" William turned on his heel and rushed to the privy passage door. He could hear Daniel's protests as he sprang down the hall.

"Annelore!" His agitated voice echoed through the passage. "Anna!"

He burst into her bedchamber and stopped short. He could smell fear in the room. All Anna's ladies, save Mary and Yvette, stood in a semicircle, blocking his view of the bed. They bowed, the candlelight making them look like herald angels.

"Your Majesty," they said.

Scowling, he looked about, trying to figure out who was in charge. His gaze landed on a bucket by the door of the queen's privy. It was dripping with sodden rags, seemingly tossed there in a hurry. Perhaps they had been giving her a sponge bath. But his instincts said otherwise. Without a word he pushed past the ladies, stopping at the foot of Anna's bed.

She was propped up on many pillows, hair spilling about her shoulders, her face pale in the candlelight, turned away.

"My queen, are you unwell?"

Anna's lower lip started to tremble, but otherwise her face was taut. He wanted to swoop down and engulf her in his arms. She looked so small, so weak. He rounded on Mary.

"Matron Mary?" His voice sounded angrier than he expected. She rushed toward him. "I'm so sorry, sire," she said in a low voice. "The babe . . . there was nothing anyone could've done—"

This couldn't be. Not his heir. Not the country's future hope, and his.

"Why was I not informed?" He was shouting. He could not help himself. Here he was, the king, yet impotent to stop this nightmare. "What the hell happened?"

"I lost him," came a scrabbled voice. "I've killed our child." William stumbled back as if struck.

Mary clasped her hands in supplication. "She was sleeping peaceful and woke bleeding. We're lucky she survived! Highness, please, she fears your wrath—"

William barely heard her. The room reeled. This could not be so. Not now. Not when so much depended . . . oh merciful God, she had almost died. He gripped his head.

"Out!" he bellowed "Out! All of you out!"

He stood stock still at the foot of her bed, head in hands, while her ladies fled, the heavy wooden doors finally clanging shut behind Mary, who had continued to entreat him as Yvette dragged her away. He looked down on his terrified wife.

"Anna . . ." His voice was barely above a whisper. The horror in her eyes stung his heart. He moved to the side of the bed. She gave a gasp, pulling away from him, her face wet with tears. He melted to his knees beside her, clenching her hand as all the rage, all the pain came swimming to his eyes.

"I could have lost you. Don't you know what that would have done to me? And to be away? To not have a final moment?"

"I—"

"Not after mother. Not after my sister. And you—" He searched her face.

"I thought you would send me away."

"Shhhh, my Anna, shhhh." He kissed her palm over and over, then climbed into the bed, wiping away her tears with strong thumbs. Folding her into his lap, he rested his cheek on the crown of her head, grateful for its warmth, her body shaking as she wept into his chest.

"I could not bear my life without you in it." He cradled the side of her face and wiped away more tears. "If only I had been here. You shouldn't have had to go through this without me."

"You couldn't have done anything," she said, voice barely a whisper. He held her close, so close. They breathed together in the silence.

"Was it . . ." His voice cracked. "Was it a boy?"

He felt her nod.

"God help us." Caving into her, he rocked back and forth, his own rare tears wetting her hair and no one to wipe them away.

CHAPTER 4

Truth Will Out

"As much as I'd like to accuse her," Yvette said, running her slender finger along the blade of Robert's seal opener, "the miscarriage wasn't Margaux's doing."

Robert lay sprawled on his settee, watching his mistress, feeling the tension of her movements in his loins. It had been a fortnight since the baby heir was laid to rest in the royal tomb. He had seen barely hide nor hair of king or queen since, leaving him overwhelmed with court politics and nary an opportunity of meeting with Yvette.

"And why are you so convinced?"

Yvette stopped, pressing the point of the knife into the tip of her finger.

"Because you scared the holy trinity out of her."

It was true. Even though his sister flaunted his orders to stay away from court, since her return she'd acted like a scared spaniel anytime he came near.

"Besides, any aborticide she's making is for herself." Yvette put the knife down and surveyed his disordered desk. "I've watched her and those herbs have gone nowhere near the queen. I would have killed her myself if they had."

Robert snorted. He highly doubted his sister was having relations with her fourteen-year-old husband, even if her marriage had given her a title. While the boy's mop of orange hair had burnished and muscles had started to replace his childish pudge, the bastard Earl of Mohrlang was still not handsome enough, nor powerful enough, for Margaux's taste.

"Don't be naïve, Robert." Yvette picked up an armored glove he used as a paperweight. "She must bed him occasionally. He may be young and unaccustomed to the intrigues of court, but he's not an idiot."

"True," Robert said, eyes grazing Yvette's taut corset. He unloosed the ties of his shirt. "But if she needs an elixir to keep a babe from coming, she's surely finding satisfaction elsewhere."

"And you want me to find out where." Yvette slid her hand into the glove and flexed it into a fist. "You've got me quite a list of duties. Following Valencia, keeping an eye on the queen, and now your sister."

"The mice will play because they don't realize you're the cat." Robert got up slowly and undid his trunks, letting them hang loose at his hips. "She wouldn't lower herself to ride anything less than a stallion, unless, of course, he was useful."

Coming up behind his prey, he grabbed the flesh at the crook of her neck. She tensed, inhaling sharply. He started to knead. She tilted her head and exposed her neck as she pressed in to his working hands. She let the armor glove fall to the floor. He bent to her ear, feeling the tickle of her hair at his cheek.

"So. Who are the stallions and who are the workhorses?"

"Don't be too hasty." Yvette thrust her arms behind her, hands grabbing his thighs. "She may be enamored with a stable boy."

"I don't think my sister knows of the existence of stable boys," he said into her skin.

She hooked her thumbs over the top of his trunks, shoving them down over his hips.

"I'm simply saying you shouldn't underestimate the power of a pair of striking eyes with long lashes." She tilted her head up and locked her own striking eyes with his. Sliding her hand to the back of Robert's buttocks, she pulled him to her, lips hovering below his. "Though he may be her undoing, she'll never regret it."

Robert's reply was snuffed out by the urgent press of her mouth.

William sank deep in his leather chair before a roaring fire. March in Havenside could be glorious sun one day and pelting hail the next. Today was hail. Outside and in. Though Anna was lying in his lap, wrapped in her robe and head against his chest, he could feel her tension seeping out.

He kissed her head softly.

"My love, you must stop blaming yourself. There was nothing you could have done."

"Why shouldn't I blame myself?" She stared at the fire. "Everyone else does."

"I don't. And my opinion used to be important."

She whipped around to face him, her head shaking in earnest.

"Don't, William, don't you ever say—don't you ever *think* your word is not important to me."

His heart swelled. He hadn't realized how desperate he was to hear her assurances. He could count on one hand the times she'd smiled in the last few weeks and two of those were for decorum's sake. Most nights she sat with him, tears were involved.

"Then why can't you believe me when I say you must put this in perspective?" He placed a hand at the nape of her neck. "Can't you see that this loss must not keep us from living?"

"Can't *you* see it was God's displeasure that brought this about in the first place?"

"How can God be displeased when we are being about our duty in making an heir?"

She climbed out of his lap, crossed her arms, and glared at him.

"It was a saint's feast day, that's why!"

"I was nearly killed that day!" He got up, squaring off. "You think God would frown upon us coming together after a day when all hell broke loose? When you thought you would never see me alive again? How could a God you say is full of mercy smite us thus?"

"He is also a God of vengeance for those who do not keep his statutes."

He grabbed her by the shoulders. "A king is put in place by God! I have tried with everything I am to keep this country together, to rule it well and true. Part of that is giving our fractured realm an heir!"

"And I feel the disgrace of failing you with every passing second." Her eyes were thick with misery.

He too had heard the murmurs about court, how God was punishing them because they flaunted his statutes. But she had never taken such gossip to heart before. Why now? He breathed in and brought her to his chest, enveloping her in his arms.

"I know you do." He caressed her cheekbones with his thumbs. "But if you fear coupling on any holy day, be it a Sunday or a saint day or a day Bartmore decides to wear his archbishop's hat, we will never be able to give the realm, or God, their due."

"I worry it will happen again, don't you see? That if we conceive on a forbidden day . . . I don't wish to defy you."

"It's not about defiance, Anna, it's . . ." He exhaled and dropped his hands to his sides. She moved to his desk and fidgeted with the wine decanter. "Please come to bed. It's Saturday. For two more hours."

She bent her head, back still to him.

"I won't force you."

Her head came up and she looked at him, face wistful. "You said that once before."

He walked toward her, arms outstretched. "And I meant it then as I mean it now."

She nodded, seemingly resigned. She came to him, lifted up

on her tiptoes and gave him a chaste kiss on the cheek. Taking his hand, she led him toward his gigantic goose-down bed. He brought her hand to his lips, grazing her knuckles.

She slid her hand against his cheek, rubbing his close-cropped stubble. Drawing her face up, he took her lips in a soft yet encouraging press. She tucked her head beneath his chin and brought her lips to his upper chest with the lightness of a butterfly.

And then they came together—deliberately, delicately. And it felt like forgiveness. It felt like communion.

Anna wandered the paths of the castle's towering boxwood maze, Mary puffing beside her. Every now and then she caught a glimpse in her mind's eye of a mousy-haired boy toddling down the trail, his doughy hands reaching out to capture a squirrel or throw the pink gravel. She had not expected this depth of pain, this depth of loss. She would do anything to keep it from happening again. Even if it meant keeping herself holier than priests themselves. How her mother had survived, losing so many . . .

"I need a distraction, Mary," she said, twirling a posy of wild-flowers between her fingers. "Something—I don't know, something to bring life back to me."

"You have something in mind, then?"

Anna reached into the folds of her skirts, pulled out a parchment, and handed it to Mary.

Dearest Majesty, The Queen Annelore,

I bring tidings from Thy Royal homeland. May it please Your Majesty to know that Beaubourg is in the best of hands, for Auntie and my cousins have stepped in as town midwives. Though none could match the kind hands of Mistress Mary and Thy Royal Self. My brother Thomas continues to help in Your Majesty's father's, His Grace's, stables as well as manage the merchant faires, which Your Highness used to do with such skill.

I humbly submit my earnest desire that Your Majesty remember that my family and I hold no ill will toward His Gracious Majesty or Your Royal person in regard to our dear Bryan. Indeed, we thank His Majesty for allowing my brother to live, even if that life not be a free one. Thus, I hope you will not find it disrespectful that I most humbly ask on my knees that Your Majesty might allow me to bring my brother some succor and news of home by way of my own person. It would do my Mother heartily well if I could see him with mine own eyes.

We pray for you and His Majesty and hope you will think fondly of us.

Your humble servant and friend,
Charity

Mary sat on the nearest bench as one of the king's speckled spaniels pawed her skirts, begging to be put in her lap. Absently, she picked the pup up and put it on the bench next to her. She opened her mouth twice to speak but stopped, frowning each time.

"I rue the day you taught that girl t' read." Mary harrumphed.

"She had an interest in healing, and you were the one who insisted." Anna saw Mary frown. "Come now, you look as if she's asked to come set Bryan free,"

"I'm only wondering what you're up to." Mary squinted up at Anna. "Like if you be planning on visiting a certain imprisoned lad yourself."

"How on earth could you think such a thing?" Anna stared at her. "He tried to kill my husband. I have no wish to set eyes on him ever again."

Mary clucked. "Don't be getting all high an' mighty 'bout it." She gave the spaniel a swat on the bottom as she rose. "You've been known to do sillier things."

"I'm not that girl anymore." Anna lifted her chin, bidding her heart to stop pounding. Mary handed the letter back then threaded her arm through Anna's, patting the queen's hand as she always did.

"I know yer not, dearie." She gave Anna's hand a motherly peck. "But sometimes I miss that foolish girl."

Mary whistled to the spaniel, who had wedged herself beneath the hedge, brown bottom sticking up in the air and wriggling with excitement. The dog made a snuff and a whine but came as called, bounding down the path in front of them.

"I shall not only allow Charity a brief visit with her brother, Mary. I also want to bring her to court. To become one of my lower ladies."

Mary stopped in her tracks.

"Bernard will have a fit! She's not of rank and more to the point she's the sister of a criminal—the sister of your former beau. Gracious, Anna, be sensible!" She didn't mention what they both knew was the important question: would the king object?

"She'll be a breath of fresh air," Anna said, "something to lighten all our spirits. And the king allows me to keep my own household, a stricture Bernard knows all too well by now."

Anna sounded more confident than she felt. While Charity was not gifted in sense, she sang like a sparrow and her freckled cheeks were always dimpled from a smile. And Anna longed for a sense of home, something to remind her of where she'd come from to help point herself to the future.

"Besides," Anna said, "the giggles of a girl just sixteen will brighten our dreary castle."

Mary let out a heavy sigh and shook her head.

"Well, with you a proper queen now, I suppose I be needing someone new to scold."

That night Anna was restless. Even though she and William had a pleasant evening together—more than pleasant, really—she could not sleep. An aching need welled up inside her to simply be with him, to lie with his body curled around her like a comma. She needed to feel safe.

Not wanting to disturb any of her ladies, she crept out of bed. Halfway to the private hall that connected directly with William's chamber, her stomach rumbled. Certainly Yvette would have left out sweet rolls and fruit. She tiptoed toward the buffet, and, reaching for a pear, she heard whispers. Her hand froze, grasping the fruit. She closed her eyes to hone her ears.

"Why do you care anyway?" Anna would recognize Margaux's disdainful voice anywhere, but she could not hear the muttered response. She slipped to the edge of the ladies' hall and peered down its length. Margaux, standing still fully dressed at the chamber door, was speaking through the peep-door.

"I will see who I want, when I want, where I want." Was she scolding Bernard? It sounded like whoever it was had caught Margaux in an illicit rendezvous. She heard the cadence of a man's voice and though she couldn't make out the words, he was none too happy. Bernard would never take that tone with a woman who outranked him. Anna strained her ears to hear more.

Margaux cackled. "Don't try to act loyal for me, brother. I know what you want and it's not to remain the Duke of Norwick."

Robert! She must discover what deceit was afoot. Daring another glance down the hall, she saw Margaux pull her head away from the peep-door. Finally Anna could clearly hear Robert's words.

". . . if you get in my way!" A foot or fist slammed against his side of the door. He looked up, his black eyes flicking down the hall toward her hiding place. She ducked again behind the wall, trying to steady her breath. What was she to do? She had no proof of anything. Only Margaux's insinuations, and those surely would not go far with the king. She hugged herself, aching even more to go to William's side. But she needed to be alone. She needed to think.

She heard Margaux lock the peephole and rustle her way to the ladies' garderobe. Anna waited until she was convinced Margaux was fully occupied, then crept back to bed, wrapped herself in her cooled comforter, and stared at a slit of moonlight on the stone floor. She would have to investigate. But how?

William startled awake. It was still dark, save for the dying glow of his fire seeping through the half closed bed curtains. He rubbed his eyes, sat up, and gave a mighty yawn. Blinking through the soft light, he saw a figure in his leather chair, sunk low, feet on the chest, staring into the flames. He rubbed his eyes again.

"Trouble sleeping, cuz?" Robert said, a melancholy look on his face.

"What are you doing in my bedchamber in the middle of the night?"

"'Tis my turn at the night watch." He raised his thin black brows.

"I'm not the queen," William said, crawling to the end of his bed and swiping his crumpled trunks off the floor. "I haven't had an in-chamber watchman since I was ten."

Robert leaned forward and poured himself wine from the half-empty decanter on the chest.

"Let's just say I was feeling nostalgic."

"You, sentimental?" William guffawed. He climbed out of bed, pulled on his trunks, and plopped in the chair opposite, usually reserved for Anna. He could smell a faint scent of her there, lavender and a hint of vanilla. He pictured her snuggled beneath her robe, eyes dancing, lips curved, her breath quickening as he—

"Would you like some wine, Majesty?" Robert poured a goblet near to the brim and slid it over to him.

"So it shall be like old times indeed," William said, taking the cup, "drunkenly waxing poetical, political, and theological until the wee hours." Robert raised his glass and took a long swig. "Come, Robert." William ruffled his hair, sending it at all angles, scalp prickling with relief. "Out with it."

"Do you remember that time in Florence?" Robert stared back at the fire. It was rare to find Robert in one of his mulling moods, even more rare, these days, that he would share it with William.

"Which time? We were there for two years."

Robert's eyes twinkled. "The players?"

"How could I forget?" William laughed. "And you're a bastard for bringing it up."

"We all thought she was a woman, Wills." Robert grinned. "Though I'll never forget the sound you made when you figured it out."

"She—he—was quite convincing . . . until his balled-up breasts popped out onto the floor." Though William smiled, his cheeks heated.

"The look on your face." Robert slapped his knee, hooting. "I've never seen a man so crazed."

"All right, all right." William took another drink to hide his embarrassment. "At least I didn't have to see an apothecary after. How's your pecker, by the way? I assume it's well recovered after all this time."

"Would you like to see for yourself?" Robert opened his arms.

"I suffer enough nightmares, thank you very much."

"Suit yourself." Robert took another sip of wine and looked back to the fire. A companionable silence overtook them. "I was actually thinking about that priest," Robert said, breaking the spell, "at Palazzo Pitti."

"The one who accused your mother of witchcraft?" William's face grew grim. He shuddered to think how close he had come to losing his friend. How Robert had brought the hounds of hell down on the smug little cleric, how the Medicis and foreign dignitaries stared at the scene.

"I was wondering why you didn't let me kill the bastard." Robert's face looked calm but his eyes burned.

"Robert, why—"

"I finally figured it out." Robert said. "For so long I thought it was because you didn't want a diplomatic incident on your hands." He set his wine down on the chest and looked at William straight on. "Then I realized—you dishonored yourself in front of important people to save your foolish friend's head."

William shrugged. "You would do the same."

Robert's face softened. "Yes, well, I never thanked you for it."

"You're welcome, I suppose." He met his cousin's black eyes. "But why all this now?"

"I don't rightly know." Robert sat back in his chair with a sigh.

William studied him. He certainly knew that Robert had a

long and detailed memory . . . But wait. It was March fifteenth—
the day Robert's mother was burned. William swallowed, then
fixed a smile on his face.

"If you're still feeling nostalgic, shall we play a hand of cards
so I can win back all the money I lost in our youth?"

Robert smiled at him, a shine in his eyes. "There's a first
time for everything."

"Now, now. It wouldn't be right to beat the king." William
rose and offered Robert a hand up. "Or the man who saved
your life. More than once, I might add."

Robert clasped William as they walked to the table.

"I guess it's fitting I repay you, then."

"With interest," William said.

The king was entertaining the Spanish again. It was St. Joseph's
Day, a lively celebration in Spain, especially in Valencia's namesake city. William even ordered the traditional bonfire, in which
courtiers burned effigies of animals or silly looking people.
And, despite his distaste for Valencia, Robert had to admit he
was enjoying himself. The feast reminded him of the summer
he spent with William and Daniel in Barcelona, pretending to
be young apprentices. Of course they fooled no one, renting
out three apartments above the sea, drinking sangria on their
balcony, popping fresh mussels and squid down their throats.
For what apprentice could afford all that?

And the women . . . well, there was a reason Robert was
drawn to Yvette. She reminded him of that time, she smelled

of it. A time when the only intrigue was seduction, the only worry oversleeping, and the only quarrels Daniel's complaints of William and Robert's slovenly ways.

He exhaled, bringing his mind back to the present. Yvette had told Robert that Valencia was taciturn in her presence, but she would crack him eventually. Robert's eyes sought her out and he smiled across the vast table at her. She raised one perfect brow and looked away, flirting with the Spaniards, cracking them nut by nut.

"And now we shall dance!" The king called to the party at large. "Minstrels, a sarabande." He clapped and turned to the queen, an alluring look on his face. Robert hadn't seen him so relaxed in a long while. Perhaps the queen had put away her foolish superstitions and was getting into his bed more often.

The royal couple took the floor and many courtiers followed, Robert among them, though he was forced by duty and decorum to dance with his sister, her husband ill with a cold.

"Countess." He slipped her slender fingers into his hand. She set her lips in a line. "You seem recovered from your midnight excursions." He weaved around her, keeping his eyes on her face. "Why, you're positively glowing."

"No thanks to you, brother." She spoke through clenched teeth.

He spun her, catching a whiff of roses. He closed his eyes and breathed the scent in again. When he opened them, Margaux was glaring at him with ice-blue eyes.

"Did you burn me in effigy tonight?" His mouth twitched.

"If only that were efficacious." She frowned as she took another spin.

"Tush, tush, my dear." He clucked his tongue. "With our parents gone, it falls to me to look after you."

"I am well past the age of needing a guardian."

"And yet the last time you got up to something, we both could have lost our heads."

She scrunched up her beautiful face, almost as if she were about to stick out her tongue at him, but caught the king looking their way, and her mouth melted into a demure smile.

"Remember this, sister," Robert brought her close to him again, breaking the steps of the dance. "If father couldn't save our mother from the stake, there's nothing I could do to save you."

"Don't drag Mother into this." Margaux searched Robert's face, her upper lip curling. "Besides, I'm smarter than her—"

"You are not her match in anything." He grabbed her arm and pulled her farther from the crowd. "And you stoop to insulting her memory?"

She wrenched from his grip, cheeks red, tears gathering at the corner of her eyes.

"You think because I was younger, because my memories are less clear, that I don't miss her? That I don't wish every day I had a mother who loved me as she did you, who could teach me the ways of women?"

Robert scowled and looked away. Margaux pressed closer, words spilling out.

"The queen mother couldn't bring herself to look at me— not after she did nothing to save Mother. And then you! Off gallivanting with William and Daniel, leaving me here to fend for myself with my only family our spiteful father and a leering king. So take your lectures and your brotherly concern and leave me be!" She wiped her cheeks, and marched toward the Great Hall doors.

It had never occurred to Robert that her hatred of him might not be entirely without reason.

"Norwick!"

Robert startled. It was the king, the queen by his side.

"You look as if you've seen a ghost, my friend," William said, pressing his shoulder. "Come, some sangria and orange spiced cakes should set you right."

As they walked toward the table of towering pastries, they were intercepted by Valencia, red-cheeked and smiling.

"Majesties," he said, his words a slur, "I have never been so comfortable in court as I have here this night."

Robert saw the queen cover a smile with her black lace fan. She was dressed in red and black silks, with ruffles of black and gold embroidery on her skirts and a high gold-spiked crown jutting from her curled and pearled hair. She could have stepped out of a Spanish painting.

"I'm glad to hear it, Your Excellency," William said. "The sangria in particular is quite delectable, no?"

Now it was Robert's turn to hide a smile. Was the king truly teasing the drunken ambassador of their strongest ally?

"Yes, sire." Valencia grinned again. Then Robert knew why the man rarely did so—it made him look like he was straining on a chamber pot. "I was just on my way to find more."

"Oh?" William put a hand on Valencia's back, steering him toward the pastries. "And we were about to partake of cake. Would you like to join us?" He glanced back at Robert and the queen and tilted his head in the direction of the table. "My queen, Your Grace?"

"We'd better rescue him," Anna said, eyes never leaving her husband, a secret delight dancing on her face. She surely was beautiful, though Robert hated to admit it. It made it harder for him to loathe her. He took her arm and trailed behind the king and the bow-legged ambassador.

"If I had a coin for every time I'd said that . . ."

The queen's pleasant mood vanished. "I hear 'tis quite the other way round, Your Grace." She gave him a pointed look as they made their way through curtsying courtiers. "Quite the other way."

Robert took a deep breath through his nose. So he hadn't been mistaken the night he accosted Margaux. He had seen her there, hiding at the corner of the wall. Dammit.

"About the other night," he said, facing her.

"I'm sure you and your sister had much to discuss." She gestured toward the spot where he and Margaux had been standing moments before. "Some intriguing plot, no doubt."

"If I were hatching a plot, it would certainly not involve my sister." The crowd pressed in behind, forcing him closer to the queen, close enough to smell her—that sweet vanilla scent of comfort and cakes, the lavender hint of summer in the wildflower fields. "I must keep watch over my little chick of a sister. For her pecking often leads to drawn blood."

"Whose blood, exactly?" Her face was pleasant, but it was only for those who stumbled and swirled about them.

"You question my fealty?" He gave her his most dashing smile.

"When I hear whispers in darkened halls about plotting for the throne, how could I not?" She moved closer. He took her hand, pulling her right against him, and lowered his lips to her ear.

"Where my sister is concerned, perhaps it is not his throne you should be worried about."

Her lips parted, her breath quickened, lifting her cleavage. In that moment he knew what drew William to her so urgently, so incessantly.

"Do not try to twist this back to Margaux."

"Even though it is her words you use to damn me?" He lowered his voice, drawing his eyes away from her lips. "If you had cared to listen further, you would have heard me throwing her words back in her face."

"So you claim she alone plots for my husband's bed, and for you to have his throne? And you an innocent?" She laughed.

William glanced toward them, eyes narrowed, still guiding Valencia around the delectables. Robert jutted his chin up and smiled. William made a quick strangled-looking face, then went back to Valencia.

"I believe our services are needed, Majesty," Robert said, smiling as if she had not just insinuated treason.

"You have yet to convince me of the need of your service, Your Grace."

Robert took the queen's arm. Her eyes grew large at his impertinence.

"I do not serve the king because he is king alone," he said. "I serve him because he is my friend. And as I've told you before, I will stand with him till the end of my days. Nothing will hinder that vow."

"Even your own sister? Your own blood?" The queen stared straight into his soul and it flinched.

"The king is also my blood, Highness. And dear to me, as my sister is not."

She pulled her arm free, straightened herself, and left him standing there. Watching her go, Robert put a hand to his chest, oddly shaken.

A month later all the arrangements had been made for Charity's arrival at court—all, it seemed, save one.

Anna stood in Daniel's office, digging her nails into the palms of her hands. While she and Daniel disagreed occasionally, this was the first time he'd outright questioned her authority.

"I hardly see how my choice of ladies constitutes state import, Your Grace."

He came to her from behind his desk, hands outstretched to take her own.

"It's not so much the state I worry of." His smile faded when she made no move toward him. "I do not wish to be indelicate, but . . . is the king truly comfortable with the sister of his enemy in the chambers of his queen?"

"I daresay the sister of his enemy is already in my chambers," she said. "Or has Margaux's marriage somehow cooled both her and her brother's ambitions?"

"Robert is not the king's enemy."

"So he says." She flicked her eyes out the window, where William was riding out with Robert and various chambermen for an afternoon airing. "But you know as well as I that Robert schemes for his own ends. And those ends involve him on the throne." She grasped Daniel's hands. "We must help the king to see this, so he will be on his guard."

"Majesty, I have known them both my life entire. Neither would ever move to hurt the other, regardless of circumstance. Or ambition."

Anna let his hands drop and moved back to the window. She watched the men disappear into the forest's edge.

"It's because you know him that you cannot see that he would act upon his ambition." She wished she could pinch her fingers, snatch Robert off his horse and fling him into the Orlea River where he belonged. "But I see how he watches the king. How he whispers with the Spanish and the French. I've even heard him plotting with his sister—"

"Begging your pardon, Majesty, but I feel this conversation has taken a dark turn."

Anna spun around, realizing too late she'd forgotten herself. She'd hoped to make a staunch ally of Daniel, for she felt he had a soft spot for her. But it did not stretch so far as to abandon his loyalties. And if Daniel was anything, he was loyal.

"Excuse me, Your Grace." She stared down at her hands. "You must understand my single-mindedness where His Majesty is concerned. I fear my imagination sometimes runs away with me."

"It is that singleness of mind I would like to recall you to, Highness. You should not bring this girl to court. It will be seen as—"

"It will be seen as what it is, my desire to move forward. To let the past be past. She had nothing to do with Bryan's plots, the king knows this. Besides which, he does not wish to interfere in the running of my household. He has enough to worry about."

"My point exactly, Majesty. Why add to his concerns?"

"His Majesty has not given it a second thought, Your Grace, and neither should you."

"He may not say so, but I'm sure it will trouble him." Daniel straightened an already tidy stack of papers.

"You may have known my husband for much longer than I, but you do not know him as I do." It came out more harshly than she intended. Daniel blushed, thick blond lashes shielding his downcast eyes. She placed a hand on his arm. "Your Grace, I didn't . . ." She sighed. "I've always had a hard time being told what to do, especially when the matter is so personal to me and yet of little to no importance to anyone else."

Daniel raised his eyes and gave a chuckle.

"Ah, Majesty," he said, giving her hand a kiss of fealty, "it's part of your charm."

"And part of yours is your concern for the king's interests, which I appreciate, even when I think you have mistaken them." She squeezed his hand in genuine affection.

"It's why he keeps me." He released her hand and bowed. "And I trust it will be of use to you as well."

"If that is all, Your Grace, I believe we shall be late to privy court. And with His Majesty and His Grace about the woods, I would be loathe to show any hint of slack."

She took her leave, wondering not for the first time what Daniel was actually thinking.

"A Mistress Charity of Beaubourg," the court caller announced, voice ringing above the murmurs of the smattering of courtiers allowed in the throne room.

In she came, dressed in green damask with ivory trim, red curls bouncing about her beaming face. Charity had grown out of her gawky youth and into a blooming young woman.

"Oh, Anna—I mean, Your Majesty," she said, nearly skipping to the dais. Anna laughed and came down to meet her.

"I knew it would do my heart good to see you, my dear." Anna squeezed her friend's hands, then looked at Daniel. His face was flushed, his lips slightly parted. "Your Grace, may I present Mistress Charity of Beaubourg."

Daniel blinked, then cleared his throat.

"Mistress Charity, any friend of the queen's is welcome here at court." Anna watched his eyes travel over Charity's figure, his blush deepening.

"I promise Your Grace that she shall bring much delight to the whole of court." She felt her spirits rise already at the girl's open, happy face.

Daniel cleared his throat again and shifted his weight. "Of course, Majesty, I—I mean to say, she is most welcome."

"Why, Your Grace!" Anna lowered her voice to a whisper as she returned to her throne. "Cat have your tongue? Or is it beauty?"

Daniel frowned. Apparently only William and Robert were allowed to tease him.

"Come now, Your Grace," she said, "we can all see she shall bring youth and verve to court, both of which are sorely needed."

Daniel muttered something she couldn't hear.

"I hope you are right, Majesty," he whispered, "but I fear her inexperience may breed more than mere mishaps." He met Charity's gaze with half-lidded eyes. "You will excuse me." He gathered his papers in his arms and left.

Anna gave Charity a shrug and the girl laughed. "Now," Anna said, coming to Charity's side again and interlacing their arms, "let me show you my chambers."

"Well, goodness me," Mary said, arms wide. "If it isn't little Charity, all grown up now!"

Charity ran to Mary's arms, giggling all the way. Anna had forgotten how much she laughed. At least it was not Brigitte's high-pitched titter.

"Yes, Mary. Anna—" Charity's freckles disappeared in to her blush, "I mean, *Her Majesty* has asked me to be a lady-in-waiting! Isn't it marvelous?"

Anna heard a distinct Margaux-esque snort.

"I know, my girl." Mary released her. "We must see about getting you some proper clothes and teaching you the ways of court. This ain't the country, dearie."

"By all means," Margaux said with a thinly veiled sneer, "I shall call the royal seamstress, Majesty. Or will the Havenside ladies be sufficient?"

Anna gave her a sharp look. "I'm sure the hand-me-downs of the upper ladies can be tailored to fit." Anna focused back on Charity, looking her up and down. "Perhaps even one of my own old gowns."

Brigitte seized Margaux's arm, horror in her eyes. To allow a lady-in-waiting a gown of the queen's was tantamount to declaring her the favorite. Anna knew her arrow had hit the mark.

"Yes, Highness," Margaux said, making a point of broadly displaying her own rich skirts in her curtsy before taking leave to fetch Bernard.

Anna looked over her shoulder to find Charity, mouth agape, staring at the ceiling and about to trip on the steps leading to Anna's bed.

"Mistress Charity," Anna said, "let's get you acquainted with your new companions."

Robert tickled his horse's neck as the steed drank deeply from the forest stream. He and the king were separated from the rest of William's men by an outcropping of rock. His heart boomed from exertion and nerves. He walked a thin line, befriending his papist enemies while trying to convince William to see the light of reformation, not for religion's sake but for practicality. And revenge. The only way to turn the king from Rome was to massage his compassion for his estranged people, while Robert showed a front of support for the papists. And if that resulted in William being dethroned? Certainly Robert could bring about a swift change, even if it brought more war. In the end, it would be worth it.

"For heaven's sake, Robert, speak your mind," the king said. "You've been brooding all morning."

"The Spanish feel we need to push Laureland harder,"

Robert said. "That we should force them to make a public, written declaration of their fealty to the throne and the realm. And if they don't . . ."

"I asked for *your* mind, not that idiot Valencia's." William kicked a large stone, sending it with a plunk to the bottom of the water.

Robert raised his eyes. "Remember when we were in France and got caught in that skirmish at Notre Dame?"

William flinched and looked away. "Why remind me of that horror?" The king, then exiled prince, had killed a boy, not knowing he was a boy. It had made him at once more ferocious in battle and keener to avoid it.

Robert grabbed his shoulders, forcing William to look at him, then quickly dropped his arms, aware of the breech of rank.

"The haunted look in your eyes that day . . . I never want to see it again."

"And what of the Spanish and their desires would crush my soul?"

"If you push Laureland, it could mean civil war."

William sighed and looked to the sky for a moment before speaking.

"Though I hate to admit it, Valencia has a point. We should write up something the lords of Laureland can sign and make public, but the words must be of Troixden loyalty, not Spanish demands." He patted Robert's arm. "You and Daniel write something, then have it to me by week's end."

"As always, I am at your command." Robert gave William a wry grin, then clicked his tongue at his horse. He still couldn't tell if war against Laureland was the best course of action, but for the time being he wanted all options in play. Perhaps, with the unwitting queen's help, William could be convinced to split with Rome. With the Germans and the English in his corner, Robert was sure he could win the resulting war. In any case, there was still much to do, many strings to pull.

CHAPTER 5

To Forgive, Not to Forget

William lay in his bath, steaming, and not just from the hot water.

Daniel had warned him that this new lady-in-waiting would be trouble, but William waved him off despite a twinge of doubt. Why would Anna want Bryan's sister at her side? She obviously liked the girl, and it made him happy to see her happy about something for a change, but that didn't stop the wheels of his mind spinning.

Damn it all to hell. He thrust himself out of the tub, water streaming down his body. He snapped his fingers for a towel, held it to his face and gave a muffled grunt of frustration.

"Send for Her Majesty." Three men jumped to their feet. "The rest of you, leave me."

He paced before his open window, letting the breeze dry him, hoping it would clear his head. He felt like a pressed coil about to snap. He pulled on his trunks, trusting he wouldn't need them for long.

Soon his caller announced the queen. In she swept, a smile on her lips, followed by Mary, Yvette, Lady Jane, and Countess Cariline.

"You brought your entourage?"

Anna's smile vanished. "We were making ready for the feast . . ." Her eyes surveyed his still glistening chest. "I wasn't informed you desired a private audience."

"It takes you two hours to ready yourself for a feast?" Why did he feel like a boy being scolded?

With a flick of the wrist, she dismissed her ladies. "They're preparing for the masque." She walked toward him. "I was playing director."

"I see." He raised a brow. "I trust watching the ladies rehearsal doesn't trump the needs of your husband."

Her face flushed. "Wills, you know it's a feast day—"

"And you know I care not for these ridiculous strictures." Blood roiled through him. He could stand the chatter no longer. In a flash he was around the desk. He caught hold of her shoulders and pulled her to him, attacking her mouth. He wrapped one arm around her waist, reaching for the laces at her back.

Her lips were shut tight, her face muscles straining. She managed to wrench her face away and gasp.

"William!"

He froze, dropping his hands at the horrified look on her face.

"Anna . . ."

Her lips were set in a thin line, her eyes colder than he'd ever seen them.

"Anna, I'm sorry . . .."

Their eyes locked as they both stood, breathing hard. She broke their stare with a stiff curtsy.

"If that is all, Your Majesty."

And before he could say a word, she left his chambers, a chasm in her wake.

Robert told himself that he only had to make it through the masque, then he could finally be alone with Yvette. He shifted in his chair. Hers were the only eyes and ears he trusted—and besides, he needed a good going over.

The sound of clapping turned his attention to the floor. The queen's ladies had assembled, dressed in black and white with props that marked them as the seven virtues: temperance, chastity, charity, kindness—Margaux as humility? Who picked these roles?—patience, and diligence. Three roles had been added: victory, peace, and, since this was a feast, Edesia.

Seven of the king's chambermen, dressed in black as the seven vices, swarmed around the dancers, Bacchus chasing Edesia. The stern Countess Cariline was perfectly cast as temperance, with her severe brow and empty wine jug. Yvette played diligence, black feathers like raven's wings jutting off her head-dress and a Latin tome in her hands, while Brigitte, as Edesia, teased them all.

But it was a freckle-faced girl dressed as charity who grabbed Robert's attention. Her hair was red, not the tabby cat orange of the Earl of Mohrlang's but the red of oak leaves in autumn. Something about her face struck Robert as familiar, but he couldn't think what. She giggled the whole way through as lust and pride chased her about the dance floor, heedless of the choreography.

He glanced up at the throne to see the king's face flushed, his blue eyes fixed on the redhead. William leaned to Robert.

"Is that the new lady?"

Robert grinned. "Wonders never cease. Doth my liege's eyes wander?'

William frowned, but he still blushed. "I only ask if she's the one from Beaubourg."

Robert looked back to the girl, her chest heaving with laughter, exertion giving her cheeks and bosom a rosy glow. So that's who she was—Sir Bryan's sister, barely there a day and already in over her head.

"'Tis a better question for your wife, Highness," Robert said. "Unless you'd rather she weren't aware of your interest?"

William rolled his eyes, adjusted himself in his throne, and returned his attention to the masque.

Robert looked over at Daniel to see if he'd caught the conversation, but he too was staring hard at the dancers, his face even redder than the king's, chin resting on steepled fingers.

Surely not. . .but as Robert followed his gaze, he found the pretty red-haired girl at its end. And there was Margaux, glaring, trying to force the young girl to the rear of the crowd by parading back and forth across the floor, her "humble" purse of burlap swinging from her arm, pausing now and then to flutter her eyes at the king.

Robert stifled a laugh. This was too rich—two men lusting after the same oblivious girl, his sister intent on the disinterested king, and the queen . . . what of the queen?

He hazarded a look across William to find Annelore staring past them all, a faint frown on her face, her mind elsewhere. Had she sensed her husband's attention wandering? If so, she gave no indication. For all Yvette's reports, the queen remained an enigma.

He looked back to the floor and found Yvette standing off the center, an exotic bird with those feathers in her hair. Her eyes seared him even at a distance. Was that desire or anger? Thankfully, he'd soon find out.

"How a silly sixteen-year-old can cause so much trouble is beyond me," Yvette said as she reached across Robert and grabbed a pomegranate.

Robert slapped her bare rump. "Come now, you remember sixteen. The entire point is to be foolish."

She sat on a pillow and glowered at him. "I was never so naïve."

Robert reached a finger out and began to trace the soft skin along her thigh. No one knew Yvette's origins, including her.

She'd been orphaned as an infant, discovered in the textile market by a Lord Parker of Havenside, who'd married her when she was thirteen and left her a childless widow two years later with a title, a large household, and no income. The three years between then and her first appearance at court were a secret she was content to keep.

It had been no easy task to win her. It wasn't until he started to entertain her penchant for intrigue that she finally yielded to him.

"I like to imagine the young, fresh Yvette." He smirked. "In fact, I long to know just how you learned so well the arts of love."

He applied his lips to her kneecap and began sucking. Yvette jerked his head up rudely, his lips releasing with a popping sound.

"My, my." He clicked his tongue. "What have I done to deserve thy scorn, O lady of my heart? You were certainly pleased with me mere moments ago."

She couldn't quite hide a the twitch at the corner of her mouth. "You know I don't like to speak of my life before."

"Yet that life is why we fit so well."

"And that's all you need know." She sucked seeds from the pomegranate, not a drop of juice escaping her mouth.

He rolled his eyes. "A woman of no means must survive as best she can. Do you truly think I care if you—"

"Enough!" She scampered out of bed and snatched up her robe. "I warned you, Robert, if you ever spoke of it—"

"I'm merely making conversation!" He propped himself on an elbow. "Since when is it a crime for a man to want more knowledge of his beloved?"

She drew a silk shift over her head. "I'm hardly your beloved.

Merely your partner in scheming . . . and in bed." She pulled her robe on over her shift.

Robert sat up, aghast. "You don't believe I love you?"

She came to stand between his thighs, running a slender hand down the side of his face.

"I know you don't—any more than I love you." She brushed his lips with her own. "*That's* what makes us fit."

He watched her leave, his head swimming. How could she not love him? It was absurd. And yet, if Yvette was out of his grasp, who else might he have miscalculated?

William sat in his dark chamber, holding a candlestick, gathering his wits. Finally, he walked down the privy hallway that connected his chamber to the queen's. Upon opening the door, he saw that all was quiet and still, Anna's bed curtains shut fast and Charity sitting by the east window for the first ladies watch of the night.

She startled when she saw him, then made to rise. He stayed her with his hand and came toward her, his candle making her hair shine like burnished copper.

"I regret that we have not been formally introduced," William whispered.

"Yes, Majesty, I'm—"

"Shhhh," he motioned with his hand to the quiet chamber. "I know who you are, Mistress Charity." William could see the top of her bosom rise and fall in quick breaths.

"Beg pardon, Majesty," she said, long, light lashes hiding her eyes.

"How long has Her Majesty been asleep?"

"A good two hours, I'd say, my liege." He had to hush her again, and she brought her hands to her mouth to smother a giggle. With effort, she pressed her lips into decorum. "Is there anything I might help you with, Majesty?"

She looked him up and down in all innocence—not like Margaux, who eyed him as she would a leg of lamb. Her bright blue eyes danced in the candlelight, filled only with devotion and willingness to serve. He swallowed.

"You may help me by continuing to watch over the queen and serving her with all the strength and fealty you can muster." He smiled down at her. "For she is precious to me. And to serve her is to serve me."

"Yes, Your Majesty. Nothing would please me better."

He eyed the curtains that shut off his sleeping wife.

"I had hoped to speak with her." He glanced to her writing desk. He could not let the night pass without apology.

He strode over, grabbed a piece of parchment, and held it to his nose. Even the paper smelled like her. He wrote quickly, blotted it, melted her blue wax, and sealed it with his ring, miniature griffin winking in the signet's indentation.

He waved the note in the air, looking for a place to leave it. At her bedside table he saw an empty tankard with a glass vessel next to it, a thin layer of golden liquid in the bottom. He sniffed. Nothing. He stuck his pinky into the glass, bringing a bit of the sticky substance to his mouth. Chamomile, honey, valerian root—Mary's famous sleeping tincture. So William wasn't the only one who'd had trouble getting to sleep that night.

He propped the note against the tankard, turned back to Charity, pointed at the letter, mimed reading it, and then pointed at the queen's bed. Charity nodded. He took one last deep breath, then left the way he'd came.

Anna woke up sluggish. Her tongue felt like burlap. The rest of her felt numb. She contemplated pretending to be sick, but being left alone to wallow in self-pity held no appeal. Perhaps William would tear to her bedside, prostrating himself before her and beg for forgiveness.

A familiar giggle brought her to the present. She cleared her throat to make her wakened state known, hushing the room around her. Lady Jane opened the bed curtains, face meek.

"Highness," she said, with a curtsy. The rest of the ladies were splayed out in a pastel line like a row of spring bulbs. When she nodded they jumped to action, setting about Anna's morning rituals, all except Charity. She hung back, biting her forefinger.

When Anna finally sat to have her hair done—always by Brigitte and Margaux, for as much as these two irked her, they were the most skilled and the most likely to regale her with the gossip of the day—Charity approached with a low curtsy, a letter in her hand. She held it out for Anna.

It was a small piece of parchment with the wax seal broken.

"What is this? Who's been at my desk?"

"No one—that is to say, Majesty . . ." Charity twisted a bit of ribbon around her fingers. "The king wrote it last night on my watch."

"Why would you not wake me?" Anna struggled to reign in her impatience. It wasn't fair to expect Charity to know the etiquette of court so quickly.

"His Majesty didn't want me to." She blushed, looking at the crimson ribbon woven in her hand.

"And you opened this?" Anna frowned.

Charity inclined her head to the side. "He wanted me to, Majesty."

"The king wanted you to read a private note addressed to me?" Anna waved away the sniggering Brigitte and Margaux.

"He pointed at it and made a gesture—he wasn't talking because you were asleep."

"How could you think that would be appropriate?" Margaux said, shaking her head. "Of course, when someone of no rank comes to court — "

"That's enough, Countess." But Anna knew Margaux was right. She took hold of Charity's shoulders. "It is entirely improper to read anything addressed to another, especially if that correspondence is between your betters."

Charity's blue eyes looked into Anna's, void of any guile, wetness starting at the corners.

"I thought . . . he—he was so kind to me."

Anna's gut clenched again. She had seen how William watched Charity at the feast. Kind indeed. She pursed her lips and sat back in her chair, allowing Margaux and Brigitte to finish their creation.

"His Majesty is quite kind," Margaux whispered into Anna's ear.

"Attend to your work, Countess," Anna said, trying her best to appear unfazed. She opened the note.

> *Can you ever forgive your fool of a husband?*
> *He loves you. He loves you.*
> ~ X, WR

And to think that Charity had read something so personal, so intimate. She looked at the girl, who sat near the window, face hangdog.

"I was young and imprudent once too, Charity," Anna said, giving her a motherly smile. "You will learn." And Anna hoped that were true.

The first time Anna could see William would be in public. Having slept through mass thanks to Mary's sleep serum, she'd have to present herself in the throne room and hope he would know all was forgiven. Not forgotten, but forgiven nonetheless.

She dressed in the royal blue damask he liked, with the velvet green piping and gold bodice. A sapphire diadem was tucked in the elaborate swirl of braids and curls Margaux had devised.

Leaving Charity behind under the tutelage of Mary, Lady Jane, and Yvette, Anna went to the throne room with the rest of her ladies. A moment before entering she pulled from her bodice the long gold chain that held its rough-cut ruby. William's heart, he had said. She'd promised she would always wear it next to hers. She clutched the ruby, said a prayer, then let the gem fall. It felt strange to wear it for all to see, especially as it was only meant for the eyes of one.

She was announced and rounded the corner of the throne dais, resisting the urge to look at him. When she came to the front of the steps, she gave him a formal curtsy, suddenly nervous and unsure of herself. She looked up, straight into his eyes. His cheeks were tinged with red, smile broad.

He bounded down to her and offered his hand. It shook ever so slightly. She slipped her fingers over his, and he covered them with his other hand. Bringing her hand to his lips, he drew in her knuckles then pressed her palm to his face.

"Majesty," he said, "you are stunning today. Is she not, my lords?"

Robert, Daniel, and various other men concurred. William led her up the steps, eyes traveling down to the ruby.

"Thank you," he whispered and kissed her hand once more. Even after she sat, he held it.

Her presence at privy court turned out to be useful, and not only for making amends with William. She was able to help a woman from the southwest, translating her pigeon French. Her husband had died, and the law said his brother should get her land, the little she had. The brother was unwilling to allow her and her five children to stay in the house they'd always known, farming the fields they knew like the backs of their hands. William ordered the brother to court, and in the meantime the woman was given a small sum so she could await his arrival.

There was also a quarrel between midwives from Duven, each claiming the other used witchcraft. William was quick to see that they both wanted to be the sole midwife in the duchy, and the competition had gone to extremes. Anna suggested they combine their services, saving money by sharing resources and tools. They didn't like the idea but could see the sense of it, so they acquiesced.

Happy that she and William were a team again, she readily agreed when he suggested she join Robert and Daniel while they reviewed the latest draft of the Laurelander's public statement.

William drew her into the window alcove of his chambers while Robert and Daniel readied the pages. Anna had read them, and by then William no doubt knew them by heart.

He held her face in his hands, almost as if he were afraid to touch her.

"Anna, my dear . . ." He shook his head. "You are good to forgive me."

She rose up on tiptoes, lips finding his, pressing in. She released him with a satisfied hum.

"You were not yourself, Wills." She circled her arms around his waist, pulling him toward her. "Shall we start over this evening?"

"Majesties?" Daniel said.

William bent down and gave her one more kiss. It was gentle and sweet, filled with longing and remorse.

"I love you," she said, snaking her arm through his as they faced the dukes, "and nothing you can say or do will ever change that."

"And may I not test that declaration." He gave her a nip on the side of her neck.

She held back a grin as he seated her next to him at the table. Daniel cleared his throat.

"Majesty? Do you have further suggestions?"

"It's fine, Daniel."

"Actually, cuz," Robert said, "I think there should be something further on swearing allegiance to any heirs."

"I agree," Anna said, shooting a glance at Robert, "there should be something more explicit about your future children, Majesty."

"You see?" Robert said. "It's already confusing."

"This is only meant to be a way for us to measure their earnestness, their desire to remain in the realm," Daniel said. "Swearing allegiance down generations may confuse the matter."

"How exactly?" Anna raised a brow.

"It's more confusing that no successor is mentioned at all." Robert sat back in his chair and crossed his arms. "Do they swear allegiance only to William, or to whomever is king?"

Was William not listening to this? How could he hear it and still claim Robert had his best interests at heart?

"And with you next in line, Your Grace," Anna said, "does it not confuse them the more? It should clearly say King William and his issue."

Robert stared daggers at her. "The issue," he said, "is the lack of issue."

"Robert!" William shot out of his chair, fist banging the table.

Daniel sighed. "This is why I left the whole heir line out in the first place."

"And yet," Anna said, "this is what happens when it is brushed aside. Wars start, even amongst old friends."

"The difference is that Wills and I always kiss and make up," Robert said.

William threw a balled-up paper with swift accuracy, hitting Robert square in the nose. Though they acted playful, Anna caught the glint of anger in both men's eyes.

"The queen is right," William said. "There should be a clause about my heirs. I don't see why this oath should not be permanently binding down through my grandchildren's grandchildren."

"I thought you approved of it as written," Daniel said.

"Indeed, but the queen makes a valid point." William squeezed her hand. "Show me some new verbiage including the heirs, and we can give it another airing at council tomorrow."

"Of course, my liege." Daniel started to gather his papers. Anna noted the tips of his ears reddening.

"Good man." William got up and slapped Daniel's shoulder. "The English ambassador has asked for an audience before supper. Shall we?" He bent over, lightly kissing Anna's forehead. "Until tonight, my dear."

She met his eyes and they fired with his desire for her.

"Tonight, my liege."

Weeks later, Anna woke in the early morning, contented. While she and William had not regained the full ease of their early days together, she felt those carefree days had bloomed into something more genuine, more full, more unifying.

She heard the soft puttering of an early rising lady and peeped through her curtain to see who shared her wakefulness. She saw the back of a golden blond head, bowed over something. Anna could only see the profile of her face, but when Margaux looked up, she was smiling. She tucked a piece of paper in her bosom, pinched her already rosy cheeks, and tiptoed over to the plates of food. Glancing around, she grabbed a woven basket and snatched two sweet rolls and a pear, a bushel of grapes, a hunk of cheese, and a carafe of wine.

Anna crept closer to the slit in her bed curtain, entranced by Margaux's clandestine activities. It was the first time she had ever seen the woman genuinely happy.

Margaux silently walked to the door, pinched her cheeks one last time, looked around again, and slipped out.

Anna lie back against her pillows, mind a whirl. Where was Margaux going with that load of food, and why was she smiling so?

Chapter 6

Time Opens All Wounds

*R*obert stood silent in a sunlit alcove of the near empty Great Hall, the rest of court having joined the king and queen on a late winter picnic in the woods now that the snow was melted. It was already almost a year since the queen's miscarriage, and while the royal couple gave an outward show of joviality, Robert knew tension continued between them.

Bartmore and Valencia stood twitching at Robert's left, whispering to Daniel. Robert was only half listening. He loathed playing conspirator with the archbishop and the Spanish ambassador, but play he must. Play and spin, spin and weave.

"'Tis absolutely God's judgment upon them," Bartmore said. "First the miscarriage and now her continued barrenness."

"Daily I see how His Majesty's devotion to the Holy Father withers," Valencia said, trilling his r's, "and how she whispers to him. They've even invited that upstart Franciscan to say mass. My Lord Duke, I do not demure when I say King Philip grows uneasy. With the false Queen of England offering a hand of friendship to Troixden, and the king's lenience toward the heretics in his own land . . ." He trailed off, as though the prospect were too grim to put into words.

Bartmore grabbed Daniel's arm. "We would hate to see our precious realm fall prey to the religious wars of our neighbors in France, let alone England."

"Gentlemen," Daniel said, "this is nothing I have not heard before, and I tell you again, the king—and the queen—are constant in their devotion to the true faith."

"Then how do you explain their lack of child?" Bartmore said. Robert snorted. While Bartmore was imbecilic, he knew better than to trade in superstitions. "Norwick, surely you agree? Something must be done about the queen."

Robert stopped inspecting his nails and gave a noncommittal shrug. Why was he so listless? Normally he would be right in the middle of this, working it all to his advantage.

Daniel addressed Valencia. "Milord, might you excuse us if you please?"

"Of course, Your Grace," Valencia said, "and what shall I tell My Majesty of Your Majesty's state of mind?"

"His Majesty is, as always, true to his friends and to the church." Though Daniel still smiled, his eyes were sharp, unyielding. "That will be all." Daniel waited for Valencia to take his leave before turning on Bartmore, all grace gone. "Archbishop, I

continue to be surprised at how willing you are to air the private
business of the king with our fair ambassador."

Bartmore waved a bejeweled hand. "'Tis common knowledge
the queen is barren."

"One pregnancy in two years is hardly barren." Daniel looked
out the window, sun reflecting off his pale hair, face stony.

"This marriage was doomed from the start, as you well know,
Cecile." Bartmore sniffed like he smelled rotting trout. Robert
could have slapped the man. He never missed a chance to
diminish Daniel.

"Common knowledge or no," Robert said, "'tis unbecoming
to speak ill of your sovereign to the ears of a foreigner—and to
speak of it as a judgment of God even worse."

"I will not be spoken to like a common courtier!" Bartmore
said. "You forget that I serve God and 'tis I who speak on his
behalf."

"I didn't realize that idle gossip had become pronouncements of God," Daniel said.

Bartmore's frown deepened. "Just because your own grip on
the king's affections is waning," he said, "don't take it out on
me." The archbishop left in a swirl of purple.

"Bartmore's an ass." Robert nudged Daniel with his elbow.

"That may be," Daniel said, staring after the man, "but he's
an observant ass."

Annelore arrived in William's chambers at ten o'clock that evening. While he was expecting the news, she knew it would still

disappoint him. She felt as if all she had given him in the past year was disappointment, though he showed no sign in his manner, his care, or his words of love.

"Again," he said. His hands rested on the windowsill, an untouched glass of wine on the desk.

"Let's not let it ruin the evening, Wills," she said, coming up behind him and wrapping her arms through his. He covered her hands in his and brought them to his lips.

"Nay, my sweet. 'Twas a pleasant picnic to be sure." He embraced her, lips to her forehead. "I should've known when you ate so much cured meat."

"Cured meat?" She laughed.

He gave her a funny look she couldn't decipher. "Don't you know the peculiarities that signify your courses?"

"'Tis dear that you observe me more closely than I do myself." She searched his face. Her own mother had taken ten years to bear a healthy child, yet with each month Anna grew more anxious.

William picked up his wine and sat in his customary chair by the empty hearth.

"Come, dearest." He patted his thigh. She joined him, curling in his lap, feet dangling over the chair's arm.

"I still think we should do something more," she said. "Perhaps if we went to visit the Holy Father in person to get his absolution."

William grimaced. "We've both confessed every minuscule transgression. Even if conceiving the babe on a feast day brought all this about, the loss of him was certainly punishment enough."

"Then why do we fail to conceive another?" She knew such talk frustrated him, but with every start of her monthly bleeding she could not help but wonder what might be keeping a child from her womb. Every day she turned over her actions—what had she done or eaten or said? And the court gossip did not help. Try as she might to ignore the likes of Bartmore and his stooges, the thought that God may have turned his face from her, from them, struck her soul in ways she did not think possible.

"Why do you try me so?" William sounded more tired than angry. "Please, Anna, heathen couples have children all the time! As for you, you've been so fastidious about keeping every possible holy day we barely have opportunity to plant the seed! And now you're bleeding again on the first day in weeks that has not been a feast day, a saint day, or a Sunday. Easter may be a joy in our faith, but nothing is rising again for me."

"Wills!" She could not help smiling. She caught the twinkle in his eyes and relaxed, pulling at the chain that held the ruby. She fiddled with the jewel, squeezing it in her palm, running her thumb over its bumpy surface, feeling the residual heat it held from her breast.

"I don't mean to try you," she said. "And of course I miss the frequency of our coupling."

The corners of his lips curled. "And here I thought it was only a means to an end."

Suddenly he tickled her rib cage, sending her into convulsions.

"Stop, I surrender!"

He halted as quickly as he had started. Bringing a forefinger to her face, he traced her features with a light caress. First her eyebrow, then her nose, the hilt of her cheek, her jaw, resting finally on her lips. She bit his finger.

"And what about the arts Lady Yvette spoke of? Shall we give them a go again?" His voice was pitched low. She was sure her face was scarlet.

"Oh, well, I ..." She could not help feeling, even amid the pleasure these acts brought them both, that she was somehow lowering herself in his eyes each time they performed them.

"Come now, my love. 'Tis better than my seeking comfort elsewhere, is it not?"

She stiffened. "How could you even jest of it?"

"Anna, I beg of you," he said, exhaustion in his voice. "Everywhere I must watch my words, curb my humor, ignore my desires. Shall our bed become one more place where I am not free to be myself?"

She rose from his lap and began pacing by the hearth, arms crossed.

"But I must be myself as well. To pretend we have not suffered loss, to pretend I don't fear your succumbing to the arms of another? I promised you a place to forget you're king, not forget we're human."

He rose as well. "How can I forget I'm king when you drag it before me each night? How can I cast out the demons of court when they follow me here through your admonishments of sin?"

She shook her head. She was so weary of this. "I accuse you of no sin. I am not your confessor."

"Nay, you are my wife," he said. "I beg you to be that—only that. Have I ever—ever!—given you cause to fear another?"

She closed her eyes and remembered the night of their consummation, how she had scrambled to his chambers in the desperate hope she would find him alone. She smiled.

As if reading her mind, he said, "After that, I mean."

"I'm sorry." She walked to him, his arms enfolding her. "I miss you. I miss *us*. I miss our easy times." She relaxed into his arms, reveling in the warmth of his chest, feeling his heart beat against her cheek.

He drew her closer, stroking her hair. "Ah, my Anna. Why is it those we love can sting us the most?"

"Forgive my silly heart," she whispered.

"You're still the only woman I ever want to be with, even with your stings."

Her fingers crept up to the ties of his shirt, unlacing them to reveal a sweaty clavicle. She brought her mouth to its rounded end, then worked her way up to the nape of his neck with slow, moist lips. He groaned as she felt his urgency rising against her. He grabbed her face in both of his hands, brushing, then opening her lips.

"All is forgiven," he breathed. He lifted her in his arms and carried her to his bed.

A week later, Bartmore swept in to supper, red-faced and glaring at Anna. But by the time he raised his hands to give the blessing, his hooked nose high in the air, he had gathered himself.

Anna had invited Multman, the young Franciscan priest of Havenside Church, to a private supper. Both she and William were curious about his work, for where the city governance had failed, it seemed this lowly priest had succeeded, helping the lame and the orphaned to find work and homes. While some muttered about his "reformist zeal," Anna believed his actions sprang from deep devotion to Christ and his church. She eyed the archbishop over her wine. Let him sit and stew along with his lamb.

The talk was pleasant, the king showing interest in Multman's ideas about the poor in the city and what could be done to help them, while Bartmore occasionally harrumphed to himself.

"And what say you on the question of sin and absolution?" The king said with a hint of a grin. Annelore met his eyes. So he would resolve their argument not by consulting the pope but by asking this novice priest? What could this man say that had not already been hashed out between them?

"Majesty," Multman said, "that is quite a lengthy topic."

The king laughed. "Then I shall rephrase. If one has sinned, confessed and paid his penance, what then? Does God exact punishment in perpetuity?"

The priest stared at his plate, soft brow furrowed. After a moment he looked up and met the king's gaze.

"Highness, begging your pardon, but it seems to me inherent in the question is a misunderstanding of sin and of penance." Bartmore cleared his throat, about to speak, but William raised a hand to stop him. "While the Lord does forgive our sin— indeed, flings it from us as far as east is from west," Multman said, "the consequences of that sin may still manifest in one's life. Say a man steals from another. He may confess and be absolved by the church and God yet still be jailed for his crimes, perhaps lose his hand. Those consequences are not removed simply because one is forgiven by God. Remember, 'tis Christ Jesus who takes sin away, not one's confession."

"Surely," Bartmore said, "you are not suggesting confession is unnecessary?"

"Your Eminence," Multman said, "as you of course know, priestly absolution is merely an acknowledgement of the fact of Christ's atonement. 'Tis not we who hold the power to cleanse men of sin—it is Christ and Christ alone."

"And priests act in Christ's stead," Bartmore said.

"It's more that we act on Christ's *behalf*." Multman said. "Lord Jesus is the one who has washed us clean, Your Grace."

"But still," Anna said, heart racing, "when one has done one's penance, why does it seem God has turned his face away? I speak not of consequences but of wrath."

"When one's penance is done with pure heart, God sees and knows. And while it may seem he has turned his face, be not despaired." The priest stretched his hand across the table as if to take hers. "He will not be long from thee."

Annelore sat back, startled at his informality. She stroked the ruby's chain at her neck, feeling its snake-like links. William glanced at her with a brief smile.

"Our faith," Multman said to the table at large, "is not about sin and penance, reward and rebuke. Out of our love for Lord Jesus, and his for us, we strive toward holiness. We are not dogs who must be taught the same lesson over and over again."

"My dear vicar," Bartmore said, "if only that were all it meant to follow God."

"What more is needed then, Your Eminence?" Anna said,

captivated by the beautiful simplicity of the vicar's words. Who was Bartmore to crush them like spring violets under his foot?

"Majesty," Bartmore said, "you forget the duties involved in such striving."

"And the church is right there to help us dogs along?" William arched a brow at Bartmore.

"As His Majesty knows," he said, "church law and custom are instituted by God and the holy church to guide and edify—"

"Don't get Her Majesty started on church law," William said, "for she knows them more fully than any cardinal."

"And what a cardinal she would make!" Multman said with true mirth, clapping his hands. "I can just see Her Majesty instructing her students in Greek. They'd swoon at her feet and hear not a word—much to their own detriment."

"More peacock than cardinal," she heard Bartmore mumble as the rest of the table toasted her loveliness in appearance and mind.

"I have not even heard of this saint, Anna," William said, coming up behind her, his lips finding the base of her neck beneath the chestnut curtain of her hair. She felt the tip of his tongue flick the knob of her spine. "Surely you shan't refuse me on his obscure account?" Her shoulders shuddered as he made to push her nightdress down, but coming to, she grabbed his hands.

"Do we not honor God more when we are more tempted yet resist?"

His mouth stopped its progression but he didn't move away,

his hot breath sending shivers all the way to her toenails, her groin starting to pulsate, his hands moving to her front.

"You heard Multman. Besides, there's nothing of marital restriction in scripture, other than St. Paul's—and that only for a time of prayer and fasting."

"Yes, but . . ." A thumb traced the skin under her breast.

"Are we fasting?" He lightly bit the side of her neck.

She shook her head.

"And, dear lady, are we praying?" A hand pulled her flimsy gown down.

She trembled, knees about to give way. He spun her to face him, his eyes drowsy with desire. He drew her against his warm body.

"So this saint you speak of . . ."

She grabbed the back of his head, bringing him to her. She kissed him hard and long, her tongue finding his, finishing with a leisurely suck on his lower lip.

"What saint?"

Robert had never seen Bartmore look worried. And to see him thus was amusing, though the cause was not.

He glanced down again at the tract the archbishop had presented, a caricature of the king laughing, grotesque, as flames consumed an old man. The anonymous Laureland author claimed it depicted the death of the stonemason Fitzroy.

Robert remembered Fitzroy's case vividly, as it brought into his collection a rare and contraband Lutheran Bible. The mason had received it as a dowry, and being illiterate, did not know of his crime until the archbishop dragged him to the dungeon. Bartmore wanted him burned, but William showed mercy, and Robert took the book. That was the last he'd heard of the man until Bartmore hurried into his office, face the color of moldy cheese.

"This should be welcome news to you, Eminence." Robert sat back in his chair, arms crossed over his chest. "You've wanted an excuse to clear out the heretics of Laureland for quite some time."

Bartmore crinkled his nose. "Wars are bloody things."

Robert's mouth twitched. "Don't tell me you're squeamish?"

"There's a reason I'm a churchman."

"So you prefer burning people to stabbing them?"

Bartmore's eyes bulged. "We burn heretics so they get a taste of hell before they die, that they may fear it and repent!" He hit Robert's desk, toppling an ink bottle. "The burning is a mercy to save their souls."

"Did it save my mother's?"

Bartmore frowned.

"I apologize, Your Grace," Robert said. He must remember not to insult Bartmore, even though the man had stood by chanting useless Latin as Robert's mother roasted. "This tract has got my hackles up. You say it came to you anonymously?"

Bartmore nodded. "Why did you not bring it to the king immediately? Why come to me?"

"You know the king doesn't take kindly to me." Bartmore's lips thinned. "He would think it was my doing."

"Was it?"

"What earthly benefit could this be to me?"

Robert looked long at the archbishop. They both knew that keeping Troixden firmly in papal hands would earn the man a cardinal's hat. And they both knew he would stop at nothing to get it.

"This is utterly ridiculous." William glowered at his councilmen, the tract crumpled in his hand. "The stonemason died of pneumonia months after his release."

"Regardless, Majesty," Daniel said, "the people in Laureland are up in arms."

The grand master general stroked his beard. "The question is, do they march?"

"The question," Timothy, Earl of Ridgeland, said, "is when do *we* march?"

"Ridgeland, we've been through this before." William started to pace. "They proclaimed and signed the statement of fealty. We must wait until we have convincing evidence of their ill intentions."

"But, sire, why must we always be on the defensive?" Ridgeland said. "Why not hit them straight on, teach them a lesson?"

William stopped in front of the wall of windows which overlooked the stables, Stone Yard, and the sodden hills beyond. The only sound in the room was the late winter wind whipping sleet against the panes. He drew a deep breath.

"We shall not take up arms against our people." He faced his councilors, none of whom dared meet his eyes. "If war we shall have, it shall not be commenced by the crown."

"And yet," the general said, gesturing at Daniel, "this diplomacy His Grace is so fond of has gotten us nowhere."

"Send me," Robert said.

Glances shot back and forth across the table, but William kept his eyes on Robert. He chuckled and resumed his seat.

"Our dear Norwick, why would we send such a handsome face into harm's way?" William said. "And yet . . .'tis not a terrible idea." A flutter of objections met this. William held up a hand. "We shall send you and the mason's widow," he said, "at the head of a sizeable train of knights and men. You will show Laureland their fallacy and calm their fears."

"Majesty," Ridgeland said, "clearly they have no wish to respect the declaration we sent them. The time for peace and reassurance is at an end—"

William surged out of his chair. "The time for peace will never be at an end if we can help it." He held Ridgeland frozen with his gaze. "We have seen enough bloodshed! We will not doom our people, no matter how bloodthirsty my council."

"Then it's settled," Robert said. "I'll ride to Laureland with my men and return with a declaration of abiding peace or the earl's head on a spike, yes?"

"Your Grace," Daniel said, "that's hardly the attitude—"

William's laugh cut him off.

"Norwick, you're always the man for the job."

CHAPTER 7

Sticks & Stones

*R*obert left council in a jolly mood. William was sending him—and him alone—to have it out with the Laurelanders. He could negotiate a final peace on conditions William would have to agree to, or . . .

Glancing up he saw his sister, clutching her damp cloak about her as she hurried along the sidewalls of the Great Hall. Her cheeks were red, lips a bit swollen, tendrils of hair loose about her face. He strolled toward her.

"Why, sis, you seem flushed."

"I bring sustenance to the poor and imprisoned as Christ Jesus admonishes us." She hoisted up a large basket for his inspection, gesturing with her other hand to where Stone Yard and the outer keep stood.

"Has your pregnancy turned you benevolent? Or religious? Or is there some other cause for your . . . glow?" He smirked as her eyes narrowed.

"What I do is no business of yours." She made to continue on her way, but he took her arm, escorting her toward her rooms. Her cloak was indeed damp, but she was warm beneath it. She hadn't been in the weather for long. She smelled of dank earth with a tinge of animal sweat. Perhaps there *was* a stable boy.

She stopped and yanked her arm out of his. "Why can't you just go away?"

"You'll be happy to learn that I am," he said. "I head to Laureland in two days' time. And I expect you to be the picture of obedience while I'm gone."

She made a face. "Do enjoy your journey."

Her eyes roved over him, then gave him a brief curtsy and hurried off.

He frowned. The day just got more interesting.

Anna's hands absently worked her needlepoint as Margaux continued to prattle.

". . . and my brother is to lead the way," Margaux said, squinting at her stitching.

"Norwick?" Anna's mouth turned down, the pleasant afternoon soured. "He is to negotiate in the king's name?"

Margaux's lovely skin turned scarlet. She inspected an imaginary knot in her string.

"I suppose His Majesty felt my brother is the appropriate messenger, being next in line." Margaux's hand went to the minuscule pouch at her belly. She was three months pregnant and radiant. Many whispered it was William's child.

Anna's hands trembled on her own needlework. If she didn't know William as she did, she might believe it. But no matter whose child it was, royal blood flowed through it from Margaux's line, both an affront and a threat.

None of Anna's other ladies spoke. Even Charity kept to her work, mouth clamped shut. The sound of the minstrels' flutes lapped over them. Anna let out a slow exhale.

"I see." She yanked her thread through one of William's shirt collars, tearing the delicate hem. "Well, I'm sure he'll do His Majesty proud."

Margaux flicked her eyes to Anna then returned to her work. Yvette rose from the silk floor pillows.

"Refreshment, Majesty?"

"Lovely, Yvette. Wine and a sweet roll, if you please."

"And some for me too, Lady Yvette," Margaux said. "Growing a baby surely gives one an appetite." She gave Anna a honeyed smile.

Anna threw the ruined shirt in a heap.

"On second thought, I've lost my appetite."

"William, how could you?" Anna's hands were white fists at her sides. "You should have at least discussed it with me!"

William had sent for her later than usual that evening, which made her even more agitated. The fire roared in the hearth, casting shadows across his face, darkening his eyes. He stared at her, then looked at the fire.

"I daresay it isn't your decision to make, my dear."

"So I have no say in your losing your head to Robert's sword?" She put her hands on her hips. "He'll come back with an army of Laurelanders—"

"Anna, please. These conspiracies are exhausting." He leaned his head back and closed his eyes. She knew his day had been long and fractious, knew she should offer him some distraction, some comfort, but the way he ignored Robert's machinations was dangerous.

"You forget how much we depend on you."

His eyes matched her ire. "And you forget that you aren't the only one who cares for our realm."

"I care about *you*, damnable man!" She took two steps toward him. "Can't you see he wants your throne? I told you I heard him plotting with Margaux—"

"So the nattering of Margaux is what you have to go on?" William ran his hands through his hair, shaking his head.

"It's not only that. The way he works everything—even a cut of meat—to his advantage—"

"You don't know him as I do." He stood and brushed past her, walking to the desk. "He would never betray me."

"We never found out who wrote those queer letters to Bryan.

And now this 'anonymous' pamphlet, the perfect excuse to send Robert to Laureland—"

"Stop!" He slammed his palms against the desk, upsetting a candle and setting a parchment to burning. He pounded out the flames with his fist. "I'm sick to death of this, do you hear me? Robert's not the villain in some drama you've created." He winced, bringing the side of his hand to his mouth and sucking on the burn.

"Let me get some salve—" She reached for his hand. He jerked away.

"No, just . . ." He sighed. "Just go."

"But, Wills—"

"Dammit, Anna!"

She crossed her arms to stop them from trembling.

"Fine, *Majesty*," she said. "But don't be surprised if the next time you see me it's looking down at your grave, dug by your trustworthy Robert. Until then, perhaps *he* can keep you warm at night."

She left, head high. As the great wooden doors closed, she heard a heavy thud against them, followed by the clang of metal falling on stone.

Anna woke the next morning to the sounds of the stable making ready for a large party. She didn't recall there being an outing today. The memory of her fight with William hit her with full force, churning her stomach. With half-open eyes, she spied her ladies starting her morning toilette. Mary came to wash her hands with rosewater. If only they could wash away this unresolved tension.

"Mistress Mary," Anna said, trying her best to sound ambivalent, "who rides today?"

"The king rides, Majesty."

What on earth? Had he decided to ride out to Laureland himself? Without telling her? Certainly they'd fought, but ... She let Yvette dry her hands, and with all the dignity she could project, she walked to the east windows and peered down at the men gathered outside the stables.

Horses nickered and pawed the ground, plumes of white breath shooting from their noses. The men huddled around a fire warming their gloved hands, all clad in thick fur capes and leather boots. William stood amid them, cheeks reddened by the wind, laughing at some comment, but the muted sound rang false to her ears. Pages and chambermen darted about, some carrying bows, others food. So it was to be a hunt.

William made comment to his companions, rubbed his hands together over the fire, and looked up to her window. She backed away. What did they think they would catch in this weather other than colds?

There was a quick pound of staff at her door. "The Duke of Cecile to see Her Majesty."

"Tell him I am indisposed at present."

A brief conversation transpired at the door. "His Grace begs to wait outside chamber."

"As he pleases."

If Daniel was waiting, that meant William had left her with duties to perform while he pranced around the countryside seeking his pleasure. Served him right if he did catch cold.

Anna's prediction was correct. She had a full schedule that day, presiding over petty grievances and requests for alms and other small sums. The fiercer the weather the longer the line, and by the time she returned to her rooms to ready herself for a late dinner with the archbishop and Daniel, she was exhausted and out of sorts.

She slumped onto the bed. While Lady Jane removed Anna's shoes and began to massage her feet, Anna heard the sounds of the hunters' return. She expected them at nightfall, but the wind and poor weather had likely driven them home early. Well, William could rub his own cold feet.

"Majesty," Jane said, looking down, "I—I was unable to attend petty court today."

"'Twas not your duty, Lady Jane. Don't fret." She smiled at the most sweet and petite of her ladies.

"I mean to say, Majesty," she said as she placed slippers lined with rabbit fur on Anna's feet, "that I wished to bring a request."

"Why Lady Jane, you needn't wait for court to ask me a favor. Surely you know I would do whatever I could to help you."

"Forgive me, Majesty." She was so quiet Anna could barely make out her words. "It's my son. He's . . ." She brought her hands to her mouth.

Anna drew her up to sit on the bed. "Tell me, my dear."

Jane stared down at her trembling hands. "He's ill. He's had a cough that lingers on and on."

"I'll send Mistress Mary right away."

Jane shook her head. "Please, Majesty, I don't think you need spare Mistress Mary. But perhaps, if she could mix a concoction?"

Anna smoothed Jane's hands. "Mary will make an appropriate serum, and I'll pay out of my own purse for as much of it as you need until he's on the mend."

Jane looked up, her hazel eyes wide. "Majesty, I can't—"

"Tush, Lady Jane, it's settled."

Anna heard men bustling toward William's rooms. She hoped he would change quickly enough to join her at dinner. She hated attending on Bartmore without William's support, especially after his performance with Multman. Come to think of it, she should have been called to dinner by then.

"Fetch Bernard," she said to no one in particular. "And a little music and some wine, I think." Margaux hurried to fulfill the requests, beating eager Charity to the task.

Anna got up from the bed and paced. She found herself staring down at the stables. Two cloaks lay crumpled on the ground, trampled by the horses, bows were tossed aside like sticks. The stable hands scrambled to keep their charges in check. Her stomach clenched with hunger and something else she couldn't place. Ugh, where was Bernard and the call for dinner?

To her relief, her chamber doors flew open, Bernard charging in, Margaux hot on his tail. His hands were empty.

"Majesty," he said, face splotched with exertion, "despite

what others claim, I thought you would want to know—"

"Bernard!" Margaux grabbed his arm. "Don't trouble Her Majesty when there's nothing to be done."

Bernard shook her off. Another one of their tiffs. Anna swallowed a groan.

"I would rather be wrong now and face censure later than keep silent and lose Her Majesty's trust."

"Whatever is the matter?" Anna said.

"His Majesty has had an accident—"

Every fiber in her snapped to attention. It couldn't be. She pushed past Bernard and charged down the hall.

"But they won't let you in, Highness!" Bernard called after her.

"Mary!" she yelled, her call reverberating off the stones. She lifted her skirts and ran.

"Protocol be damned, you will open these doors at once!" Anna was past caring what this gathered group of guards and councilors thought of her. Her husband was lying, perhaps unconscious, surrounded by people more concerned with their positions than his welfare.

"But, Majesty," Halforn said, "the doctors need as little distraction as possible. And Norwick and Cecile will—"

Anna grabbed Halforn's hand and yanked him toward her, his round, pink face shocked.

"Your Grace, if you don't let me in this instant, I'll make King James's reign look like a spring festival."

He swallowed, then nodded. The men parted, and a guard

opened the great wood doors. She edged her way in, Mary close behind.

Men talking in hushed tones crowded around the bed, hiding William from view. She started toward the dais. Robert caught her eyes and moved to intercept her.

"Highness," he said, voice barely above a whisper, "of course you want to see him, but the king needs rest."

She could see out of the corner of her eye, her husband's boot. They hadn't even bothered to undress him.

"He needs his wife." She shouldered past Robert and beheld William lying on the bed, still in his hunting clothes. His eyes were closed, but he was breathing steadily. A quick glance revealed that there was no blood on him. She fell to her knees at his bedside, seized his hand, and stroked the hair from his forehead.

"Wills, my love."

His mouth twitched and he opened his eyes halfway.

"Too informal in public, my dear."

"I could give a gnat's arse at the moment."

He chuckled but winced, grabbing his shoulder.

Thank God and all his angels. He was alive, he was whole. She pushed back relieved tears.

"What in heaven's name happened? And why aren't you under the covers?"

He waved a hand. "I had a coughing fit from the cold. Startled my horse. He reared, and I fell. Smashed my shoulder on a rock. Next thing I know I find a smartmouthed angel at my bedside, so I suppose I'm dead."

"This is no heaven." She frowned at him, cradling the side of his head, thumb brushing his temple. "Where's the doctor?"

"You're the doctor." He patted her hand dreamily.

"If anything had happened to you—"

He squeezed her other hand, kissed it, and brought it to his chest.

"Pull yourself together, my queen," he said with a wink. "You're doting over me as if I lie in a nursery."

"When you behave like a child, I shall treat you like one."

"I needed to release some pent-up energy." He gave her an impish grin. "My preferred method being unavailable."

"I wonder why that was?" She grabbed his face again and looked into his blue eyes. "If you were harmed . . ."

"Majesties." Daniel cleared his throat. Anna straightened. "The royal physician wishes to check His Highness once more."

William rolled his eyes and hoisted himself up with a wince. Anna studied the black-cloaked man at the bedside and shuddered. He reminded her of death itself.

"If you please, Majesty," the man said.

Anna beckoned Mary, who came to stand beside her, eyes trained on the doctor. He looked in William's eyes, bent his legs, listened to his chest, felt all around his head, manipulated his left shoulder.

"Does your chest still hurt, Majesty?"

"Why would his chest hurt?" Anna said.

William waved a hand. "Just the fall. I'm fine."

The doctor pressed the sides of William's neck.

"His Majesty's shoulder is merely strained," he said, rising. "It will be sore for some time. I worried there might be effects on his heart, that being an issue with his brother—"

"I'm *fine*."

"If it please Your Majesty, milord," Mary said, "might I have a look?"

The doctor reared away from her as if she were a rabid dog. William waved her forward and chuckled, which turned into another coughing fit.

Mary's hands moved about William's shoulder, pressing and nudging. She gave a curt nod, then placed a hand over his heart.

"Do ye mind if I listen, sire?"

"Be gentle, Mary," William said, "for your mistress has bruised it of late."

Mary scowled at Anna, then laid her head on his chest and closed her eyes, ear to his heart, thumb on the pulse at his neck.

Robert started toward the bed. Anna stepped in front of him.

"Hmph," Mary said, straightening. "Majesty, you be fit as a fiddle and merely wanting of rest from this gaggle."

"It would, of course, be best to monitor the situation," the doctor said, looking down his nose at Mary, "in case there's a tear or fracture."

"We'll take care, Her Majesty and me," Mary said.

"Can I be of assistance?" Daniel asked, approaching them.

"It seems," the doctor said, "the midwife wishes to wait upon the king."

"She is more than a midwife, sir," Anna said.

"Mistress Mary is renowned for her healing," Daniel said, "though I believe a physician's watchful eye would not be remiss—"

"I do wish everyone would quit wringing their hands over me," William said. "I'm fine, Cecile, doctor. All I need is some rest and my pretty wife."

"I will come again later this evening then." The doctor gave William a stiff bow. Daniel escorted him out, apologizing all the way.

"In fact," William said, "if you could all leave me be, I would like nothing more than to rest, as Mistress Mary has so wisely prescribed."

The men took their leave, Robert last, giving William a long look that Anna couldn't decipher. Whatever it meant, it made William smile.

"Mary," Anna said as she began undoing William's boots, "please mix the tincture you think best and send for some wine with it." Her stomach growled. "And perhaps a light plate for sustenance."

When she had him down to only his shirt, she climbed onto the other side of the bed and nestled under his uninjured arm.

"Don't scare me like that again."

"Or what?" She heard the teasing in his voice. She kissed his chest, then laid her ear next to his steadily beating heart.

"Or else I'll sic Mary on you—permanently."

Hours later, Anna still lay curled up with William, her head on his chest, he in a clean nightshirt and snug in bed. He didn't eat much but drank Mary's medicine with two glasses of wine. Anna watched the steam from her own mulled wine rise in wafts.

"I am sorry," she said, "but I still don't trust him. I can't help it."

"Robert will harm nothing but my pride on occasion." He combed his fingers through her hair.

"All the same, with me not pregnant, and Margaux . . ." She struggled to keep the tremor out of her voice. "I just worry—what's to keep me from being sent to a nunnery, so you can marry another to get an heir?"

William wrapped his good arm around her, drawing her in close.

"Oh, my sweet."

He wiped the tears from her cheeks with his thumbs and tipped her face toward his.

"No matter what Robert does, no matter who Margaux beds, no matter what council demands, no matter if the Germans or the French or the English steal our lands, no matter who sits on the throne, *you* will always be by my side." His eyes bored into hers. Her heart swelled. "Do you understand?"

She sniffed and nodded. "And yet, you must know I will do what's right for our realm. The people need you as their king, not simply because you've been deemed so but because you're good and noble, and you love them." Her throat caught. "And if I need to see you with another queen to keep our country whole—"

"Anna." His blue eyes flashed. "I love this land and its people, but I will not be parted from you. For any reason. Ever."

"Even when I rail at you?"

"Especially then." He gave her a sly grin. "For I like the making up part."

"Certainly not now." She frowned at him. "You've been in an accident—"

"Hence I should start living again, aye?"

"Wills, I'm serious. You've got to rest your shoulder."

"I know a lot of things that don't involve shoulders—not *my* shoulders."

She smacked his good arm and shook her head. "Have some more wine, dear, and go to sleep."

He smacked her bottom in return. "Fine. You should make an appearance in court anyway, lest they all think me dead." He grinned. "But after that . . ."

Her own smile turned devilish. "Then we shall see."

Chapter 8

Birds of a Feather

Just after the first sprigs of spring, Robert returned from Laureland. He'd finally convinced the earl and lords that stonemason Fitzroy had not been burned and had, in fact, been shown great mercy by the king.

But it was too little too late. The common folk were convinced the king was on the verge of an inquisition that would put the Spanish to shame. Everything they said was a jumble of lies, half-truths, and fear-mongering, no doubt stoked by Germans and fanned by lords hoping to gain more lands if the throne changed hands.

"They will march on the crown," Robert said at council. "I'm certain."

William's heart sank. Though he'd heard Robert's report in private, something about it being said before council made it real, made it true.

"What are their demands?" Daniel said. "They must have reasons to march on their king."

"Since when are angry men reasonable?" William said.

"They claim it's all to practice their own faith in peace, even though they already do." Robert said. "They do not trust His Majesty."

"But they trust the Germans?" William gave a mirthless laugh.

"The laws of our land are the laws of Rome, and they have turned against Rome. They wish to break from the realm or bring the throne under Protestant rule—or die trying."

"And if they march, they'll die in droves." William held his face in his hands, stomach twisting at the thought of laying his own people low. "They must believe they'll have help."

"Majesty," the grand master general said, "there is nothing more to be done. We need not wait for a formal declaration—their words alone convict them of treason."

"We still have almost two months until the roads are clear enough," William said. "Surely if we—"

"Begging your pardon, Majesty," the general said, "but the danger is too great."

William grumbled, staring out the window.

"Apologies, Majesty," Robert said, "if you did not feel my diplomacy was up to par."

William waved Robert off. "Nay, Norwick, you know 'tis not what we meant." He dropped back in his chair, head hitting the wood. "But assuming you are right, we will not attack our people based on one opinion—wise as it may be. And surely there's still time to try and get them to see reason."

"Majesty," Halforn said, "even I don't see much hope in more talks."

"We should be on the offense," Ridgeland said, with his characteristic fist-pound. "The thaw has come—why not ride out now?"

"We've told you again and again," William said, "we will not attack our own people."

"Even if they declare war against you?" the general said.

"Which they have not done." William had seen too much of war up close, the burned towns and raped women. He shook his head and turned back to the table. "We will use all the time God gives us to make them see aright." Protests erupted from everyone but Daniel. William raised his hand for silence. "But in the meantime, we prepare for war."

Bernard stood stiff, fingers fidgeting with his rings, looking anywhere but at Annelore.

"Majesty," he said, "I wish you wouldn't make me say. 'Tis indelicate—"

"I will decide what is appropriate for my ears, Bernard." Annelore sat amid her ladies, all ensconced in their needlework. They were filling in a section of a new tapestry for the Great Hall, depicting a unicorn in an Edenesque setting. They had been chattering about court gossip, and when Bernard's face turned the color of a turnip, Anna knew she was on to something. She looked up from her work.

"Out with it, sir."

"In front of your ladies?"

Charity bit down a giggle.

"I daresay I'm the only one who doesn't know this juicy morsel."

"But Majesty, most of it was in Spanish, so I—"

"Bernard!"

He gave a groan and cleared his throat. "His Excellency said you were nothing but a painted peacock, Majesty."

"He did, did he?" Heat rose to Anna's cheeks, but she kept at her work. "And how exactly am I a peacock?"

Bernard's answer was another strangled groan.

"I heard it as well," Margaux said.

"Then perhaps you can enlighten me, Countess," Anna said.

"Valencia and the French were talking about the lack of an heir." She leaned over to pick out a bright blue thread, making a production of not squashing her blooming belly. "That's when Valencia said you were just like a painted peacock."

"We've established that." Anna stopped her work again to glare from Margaux to Bernard. Brigitte whispered into Margaux's ear then tittered.

"He said you were just like a peacock," Margaux continued, looking straight at Anna, "because you are pretty, small-brained, and infertile."

Anna yanked at her needle, sending it right into her left forefinger. "Dammit," she said under her breath. She sucked on her finger, tasting metal. It was as she feared. People were not only beginning to talk, but they'd also become bold, insulting her in public. It was only a matter of time before they demanded a new queen.

"If it makes you feel better, Majesty," Yvette said, handing Anna a kerchief, "he called all your ladies your hens."

"Hens?" Charity wrinkled her bespeckled nose.

"And it's all over court," Margaux said, examining her embroidery. "How dare he, really?"

Anna took a deep cleansing breath, then smiled at her master chamberman.

"Bernard," she said, "could you please send for as many seamstresses as are available?"

"That skunk of a Spaniard insults you thus," Mary said, scooping up discarded thread and scraps, "and yer thinking 'bout clothes?"

"Is not the best revenge to care not a whit?" Anna picked up her needle, and began again, a tiny smear of blood marring the unicorn's throat.

William could not relax. Never mind that Anna was making his feet mush with her kneading fingers. Never mind that the fire was warm, the wine well spiced, and the castle quiet at last. Never mind that he anticipated a languid night in bed with his wife. His worries refused to stop churning.

". . . and I do think Brigitte and Sir Markus might make a fine match," Anna said.

"Hmm?"

She let his foot drop.

"Wills, have you heard a word I've said?"

"I'm sorry. I'm just . . ."

"Distracted." She kissed his forehead, and moved behind him to start on his shoulders. He gave a grunt of satisfaction.

"I keep trying to figure out how I can keep out of this war."

"Don't let council bait you into it. When push comes to shove, Laureland won't fight—why would they? They've not been persecuted in the least, they had a bountiful harvest last season . . ."

"Robert's convinced they're thirsting for blood."

She gave a none too gentle press with her knuckles at the base of his neck.

"Why not send my father? He's known, and I daresay liked."

"He's my horse master. It would be seen as an insult, especially after Robert just returned."

"It needn't be official." She wrapped her arms around his neck, bringing her soft, warm cheek next to his. "Any duke worth his salt would ride to his neighbors if he'd heard rumors of war. And he's been in Beaubourg this winter, negotiating with some lord in Laureland for a pregnant filly's colt. He's every reason to go there unofficially."

She had a point. But the duke, like his daughter, was compassionate to a fault. No matter what Anna said, her father's kind heart would color his opinion. At the same time, William was out of ideas.

"All right," he said. "I'll send him on the pretense of this filly, and wish him Godspeed." She leapt up and hugged him, falling into his lap. He warmed to see her so happy.

"Now, my queen." He captured her fingers and nibbled them. "If we are to put all our efforts to avoiding war, I must ask you . . ." He sighed. He didn't want to lose their playful banter, not again. But he must warn her. Her pretty face formed a question mark.

"What is it?"

"There's been talk—"

She looked away. "Peacocks?"

"'Tis more than that." He gently pulled her chin to face him. "The rest of the realm wants us to put Laureland in their place. The more we seek peace, the more they call for blood. If the crown doesn't take up arms, I fear the rest of our people will. Especially as word spreads that the Queen of England has been sending me letters—"

"Queen Elizabeth has been sending you letters, has she?" Anna crossed her arms over her chest.

"She pledges her support of my claim to the throne if I am lenient to Laureland."

"In other words, she wants to make nice so she can use Troixden to invade France? Not to mention keeping the Spanish from having another port by which to attack her."

William laughed. "My dear, you should have been an ambassador. Even Daniel didn't figure that out at first."

"Well, certainly at court they will have to stop calling me brainless, though I suppose pretty and infertile still stand."

He took hold of her face, rubbing her cheeks with his thumbs.

"Anna. Annelore, look at me." Her eyes looked straight into his. "Anyone who speaks of you thus is an ignorant ass. I would rather have you by my side than a million heirs."

Her eyes brimmed as she bit the inside of her cheek. "Seeing Margaux grow bigger every day, hearing the whispers about you and her . . ."

He frowned. "Why didn't you tell me how horrid this has been for you? You've but joked about it."

"You have enough to worry about besides childish gossip."

He brought her face to him and pressed his mouth to hers, long enough to feel the weight of the world drop away, to feel her breath quicken and her body arch toward him. It took all his strength to break away.

"Far be it from me," he said, "to censor your passion. But the talk I speak of is more injurious." She gave him a quizzical look. "There are rumors that you sympathize with the Lutherans. Not out of queenly pity, but in their faith."

She sat up fast, wide eyed. "Who dares call me a heretic?"

"When they hear you praise Elizabeth for ruling without an heir, when they hear you argue with Bartmore, when you honor Multman for his ideals of shared wealth . . ."

"So Bartmore's got his purple feathers in a bunch?" She was up out of his lap then, pacing in front of the fire.

"Perhaps it started there, but the rumors have spread to the countryside. He's not the only one who bristles at your bold faith."

She turned her blazing eyes on him, and he couldn't help shuddering. She was a terrible beauty when crossed.

"Perhaps instead of wagging tongues in vicious lies, they should wag them in prayer!"

William held up his hands in surrender.

"I don't disagree. But you must be careful. We must be careful."

She gave him a withering look. This was not going well.

"So it's back to 'look pretty and shut up,' is it?"

"Why must you always jump to extremes?"

"Bartmore's nearly got me strapped to a stake, and you're calling *me* extreme?"

He sprang out of his chair.

"Extreme is half our people being slaughtered on the rumor of a queen gone heretic!" He knew he should get a shovel and dig himself out of this, but he couldn't help himself.

"So I'm sending our country to ruin with my empty womb and wrongheaded religion?"

"Dammit, Anna!" He threw up his hands. "This isn't about you, it's about people's *image* of you!" He watched her take several long breaths.

"I—" she opened her mouth as if for more protest, but instead shook her head. "I . . . will try."

He relaxed and embraced her. "I would never diminish your spirit—not that I could, even if I wanted." He gave her a wry look. "You just . . . you just need to be careful."

She smiled sweetly, but he knew that look in her eye. She was scheming.

"Don't worry, Wills. As you say, I should have been an ambassador." She kissed him then, twining her fingers in his hair, pulling him to her. She was trying to distract him, but he didn't care.

He hoisted her in his arms and carried her to bed.

A week later, Anna returned to her chamber after morning mass to find Bernard standing beside her bed, the curtains closed, a supremely satisfied look on his face.

"Majesty," he said with his jig-bow, "your order has been delivered." He pulled back the curtains with ceremony to reveal a pile of gowns, exactly as she'd specified. She hastened to the bed and touched the white plumes of fabric.

"They're absolutely perfect!" she said. "And right on time. Be sure to pay them more than usual." Her ladies gathered around the bed as well, all marveling at the handiwork of the royal seamstresses.

"Majesty," Margaux said, her hand stroking her protruding belly, "whatever are these for?"

"Why, they're for you, ladies," she said, "and for me."

She gingerly picked up the one colored gown in the center of the bed, a royal blue satin with a skirt and train more colorful than Joseph's coat. She held it up to herself.

"If I am to be a peacock," she said, kicking out the train made of genuine peacock feathers, sewn so closely together that they concealed the fabric beneath, "I might as well look like one." She handed one of the white gowns to Mary. "And you, my ladies, shall be my lovely hens."

Her ladies fluttered, holding up the white silk skirts with white ostrich feathers trailing to the floor. Charity pressed a gown to her body and twirled around.

"I feel like a cloud!" she said, spinning the other direction.

Anna looked across the bed and saw Margaux's face turn from shock to a slow, wide smile.

"Bravo, Majesty." She drew a gown from the bed and held it to her bosom.

"So you approve, Countess?"

"Highness, you know I love a dramatic entrance." She laughed that beautiful trill of hers.

Anna went to her full-length mirror, a spring in her step. It had taken two years, but she'd finally impressed her rival.

William sat back against his throne in the Great Hall, clad in black, befitting his mood. April Fool's Day. He looked over at Robert, flirting with the French ambassador's daughter. How could he be so calm, almost lackadaisical? Not for the first time, William wished he could simply hand the throne over to him. But as much as he loved his friend, he knew Robert as king would mean more war, not less.

He spied Daniel on his left, who sat grimly reading correspondence from the Duke of Beaubourg. The duke seemed to think a handful of rich Laureland lords were behind the whole of it, hoping for a land grab. If these motives were unmasked, the duke believed the people's loyalty would return to the crown. William wasn't so sure. If they didn't trust him, why would they believe him? But he clung to hope, even as his men readied themselves for war.

Valencia stood chatting with Bartmore and the French envoy near the foot of the dais, the court jester making faces behind his back. But even this did not lift William's spirits.

He heard a commotion at the courtyard entrance. He called for more wine, and by the time the taster handed him his goblet, the hubbub had progressed to the far end of the hall. Courtiers fell into curtsies and bows like a wave. Now what? William sat up straight, Robert stopped flirting, and Daniel frowned.

Then William saw her.

She had turned past the final pillar, heading straight for him, head high, face serene, a gold and emerald crown on her head, his mother Matilda's emerald necklace dripping into her cleavage, which was pushed high and tightly bound in a royal blue corset, boldly revealing her flat stomach. Her ladies, dressed in pure white, held her skirt and train. As she came closer he caught the shimmer of peacock feathers.

She finally made her way to the group of foreigners. Valencia's eyes were saucers as he stammered out a "Your Majesty." Anna gave him a quick nod as she idly twirled a bright red feather about a foot long.

"My liege," she said to William, floating to the floor, plumes of peacock feathers fanning.

"Majesty." He smiled broadly as he rose to take her hand. "You are looking particularly lovely today."

He kissed her knuckles, then lingered on her lips, and led her to her throne. Her ladies followed, fixing her train so it flowed down the stairs like a bird's tail off a branch.

"And what have you here?" he said, indicating the feather.

"'Tis a gift, Highness, for you." She bent over and tucked it in his doublet, the blood red of it jumping out against his black leather.

"Ah, am I to be the rooster? For I feel more the raven."

"Nay," she said, loud enough for all to hear, "you are the phoenix, and like the phoenix, you shall rise from the ashes, always triumphant."

Robert laughed and applauded.

"Bravo, Majesties—you make pigeons of us all."

"Oh, you could never be a pigeon, Your Grace," Anna said, deadpan, "for no henhouse is complete without its fox."

Court erupted in laughter. Robert took Anna's hand and kissed it, bowing on one knee.

And in that moment, William could not fathom loving her more.

"Your Majesty." Bartmore gave William a deep bow upon entering Council Table, then laid a large, heavily sealed parchment down as if it were a babe. As summer, and fighting season, neared, council itself was split into factions, Bartmore leading his own charge to scorch the earth with the blazing of heretics.

"Eminence," William said gesturing at the parchment, "shall you enlighten us?"

"I certainly do not wish to interrupt the proceedings." He gave William a silken smile. "However, a message from His Holiness, I believe, must supersede any other discussion."

William's brows shot up. The pope? Why was this not sent directly to him? Or was Bartmore finally getting his cardinalship?

"Please proceed Eminence," he said.

"His Holiness has written to me in regard to appointing a new bishop." Bartmore unrolled the letter, making sure every attached seal hit the table with a resounding plunk. "He feels that Havenside is large enough and influential enough to deserve one."

William relaxed. Nothing wrong with that, though he'd have to think carefully about whom to nominate.

"Very good, Your Grace. We look forward to your thoughts on the matter." He gestured to Daniel to continue with the proceedings. His forces were by no means ready to ride out, and every day of delay put them at a strategic disadvantage.

"That is not all," Bartmore said, "begging Your Majesty's pardon." He stroked the papal seal. "His Holiness adds, as an aside, that he hopes all is well for the true faith in Troixden, and he graciously asks me to tell him if there is any support he might lend in regard to the troubles he has heard of in the north."

William thrust his open hand toward Bartmore. "Give that here, Eminence."

Bartmore clucked, but passed the letter on. William scanned it. Yes, His Holiness had used the exact phrase "any support." This was no convivial postscript—the pope was telling William he'd have the full backing of Rome in any war against Troixden's heretics. And the German states.

He laid the letter down and looked at his councilmen.

"My lords, we are certainly more ready now."

That night Annelore lay with her head on William's bare chest, stroking his long fingers and fiddling with his rings.

"Well, my pretty peacock," he said, "if that performance

doesn't shatter Valencia's pronouncements, I don't know what will."

She sat up and pressed her happily swollen lips against his. The king had been insatiable that evening.

"I believe that was near a record."

"Only near?" His tongue traced her mouth. "Shall we break it, then?"

"Dearest, if a babe is what we desire, I do believe I should rest for at least a smidgeon of the evening."

A stamp of the night guard's staff interrupted them. William snarled.

"His Grace, the Duke of Cecile!"

William rolled out of bed with a sigh and pulled on his trunks, Anna grabbing for a sheet to cover herself.

"Does the man never sleep?" she said, puffing hair out of her eyes.

"No, he doesn't. I think he survives on parchment and Latin." He walked toward the door.

"William! You can't let him in here!"

He considered her. "He wouldn't be here if it weren't important."

"I agree," she said, "but wait until I've taken leave—"

"Tush, Anna, he knows you're here." He grinned. "And no doubt what we've been up to."

"Well excuse me for not wanting to rub his face in it," she said. "The poor man has no wife. I'm sure this . . . scene . . . is not exactly—"

"Let's just say I don't think your presence would be distracting to him in the least."

"Oh, really?" Anna cocked a brow. "Have you not seen how red he turns whenever Charity enters a room?"

William frowned. "I didn't think—"

"His proclivities may not be what you think they are."

William shrugged it off. "Regardless, my dear, if he comes this late, 'tis for good reason. And in any case I'm sure it's something I'd like you to hear." He stopped midway to the door. "Enter!" he called as Anna shrank further under the covers, trying to be as inconspicuous as possible.

Daniel rushed in, heading straight for William. "Majesty, about the pope's request—" He stopped short. Even in the dim light, Anna could see him blush. "I'm . . . I'm sorry Highness, I was heedless of the hour—"

"Relax, friend." William gave a good-natured slap to Daniel's arm, grinned, then poured them both a drink. "I know you work through the night."

Daniel's eyes landed on Anna, and she gave him a commiserating grimace. She didn't think it was possible for him to turn redder.

"Truly, Majesty-ties—I should come back in the morning. It's not of such—"

"Daniel." William handed him wine. "Take a long draught, then pray continue."

Daniel grimaced, then drained the goblet and handed the king a parchment.

"Bartmore has given me his list of potential bishops—only two, both court almoners with no congregations."

William snorted and brought a glass of wine to Anna, kissing her forehead as he did. She flicked her eyes to Daniel, then frowned at her husband. Why was he making the poor man more uncomfortable?

William sat by her feet. "I thought the archbishop more sly than this," he said, waving his goblet about. "He should have put a country friar in somewhere."

"Or Multman," Anna said. "He would make a wonderful bishop. And he's well loved not only by his congregation, but also by many outside."

"But not many at court," Daniel said, still averting his eyes.

"Well, he is loved by this courtier," William said, touching his chest, "for he convinced my wife to join me in more sport, as it were."

"William," Anna said under her breath.

"While he is a good man with a solid intellect," Daniel said, "I do believe his ideas would be considered too . . . broadminded. And with the current state of things . . ." He shook his head.

"What do you think, my dear?" William asked Anna.

"I believe this is the purview of God, not politics."

William laughed and squeezed her foot through the covers. "True enough, but cannot God's will be brought about through politics? Or, rather, in spite of them?"

"Perhaps," she said. "But if there is to be a bishop of Havenside, it should be a man whose heart strives after good."

"Highness," Daniel said, speaking only to William, "I've no wish to place the people of Havenside into the hands of grasping men. However, Multman's actions have been called into question—"

"As were the Lord's," Anna said.

"More to the point," William said, refilling his glass, "if

Multman's betters oppose him, the pope will certainly not select him." He turned back to Daniel. "Besides, no one will know of it save Bartmore, who needs as much putting in his place as he can get. The man's become unbearable of late."

"I had thought to nominate Abbot Carlo." Daniel put down his goblet. "He is of Spanish descent through his mother. He would not make undue waves."

"My whole life is undue waves." William guided Daniel to the door. "You may put down the abbot, but you must also put down Multman, with my hearty thanks to His Holiness for his support."

A queer look passed over Daniel's face, not of embarrassment, but of anger.

William shut the door and returned to Anna.

"Now my dear, where were we?"

CHAPTER 9

St. Bartholomew's Day

$\mathcal{S}$ ummer was upon them, and Anna started to relax. Perhaps her father had been right. Perhaps all this talk of war was simply the saber rattling of a few Laureland lords. Perhaps William wouldn't be gone and in mortal danger for weeks on end.

She took her warm wine and walked to the east windows. Rain beat down outside, battering the flowers below. The summer squalls of Havenside were cool, hard, and brief. The sun and warmth would return by the next day.

A light in the top southern corner of Stone Yard caught her eye. She thought of Bryan, alone in that stark prison. She'd allowed Charity to visit her brother twice but couldn't bring herself to go and see him. William told her Bryan sent a letter every Sunday without fail, begging to be put to death. She hated to think of William as cruel, yet to leave Bryan alive after his attempted regicide seemed less merciful now than it had at the time.

Movement below caught her eye. A woman, cloaked against the weather, darted toward the castle from the stables. At first she thought it might be Charity, but she was there in Anna's chambers, humming softly to herself while she sewed and flirted with the musicians. The mysterious woman glanced up at the castle walls, and Anna saw her face. Margaux. What on earth . . . ?

A stamp at the door drew her attention away. Daniel. Ever since that evening interlude two months prior, he'd been more distant, more formal, and she was sorry for it.

"Majesty," he said, after his bow, "the pope's decision was read at council, and the king has sent me."

"By all means proceed, Your Grace, but may I offer you some refreshment?" She motioned to Yvette, who rose to make up a plate.

"Thank you, Highness, but I come only for a brief courtesy."

Anna put down her glass and approached him. "Your Grace, may I be forthright with you?" He nodded his assent. "I feel as though I have done something to win your disfavor, which grieves me. Would you do me the honor of revealing it, so I might make amends?"

He gazed past her head. "I apologize, Highness, if it seems that way. Perhaps it is the stress of this situation with Laureland."

"Your Grace," she said, "I know you to be a politic man, but

I thought we were in some form friends. Please, tell me. I will not take offense."

His gaze finally met hers. "His Holiness has selected Multman as bishop."

"But that's good news!" she said, clapping her hands together.

"Begging your pardon, Majesty, but it's not. The poor may love Multman, but the tradesmen do not."

"Multman is an honorable choice. Clearly his standing has impressed the pope."

"The tradesmen claim the king has forced the pope's hand," Daniel said, eyes suddenly ablaze, "and that His Majesty plans to break with Rome entirely."

"That doesn't make any sense." She shook her head, almost laughing.

"It doesn't need to make sense to infuriate the masses. I tried telling the king as much, but . . ."

"But what?"

"He listens to you."

His look was so severe she fell back a step. "My apologies, Majesty, I . . . I lost my composure. 'Tis entirely unacceptable."

"'Tis all right, Your Grace." She patted his hand. He raised hers and brushed it with his lips. "Please remember," she said softly, "we're on the same side."

He gave her a wan smile. "I shall try."

The Archbishop of Bartmore sat scowling in front of Robert's desk, drumming his fingers on the black wood.

"It is inconceivable to me how His Holiness could have selected this upstart." He wiped his forehead again with a kerchief. "Unless, of course, there was undue influence."

"Really, Your Grace?" Robert turned from his windows and faced the archbishop. If Bartmore feared competition, perhaps he should get himself to Rome and start kissing more arses. "You accuse the pope of taking his cues from earthly rather than heavenly sources?"

Bartmore stared at him. "It is entirely possible that *my* selections were never presented to His Holiness," he said, "which would point to some type of interference."

"Or perhaps His Holiness thinks a servant of the poor a better choice than one of your puppets?"

"Enough!" Bartmore wagged a finger at Robert. "I know you think this instability will help your own cause. That the people will revolt and demand a new king."

"And I'm just the man for the job, is that it?"

"Indeed! The perfect Catholic, playing around as my ally."

Robert grunted and walked to his desk, hands behind his back. "I've never seen our relationship as more than transactional, Eminence. And the fact that you just rode into Havenside with a mob of over a hundred men all crying out for war with Laureland does not exactly warm me to you."

"I stand for our people," Bartmore said. "They will have their land cleansed of heresy, one way or another."

Robert leaned over his desk. "And you will have your cardinal's cap?"

Bartmore's mouth twitched. "I will have whatever God ordains."

Anna returned to her chambers after her weekly distribution of alms, accompanied by Yvette, Cariline, Mary, and Jane. The gathered poor were a small group, many of them averting their eyes from her even as they received her coins and blessings. She even heard a few passersby mumble curses under their breath.

William was right. She needed to be careful. Arriving at her outer hall, a voice interrupted her thoughts: Charity's haunting soprano, echoing as if the palace itself were lamenting an unrequited love. In an instant, Anna forgave Charity's missteps of decorum, her uncouth flirtations, her nonstop talking. She held a finger to her lips as she and her ladies entered her chamber.

When she opened the door and saw the gathered audience, her heart stopped. Charity knelt on the floor, skin pink with the exertion of song. The queen's younger ladies-in-waiting, surrounded her, and sitting before her was the king, smiling, Charity's hand engulfed in his.

Head high, Anna strode into the room. Her ladies scampered to their feet as William dropped Charity's hand and rose, brows raised. Charity flushed deep red and kept her eyes on the ground as she made her curtsy. But had Anna caught a smile on her lips?

"My queen," William said, holding out his arms. "I've been waiting for your return."

"I'm glad to see my ladies have kept you entertained." She felt nauseated.

"It was not a long wait." He came to her slowly, as if she might bite. Maybe she would.

"Leave us," she said, with a flick of the wrist. Her ladies scattered as she seated herself at the vanity. "So you wished to see me?" She glanced in the mirror and caught the king's reflection. He looked like a boy caught with a plum pudding.

"I thought you might wish to have a stroll about the gardens with me," he said.

"I've just returned from outside."

He stood behind her. "I've not known you to refuse an airing."

She met his gaze in the mirror, skin prickling, jaw clenched. "And I've not known you to have such interest in the talents of my ladies."

"Anna, come now." He looked to the ceiling. "She's been a command performer at court many a time."

"And elsewhere, apparently."

He grabbed her arm and pulled her around to face him. "What are you accusing me of?"

"I see how you look at her."

"She's a child!"

"She's not, and you know it!"

He released her and ran his hands through his hair. "You'd rather I refuse her request to sing for me? Or perhaps you'd rather I simply shut my eyes whenever a beautiful woman appears?"

"So you admit she's beautiful." She went back to the vanity. Her stomach roiled.

"Are you joking?" His voice rose. "I have always—*always*, Anna—been faithful to you. And yet you expect me to not even *look*?"

She met his eyes again, stony. "It's *how* you looked at her."

"Don't do this." He crossed his arms. "Your jealousy is neither appropriate nor becoming."

"I've spent months ignoring rumors about Margaux's pregnancy." Her throat was tight. "Now I come to my own chamber to find you swooning over my maids, and you expect me to happy about it?"

"Again—what exactly are you accusing me of?" He glared at her, chest rising and kicked a tuffet, toppling it with a thud.

She felt faint, sweaty, queasy.

"You can't simply . . . simp—" She couldn't breathe. She clutched at the vanity, the floor swimming. "I . . . William . . ."

She heard him yell for Mary, as the floor came up to meet her. Then everything went black.

Annelore woke to find William sitting with his elbows on her bed, head in his hands, a candelabrum, the only light in the room, dripping its wax to the floor beside him.

She reached out to touch his arm, and he startled awake.

"Anna, my love." He enveloped her in his arms, pressing her forehead to his lips. She inhaled his comforting scent, glad to be in his embrace. "I'm so sorry we fought," he said into her hair. "Especially—" He stopped and pulled back to look at her, hands framing her face. "I'm so glad you're safe."

She looked at him, puzzled by the anxious look on his face. "I'm fine of body, Will, but of heart—"

"Never mind that now." A sparkle brightened his eyes as the corner of his mouth twitched. "I have a surprise for you."

"Honestly, William, you have an infuriating way of changing the subject when—"

"You're with child, Anna." Wetness glinted at the corners of his eyes. "You are once again with child."

Her jaw dropped, mind flying back through the weeks. She had definitely felt sick of late, her mood more pitched, but she attributed it to strain. She'd missed her last bleeding, but that had happened occasionally.

"For certain?" she said.

"Mary told me." He held her hands. "She said she had her suspicions."

"Which she never shared with me." This should be wonderful news. Why was she out of sorts with it?

William laughed. "Perhaps she had her reasons." He tapped the tip of her nose. "Besides, it gave me the pleasure of surprising you, something I rarely have opportunity to do."

"You're right. 'Tis happy news indeed." She managed a smile and drew his hands to her lips.

"Mary said she thought you were a good ten weeks along. We may have our heir by December." He stroked her cheek tenderly then climbed into bed, slippers and all, settling in beside her.

By Advent. And now would she, too, finally be a mother? Could she be the sort of mother the realm's heir deserved, the sort William wished for his child? And if it were a girl . . . She nestled into him as if she could smother her worries in his chest.

"Now sleep, my dear." He kissed her head and leaned his own against it. "Both of you need rest."

Both of you. Despite her misgivings, she smiled.

Toward the end of August, Anna sat at one end of the privy dining room table, flirting with William. As her womb grew, so did their affection. It was as if they were newly wed again. Reluctantly, she brought her mind back to their guests. The French ambassador and his envoy would return to Paris the next day. Thus, they were enjoying a last formal meal.

"I pray His Majesty, King Charles, will allow me to seek relief from this oppressive heat," the ambassador said. "If your Havenside is this hot, Paris is sure to be sweltering. And these sporadic downpours?" He grimaced.

"We're sure he'll reward your faithful service," William said, raising his goblet of wine, "and of course you must send him all our good tidings and good will."

"Quite so, Majesty," the ambassador said, returning the toast. "We have always treasured your friendship—our little neighbor to the north."

A slight narrowing of William's eyes was all the evidence he gave of offense. Anna shot him a smile. A dour-looking French page approached the table. He whispered something to the ambassador and handed over a note.

"Please excuse me, Majesties," the Frenchman said, "but apparently this is of some urgency."

"Of course," William said. "We only hope 'tis nothing to darken the occasion."

The ambassador gaped at the note, half rising from his chair, then sat again.

"Begging your pardon, Majesties," he said, "but I must share the glorious news."

"Yes?" William raised his brows.

"It seems the king has put down an attempted coup on the royal family. They are all safe."

"Thank the Lord," Anna said, crossing herself. It was one of her worst nightmares, any attempt at the throne.

"And there is more," the ambassador said, eyes gleaming. "It is a victory not only for the king but also for the true faith. This was apparently a plot by the Huguenots, and the king has pushed them down. He has displayed the body of that heretic Coligny, and the whole city of Paris has taken up arms and driven every last Huguenot rat into the Seine!"

"Surely not all," Anna said. "That would be thousands." The thought of citizens killing their neighbors repulsed her. It wasn't righteous. It was murder.

"Every one!" The ambassador looked at her, face alight like a child's on Twelfth Night. "Entire households have been eliminated!"

Women. Children. Babies. Her hand leapt to her womb.

"But that's horrible," Anna said, unable to stop herself. She looked up to see William's face pale, his jaw tight.

"Horrible?" The ambassador laughed. "Is this not why you make ready to fight? To rid yourselves of the vile Protestant taint?"

"But to slaughter innocent women and children—"

"They cannot be innocent!" The ambassador slammed his fist on the table. "Their lies spread like the plague and imperil our very souls!"

"Ambassador," William said, rising from his seat, "the queen's heart is that of a woman. She feels all things acutely no matter their validity."

Anna opened her mouth to protest. How could William support such a thing? He would never allow the people of Havenside to murder one another.

"The heretics have received quite a blow," William said, resting his hand on the ambassador's shoulder. "Hopefully that will squelch them. And we join you in thanking God that the royal family is safe and secure."

"Thank you, Majesty," he said, rising with the rest of his entourage. "If you will excuse me, I shall write to His Majesty now and send him your congratulations."

"Please do, heartily." William returned to his seat. Once the ambassador was gone, he sent the servants away.

"I know what you're going to say," he said.

"I don't think you do."

"Anna, they would have killed the king."

That would cause her to wake in terror more nights than she cared to think on.

"But surely not every Protestant in Paris was a part of the plot."

"Sometimes matters get out of hand."

"Out of hand!" She was up in a flash, eyeing him across the spread of half-eaten supper. "You never would have allowed such wholesale slaughter!"

"Anna, please. I don't like it any more than you do, but seeing as our realm is on the brink of just such an event, isn't it better to bite our tongues and celebrate along with the French?"

She narrowed her eyes. Of course he was right in a political sense, but morally . . .

"I can't conscience killing children."

"I'm not asking you to. But your outburst was heard by ears that should not have heard it."

A picture of Margaux's smug face popped into mind, right alongside Robert's. William rose and walked around the table to take her hands.

"We have to tread carefully," he said. "We must make sure your sentiments are seen as a woman's frailty and not as sympathy for the Protestant plight."

"But, Wills—"

"I'm sorry, my queen, but it must be so. To protect our own people, our own children." He flicked his eyes to her stomach. "There's nothing to be done about those who have already perished. We must look to those who now live."

She allowed him to embrace her but felt no warmth.

Two days after the news from Paris, William sat among dour faces at Council Table. The queen was there, but she kept her eyes on her hands or out at the rain-drenched window. This matter with the Huguenots had hit her harder than he'd expected. But what did she want him to do? He must look to his own land at present. He had no leisure to worry about the bloodthirsty in others.

Timothy of Ridgeland was elaborating on the readiness and expertise of his men. "We have arches trained to use fire as well as longbows. Three hundred—"

A scuffle outside the doors cut him off. Robert burst in, red-faced, dressed in riding gear, hand on his sword hilt.

"Majesty, take heed," he said, charging into the room.

"Your Grace, what on earth . . ." Halforn rose from his seat in alarm as Robert went straight to the queen.

"We must get Her Majesty to safety," he said, reaching for Anna, other hand still on his weapon.

William sprang from his chair, fighting the urge to shield Anna with his body. "Speak your concern, Norwick."

"The city is in riot." His eyes met William's. "That's why I was delayed to council. They haven't taken kindly to the queen's pity for the French Protestants. They say she has been a Protestant supporter all along."

"Ridiculous!" Anna turned terrified eyes to William.

"They say Her Majesty has poisoned you, sire, with dogma," Robert said, "and convinced you to break with Rome. They say you claim to speak for God."

"All that from a slip of the tongue?" William said.

"It's been building for years now," Robert said. "All it needed was a match."

"We must leave at once," Anna said, face grim, "get out of the city—"

"It's too late," Robert said. "The palace is surrounded. The wall guards thought it was merely more troops gathering to prepare for the Laureland offensive. It wasn't until the crowd started yelling and throwing rocks that we realized what was happening."

"We've at least five hundred armed men with horses in the castle guard alone, not to mention the troops," William said. "That's more than enough to hold off some peasants and merchants. I'll come to the outer balcony and speak to them—"

"The Lord Mayor to see Your Highness," the door guard called.

"Send him in."

The lord mayor, his white tufts of hair standing out at odd angles, was wheezing.

"Majesty, Your Graces," he said. "The city is in chaos."

"We will not have a repeat of Paris, Lord Mayor." William stared him down. "Do you understand?"

"Then I would recommend sending guards to the Jewish quarter, Highness, for part of the mob is heading there now with ill intent." The mayor's cragged brows creased.

"Why Jews?" Halforn said. "This has nothing to do with them."

"It doesn't need to," Daniel said. "They will be harmed first, then any other heretics ferreted out." He flicked his eyes to the queen. She held herself, arms wrapped around her belly, head shaking slowly.

"Send one hundred men, Master General," William said, "and send one hundred more to surround the palace. The rest must go into the streets and maintain order at any cost."

"Lethal force, Majesty?"

William hesitated only a moment. "Yes."

He strode to Anna, reaching for her shoulders. Her face was determined, but he could feel her tremble.

"Take your ladies and go to my chambers. Stay there until I return."

"My liege, you mustn't go out—"

"I will talk sense into my people." He grabbed her head and kissed her crinkled brow. Releasing her, he returned to his men. "Cecile, we have words to craft."

The killing began with Rebekah the midwife. She was violated, strangled, and hung from her sign with a Star of David carved into her chest. William knew he couldn't tell the queen. Not yet. Perhaps not ever. So far, reports were of five Jews killed, including Rebekah, and two houses set ablaze, the fires spreading slowly, thanks to the heavy rain.

William, surrounded by six armored knights and Daniel by his side, felt his stomach lurch as he heard the mob's yells through the knife-thin archer slits in the stone walls. He would speak to the people from the balcony above the castle's main gate. He'd make them see reason. He'd stop this killing, this madness.

His guard opened the door to the balcony. Three knights moved out in front of him. William followed his men. The noise of the crowd subsided.

"Heretic!" Someone yelled.

"Let the king speak!" Another called.

"Good people of Havenside!" William held up his hands. "Our heart is deeply troubled by word of your disquiet." A few grunts and shouts rippled through the horde. He raised his voice. "It has come to our ears that wild rumors and falsehoods have been taken as truth—"

"The queen's a Lutheran!" A woman yelled. "She'll have us all burned!"

"The queen is the most devout person we have ever known," William said. It seemed to be his refrain these days. "And her heart for the people exceeds even ours, if that be possible."

"She plots with the Queen of England!"

"Good people!" William looked down at faces twisted in jeers, mottled with anger, white with fear. "The queen has never strayed from the one true faith. Never. Nor have we."

"You side with Laureland!"

"She'll let them burn us!"

"Bring us the queen!"

"The queen! Bring us the queen!"

Nothing William could say would silence them. And there was no way on God's verdant earth he'd subject Anna to this.

"We do not wish to put our guards upon you!" he shouted.

The crowd took up a chant. "The queen, the queen! Bring us the queen!"

Daniel whispered something in William's ear but he couldn't hear it. As he leaned in to have Daniel repeat it, he felt movement on his right, and the crowd quieted. Through the rainy haze he saw Anna standing there, face stone, and without her crown. He moved to launch himself in front of her, but Daniel stayed him.

"Burn her!" someone cried out. She flinched.

"My people," she shouted into the wind, "I have always been

and always will be devoted to your service. From the bottom of my soul, I apologize if any words I spoke have given you a moment's grief or worry. 'Tis only a woman's weakness that causes me to grieve any violence, no matter how justifiable."

"Liar!"

A soggy projectile flew toward the balcony, falling well short. William could stand it no longer and pushed in front of her, two guards following suit. He felt her stumble back behind him and grabbed her arm. The archers aimed into the crowd as women shrieked.

"Be still," the queen said to the guards. William felt pressure on his back from her hand, urging him to step aside. "Stay your weapons."

The archers looked to William. He gave them a nod and reluctantly stood back. The archers too moved aside, arrows still quivering on lowered bows.

"I ask you to forgive my feeble heart!" she called out.

A tomato, half rotten, struck Anna in the chest. Her hand flew to her sternum as the putrid juices trickled onto her bosom, the fruit itself rolling down her gown, leaving a red streak on her ivory and gold silks. The guards raised their bows, but the crowd had gone dead silent. Anna closed her eyes and again stayed the guards.

"I ask you to forgive me," she said. "and to remember that I am here to speak for your struggles to those above you." Her voice caught, and she closed her eyes. "I ask you to believe in me, as I believe in you." She lifted her head. "And now, I ask you to pray with me. Pray for our city, our realm, that we will be delivered from fear, from division, from heresy."

At this, she bowed her head before them, clutching a simple wood rosary. Crossing herself, she began. "Our Father, who art in heaven, hallowed be thy name . . ."

A man near the front of the crowd knelt, following her prayers. And then slowly, miraculously, down they went, one by one into the mud, caps off, a sea of murmured prayers rising above the rain.

William rested his hand on the nape of Anna's exposed neck. With her free hand, she reached up and grasped it, her fingers cold and trembling. When she reached the end, she regarded the crowd. A raven cawed. The people were still. She glanced at William.

"I love you," he whispered. "So will they."

She nodded, more in resolve than agreement it seemed. Tendrils of hair stuck to her face, and her soaked silks clung to her arms. She bowed her head and began again.

"Our Father, who art in heaven . . ."

All William could hear above the hammer of rain on stone was the rise and fall of her voice. He could not tell what time had passed when she came to the finish for a second time.

"Hail Holy Queen, Mother of Mercy, our life, our sweetness and our hope. To thee do we cry, poor banished children of Eve, to thee do we send up our sighs, mourning and weeping in this vale of tears. Turn then, most gracious advocate, thine eyes of mercy toward us, and after this our exile, show unto us the blessed fruit of thy womb, Jesus. O clement, O loving, O sweet Virgin Mary. Amen."

There was a hush, as if the earth breathed. Then, a solitary old lady stumbled back to her feet.

"Bless you, Majesty," she called out. "Bless you!"

William recognized her as the widow of the fateful mason.

"Go in peace," he said.

She waved at William and toddled off, the silent crowd watching her go. Then one by one they followed, picking themselves up and bowing to the queen as they disappeared behind sheets of rain. Anna kept her hand raised in blessing until the last man left.

Then her hand finally faltered. William seized it, pulling her to him. Her knees buckled as he caught her in his arms, holding her there, pressing her to him as if she were his own skin. He kissed the top of her sodden head.

"You are magnificent."

Beyond the square, fires still burned, people still shouted, glass still shattered. How had he been so blind?

"I'm terrified, William." She shook in his arms. "What will become of us?"

"I wish I knew," he said, clinging to her. "But what hell may come, we shall face it together."

CHAPTER 10

Cleave then Leave

That evening William sat back, damp and weary, at the head of the reconvened Council Table.

"Even I," Daniel said, "believe the time has passed for negotiations. We must engage the north if we're to keep the rest of the country to heel."

"And we must go now," the grand master general added.

"Are we ready?" William said.

"We could leave Havenside tomorrow," the general said. "By the time we reach Laureland, we'd have five thousand men at arms joining us—not to mention the Holy Father's Swiss Guard enforcements. We'll have them crushed by October's end."

William looked down the table into his father-in-law's eyes.

"Highness, I know the thought of shedding your people's blood wounds you," the Duke of Beaubourg said, "but I too see that we must come to blows."

"Majesty," Robert said, "there is no one finer in battle, both in combat and strategy, than our general. And no king as brave and true as Your Highness." Robert rose, hand to his heart. "We ride under your banner as a loyal band, eager to fulfill your call, eager to save Troixden from all who would desecrate her." The rest of council stood with him, hats off heads, hands on hearts. "Lead us on to victory, for God and Troixden. We will not disappoint thee."

William looked down at the papers in front of him. The letter from Bartmore's men, demanding action against Laureland. A comic leaflet depicting the king, swordless, cowering in a corner while grotesque-looking Germans danced about with his crown. "William the cower-ed" it read.

He crumpled it in his hand. They were right. And after what he had just witnessed, as fires continued to smolder in the city, he knew there was nothing else to be done. This is what it meant to be king.

He rose, his men standing silent, hands still on their hearts.

"God help us," he said, "it is war."

Anna sat curled in William's arms in front of his fire. Even his robe over hers could not warm her. All she wanted was to stay there, wrapped in his strength.

"I wish there was some other way," she said, smoothing down the bristled hairs of his bearskin rug.

"It's part of being a king—and a queen." He covered her hand with his. "Fear not, I'm sure I'll come back so dirty and smelly you'll want nothing to do with me."

She buried her face in his chest. "Even if you rolled in horse manure and didn't bathe for a year, I would welcome you to my arms and not let you go."

He chuckled, lifting her chin. "I shan't leave you and the babe adrift. In fact, I intend to make you co-regent with Daniel in the very *unlikely* case that I don't return."

She sat up straight, her stomach dropping like a stone. Even the mention of this at court would be met with wild protest—especially from Robert.

"I spoke to Daniel at length about it after council," William said. "Since Robert will be with me on the field, he's under the same risk as I."

"You really think he'll see it that way?"

"I'm sure not, but that's the way it shall be."

She rested her hand on her belly.

"I'm glad you've taken my cautions about Robert more seriously. This certainly puts his claims—"

"That's not the point." William scowled, but his eyes remained soft. "It's not that I mistrust him, 'tis that I mistrust his rule. He would not purposefully lead us to ruin, but his tendencies dictate otherwise."

"As you say."

"And," he said, "I intend to crown you queen in your own

right—not only queen consort but ruler, regardless of what may hap with the war."

Her eyes grew wide. While she certainly prided herself on her contributions to council and had particular opinions on how many a matter should be handled, ruling as queen outright was another thing entirely. Could she do it? What's more, did she want to?

"This is all so fast," she said. "Pregnant, the riots, the possibility of ruling in your stead . . . I don't know what to say."

"After your performance today, I can think of no one more suited to the task. Especially with Daniel's help." He took her hands again. "Besides, with the pope behind us, the campaign should be over in short order."

"I wish I had your confidence."

"And I wish you could see yourself as I do."

She looked at their intertwined hands stretched across her stomach. If only it were that simple.

Robert pushed his way through the doors of the throne room, heart pounding like a charging warhorse.

"How dare you, sire?" Robert said.

William glanced up, mid-rise from the throne. "Norwick?"

"And when were you planning on telling me? Tomorrow, at council, in front of everyone?"

William looked over to Daniel. "You may leave us, Cecile."

Robert bit his tongue until Daniel and his secretaries left the room.

"Crowning the queen to rule whilst I still live?" he said. "Do you wish to make me a laughingstock?"

William crossed his arms over his chest. "How do you plan to rule if you're cut down in battle?"

"You may hide behind that reasoning at council, Highness, but I see through it."

"And what do you see?"

Robert met William's stare, head held high.

"I see that you fear me."

The room was silent for a long moment.

"Aye, cuz, I fear you," William finally said. "Not the harm you would do me, but the harm you would do the realm."

"Harm!" Robert threw up his hands. "I would lead us—"

"Right into the hands of the Germans!" William sprang from his throne and strode down the steps. "I know your inclinations, Robert, and I've looked the other way out of friendship and love, but I will not have you tearing asunder my kingdom."

Robert froze. "Inclinations?"

"Can you deny that you wish our realm to be Protestant?" William stepped to him.

"The pope is a mere puppet of the Spanish. All his dictates are to please—"

The king grabbed Robert's arm, pulling him close to his face. "Your sentiments are treason. Heresy. And you wish me to name you king?"

"'Tis true I hold no love for the pope," Robert said. "But I have never and will never wish you or the realm any ill."

"I know." William finally released him. "But that doesn't mean you won't harm it."

"I would never hand our realm over to the Germans!" Robert put his hands on his hips. "I would rather *we* rule *them*."

"Are you mad? Conquer the whole of the German states? With ten thousand men in total?" He sighed. "*This* is why I fear your rule. You're reckless—"

"And yet who rules is not for you to decide. It was decided by birth."

William began to pace. "You might as well save your breath, for she will not take the crown upon her."

Robert blinked. Why wouldn't she jump at this chance? "So . . . what? If you die in battle . . ."

William stopped pacing and faced him. "If I die in battle, she and Daniel rule as co-regents until my heir is of age."

"You can't put a bastard and a woman in charge!"

"Why not?" William near shouted. "If my father hadn't whored around so, if Daniel was begot of my mother, he would be king now. And so much the better!"

"Come now." If Robert could calm his own temper, he might yet sway William. "We all love Daniel, but placing your half-brother inches from the throne, especially when we are off to fight insurrection—"

"Do you fear insurrection, or losing your place in line?"

Robert glared at the floor, hands clenched. "Has she poisoned you so against me?"

"Leave her out of it."

"But it's true—"

"Robert!" William took a deep breath and lowered his voice. "There is nothing anyone could say, even you, that would poison me against you. I know your heart, and there's no doubt in my mind that you strive for my best."

"And yet you don't believe I would strive for Troixden's best?"

"I fear you would bring more bloodshed," William said. "And don't think I haven't heard the rumors—that you'll change sides once we reach Laureland, ride out against me and claim the crown for yourself."

Robert was speechless. Certainly he'd hoped the war would loosen the country's ties to Rome, their defeat leading to a treaty that allowed Protestants the right to worship. Just another step in turning the tide for Troixden.

And William knew all this, and more. Robert grabbed William's hand and knelt before him.

"You've had my fealty my life entire." He kissed the king's ring of state. "I now swear it to you again." His voice clutched. "God knows I've had plenty of opportunity to kill you before."

The king shook his head and hoisted Robert up, wrapped an arm about his shoulders, and guided him toward the privy chambers.

"Indeed you have." He said. "And are sure to have many more."

Robert managed to laugh, but his heart grew only heavier.

Stone Yard was exactly as William remembered: the reek of urine-soaked hay and human filth, perpetual dripping sounds, slimy stones beneath his feet. The furrow in his brow deepened as he ascended the stairs, not at all looking forward to his task. They were slick, uneven, cracked. But up to the top he must go, for it was in the so-called Noble Suite that Bryan of Beaubourg was housed.

He'd stopped reading the weekly pleadings Bryan sent, but for whatever reason, he'd read this last. All it said was: "Majesty, I am, as always, prepared to die for you. I beg you, as your most humbled servant, may it be soon."

Perhaps he'd finally found a use for Bryan.

He walked into the cell, which was not without creature comforts—a desk, a chair, an actual bed, a fireplace. Tiny trinkets, probably from his family, lined the desk and window, even a basket of sweet rolls sat on the table by the fire. He must have a friend in the kitchens.

Bryan was on his knees in the middle of the room, head down, golden hair hanging over his face, clothes dirtied yet neatly mended. He noticed Bryan's hands, fingers spread on his thighs, nails clean and trimmed. Was he somehow warned of William's coming, or was the man so fastidious even in prison?

"Majesty," he said, face still to the floor, "thank you for fulfilling my request. Yet I would like a priest for my final confession, if it be your pleasure."

"I'm glad to hear of your willingness and your faith," William said, "but today will not be your last." Bryan's head snapped up. "However, you shall have your chance to die for me at long last." He held Bryan's eyes for a moment. "Now tell me, if you please, have you any news from the outside world?"

Bryan shook his head. "All that meets my ears is court gossip, and the only letters I receive are from my mother."

"And what does your mother say?"

"M-my mother?" It was as if Bryan had woken from a long sleep and was still gathering his wits. "She—she tells me of my family. She's hoping Charity will find a good match at court."

"But nothing of the larger world? No news of the insurrection?"

"Insurrection?"

William started to rethink his plans. The boy did not seem all there.

"There is to be war," he said. "Laureland will take arms against the throne, in league with the Germans."

Bryan jumped to his feet. The guards lunged forward and held him.

"This can't be! What will become of Beaubourg? The queen?"

"We will subdue them, fear not." William strode to Bryan and put both hands on the knave's shoulders. "And you will either help us or die trying."

"I am to fight?" Bryan's blue eyes widened.

"We ride in a week." William released him and paced. "In that time, you will retrain under strict supervision. If you're deemed strong enough, you'll ride to battle. You'll either fight nobly and die, or you will fight nobly, win your freedom, and return to your family."

Bryan fell to the ground, grabbed William's hand, and kissed his ring.

"Majesty, you do me more honor than I deserve."

"Not for the first time."

"I will fight with all my strength to keep you and the queen safe and our country whole."

"If you don't," William said as he pulled his hand away,

"you'll be killed on the spot. Probably by the Duke of Norwick, which, I'm sure you realize, would not be a quick death."

William made to leave but stopped at the threshold. Bryan was still on his knees, face alight.

"Hear me well," he said. "Do not make us both regret my decision."

The wind whipped Anna's green velvet skirts, fox fur ruff tickling her neck. The gray clouds hung low, their weight pressing down on her. She stood in the castle's courtyard, Daniel by her side, the entire court standing solemn and silent behind.

William stood at the head of his troops, facing her. His black warhorse pawed the ground and whinnied. Hundreds of men shifted on their mounts, but none spoke. No one even coughed.

As was tradition, William knelt in front of the queen, chainmail clanking beneath his cloak. She remembered being wrapped in that very cloak when they lay in a meadow in Beaubourg. He'd gone to his knees there too, entreating her mother's spirit. The memory pierced her. The stupid, senseless pursuits of men that left women widowed and children fatherless. How could he ride? And yet how could he not? He took her hand, kissed her wedding ring, then pressed the back of her hand to his cheek. She felt him breathe in her scent as he pressed his lips to her palm. She willed her legs to stay strong.

"My lady," he said, holding her hand to his chest, "the honor of your favor and blessing."

Bernard, directly behind her, held out a ceremonial kerchief, blessed by Bartmore. But this kerchief she'd never held, never stowed in her sleeve or tucked at her bosom. She reached inside her corset, right next to William's ruby, and pulled out a well-worn silk kerchief, an A in her mother's hand stitched in the corner. She pressed it into William's hand. He kissed it and tucked it down his mail. She spied a glint of moisture at the corner of his eye. Oh, that God would bring him home safe.

She held her free hand over his. It looked strange, disembodied, like someone else's fingers trembling in the dull light.

"Go in the name of God," she said in a voice she barely recognized. "His hand to keep thee, the love of Christ in thy veins, the strong Spirit bathing thee, all three to shield and aid thee, behind, in front, below and above, and bring thee back victorious."

"Amen," the king said, still on his knee.

She wanted to say so much and couldn't. She lowered her voice, for his ears alone. "God bring you back to me, to us . . ."

He leaned forward, placed his hands on either side of her pronounced belly, and pressed his face into her softness.

"God keep you both," he said, a catch in his voice. He rose. "We will save our people from all-out war, and I will return to you."

She grabbed him about the neck, pulling him hard to her. He gasped. She'd be damned if ceremony intruded on her last moments with her husband.

"Make it so," she said into his ear. "For if you perish, my heart—my soul—perishes with you."

His grip tightened about her. "I will do everything in my power to grant your desire, my queen."

Her laugh was bittersweet. Looking over his shoulder, she glimpsed Bryan. He caught her eye and bowed his head.

"Lord have mercy, I love you," William said, eyes flitting over her face as if to hold this picture of her and take it with him. "Brave face, my queen," he said, looking her over once more. She released her breath, and he kissed her, lips soft and sweet.

Then he let her go, went straight to his horse, and mounted.

"My people," he called, "give the queen and the Duke of Cecile all the fealty you give your king. And pray for swift victory, for our heir, and for the speedy return of all our loyal men. We ride to victory!"

Cheers erupted. The standard bearer lifted the blue and gold griffin flag of Troixden high as the men formed an aisle for the king's party to ride through. The standard bearer was followed by Ridgeland, Norwick, and Duven, then the grand master general, and finally, the king.

She felt her knees weaken, but she locked them and stood straight, heart in her throat, eyes stinging, until the last man was but a speck on the dark horizon.

CHAPTER 11

War

Anna knew it would take William at least two weeks to reach Laureland, and probably a week or two more to reach the borderlands, where they believed the rebels to be. There would be nothing to report until then. Surely. And yet she longed to hear some word. She had written three times, Daniel frowning with the third and lecturing her about resources expended on messengers.

She had hoped her newly bestowed duties would keep her mind occupied, but Daniel had removed these tasks from her hands one by one. Though she still presided at privy court and attended Council Table, he rarely brought anything to her attention. If this was how the war would play out at home, it would be a long one indeed. But Anna had no intention of surrendering that easily.

Anna all but jumped from her seat by the window, needlework sliding to the floor, when Bernard approached.

"Majesty," Bernard said, "If you please, I have news to impart."

"From the king?"

"Yes and no." Bernard beckoned her toward the fireplace. "Highness, I don't wish to think ill of anyone, especially His Grace—"

Anna grabbed his arms. "Out with it!"

He swallowed. "It seems there has been some word from the king on their slow progress, and nothing of interest to report—"

"I will decide what is and is not of interest." She regretted her tone. It wasn't Bernard's fault she hadn't been told.

"To be sure, Majesty, but pray let me continue." She took a deep breath and nodded. "Apparently—and this is only what I heard—it has been instructed that all letters from the front are to pass through the Duke of Cecile's office. Even those addressed to Your Highness."

Anna felt a white-hot fury rise up and color her cheeks. *Her* letters? From William? How dare he?

"Majesty, I beg your calm." Bernard held up his hands. "If you attend upon him now, he may only conclude that your female mind can't handle—"

"I'll show him what I can't handle," she said, grabbing her loyal servant by the wrist. "You shall announce me."

"But, Majesty—"

"*Now*, Bernard." She looked at his red face and gave him a quick wink. "Worry not. You've taught me well."

"Highness, what a pleasant surprise." Daniel rose from behind his desk. "How may I be of service?"

"I'm so glad you asked, Your Grace." She gave him a tight smile back. "I would like to see the letters from the king." She heard Daniel's men shift behind her. His secretary studied the rug.

"Please, Highness," Daniel said, "have a seat to give you ease. I was going to bring you the letters."

"Seeing them will give me ease," she said, her facile look still in place.

"Of course." He removed a chain from around his neck, a large gold key appearing above his collar. He gave it to his secretary, who used it to open a small box at his side. Inside the box yet another key was revealed, which Daniel used to open the bottom left drawer of his desk. He extracted five letters in a bundle and handed them to Anna.

She sat in the chair facing him and scanned them. The first three, in a clerk's hand, reported the army's progress. They had forded the Orlea, taking more time than planned. They were caught in a squall crossing the Truss Mountains and again delayed. The going was slow, but spirits and supplies ran high.

Even these dry records made her heart burn, knowing William had dictated these words, touched this paper. That somewhere, miles from her, he was still there.

But the last two letters stopped her breath.

"These are addressed to me," she said, her voice deadly quiet. Daniel had the decency to blush. "These are personal letters, from your king to your queen." She rose, all trace of playacting niceties gone. "There is nothing—*nothing* in them of import to you or the realm."

She'd never seen him look so uncomfortable. "The king made it clear that all letters from the front should come through me, so as to not expose you—"

"Your instructions did not include reading my personal letters!" She slapped the letters on top of a neat pile on his desk, tipping the papers. "We're to run court in tandem. You may not unilaterally decide what I will and will not be exposed to!"

"Majesty, my allegiance is ultimately to the realm, to keeping the king and his kin on the throne. While I may agree with you personally, my higher duty is to the heir you carry." He gave her a pleading look. "Do you not see? If any word were to come that might upset you—any word that might cause you again to . . ." He looked at her belly, his eyes almost yearning. "You must know that I seek to protect your child, and that so doing means shielding you from undue pain."

"Do you think me so weak?" Her tone was softer now. Daniel was no Robert, and she shouldn't treat him thus. Still, his actions frustrated her. "Don't you think I take every measure for the care of the babe?"

"Please accept my humble apology." Daniel bowed his head, then looked straight into her eyes. "But also, please allow me to continue to read all official messages from the front so that, if any news be grave, I can inform you in a way that causes the least . . ." He came around the desk to hold her hand. ". . . grief."

"If the king were to be killed, Your Grace," she said, "no words on earth could curb my grief."

"That's what I'm afraid of."

"All the same," she said, "no words could inspire me to more resolve. Remember that. And do not do me injustice again."

"I'm sorry you felt it so." He released her hand. "I am not your enemy, Majesty."

"Nor am I yours. Heaven save us, but we are in this together."

"Yes, Your Majesty." He returned to his desk, straightening the pile Anna had spilled. He picked up the two letters addressed to her and held them out.

"I have more than enough room in my day, Your Grace." Anna smoothed the letters against her chest. "You should not overtax yourself. I am here to share the weight, but if you don't trust me, I cannot help you—or the king." He nodded. She drew closer and touched his hand as it rested on his desk. "I know that you miss him too," she said softly. "We can be a comfort to each other in this."

He kissed her hand with a reverence that startled her.

"Thank you, Majesty. I will remember."

A fortnight later, Council Table proved uneventful. No further word from the king or any other, though Anna still didn't trust that she was kept apprised. She knew someone, be it Daniel or one of his minions, would read her letters to the king and thus kept their content frivolous. William's in turn were few and too far between, but loving and candid, asking her advice, sharing tales of men at camp that made her sides hurt with laughing. How she longed to indulge him in return. She'd tried to hint that his letters were being read, but thinking more on it, she realized he wouldn't care who knew of his devotion. Still, she did not like the idea of his private thoughts being laid bare to anyone but her.

"If that is all for the agenda . . ." Daniel said, calling the small gathering to a close.

"Your Grace," Anna said, "if you please, I must be away from court for perhaps four days."

Daniel's brows seemed to merge into his hairline.

"Away, Majesty? Why did you not speak with me?"

"I would have, Your Grace, but was only made aware of the need myself moments before council."

"I see." He looked down, collecting his papers. "And where, pray tell, are you going and why?"

"My Lady Jane's son has taken ill again." Halforn seemed only half listening. Bartmore, per usual, was frowning at her. "She believes it may be something serious, and Mistress Mary and I would offer our help."

"She is of Cecile, is she not?" Daniel said, a hint of reproach in his tone. "I know many healers there, it being my duchy. I shall send for them most happily."

"She is one of my ladies, Your Grace," Anna said, "and I shall be most pleased to attend upon her."

"Highness." Daniel looked earnest. "If it is true the boy has an illness, His Majesty would never forgive me if I allowed you in harm's way."

Anna rose, descending the dais she sat upon. "Your Grace, I do not believe he has anything I might catch. Indeed, Lady Jane has always been the picture of health."

"Majesty, His Grace's caution is not undue," Halforn said. "With the king at arms, you and Cecile running court . . . even if you were not to fall ill, having you gone is surely unwise."

"My dear Halforn," she said, smiling sweetly, "I believe His Grace Cecile has everything in hand and shall not need me for a few days."

"And what of the babe?" Daniel said.

"As I have said before, Your Grace, I would never do anything to risk the life of my child. I hold it higher and dearer than my own."

"If you are set on it, Highness," Daniel said, "Certainly none can stop you. But for all our sakes, take care. We do not wish to engage our sorely missed king's wrath."

She put her hands on her hips and gave them all a wry smile. "And will you not miss me?" All but Daniel erupted in flattering vows.

Cecile was a minor duchy half a day's ride south of Havenside, tucked between rolling wheat fields and pastures dotted with pillowed sheep. Lady Jane's manor, or rather, her husband's manor, stood at the end of a lane lined with cypress trees, the building's pink stones brilliant in the noonday sun.

Anna's carriage bumbled down the dusty road, halting before the wide stairs, where Jane stood clasping her hands, surrounded by servants. Her husband, Baron Thomas Burn of Cecile, was away at battle. Whether Lady Jane felt the pang of his absence as Anna felt William's, she did not know, but she did know that a woman with a sick child and a household to tend to would be missing her husband's service, if not his embrace.

Bernard, who had stubbornly insisted on accompanying the queen, sprang forth to open the carriage. With his typical flair, he called out, "Her Majesty the queen!" and helped her to the pebbled ground. Mary and Yvette followed her.

Lady Jane, so shy at the palace, ran down the stairs to greet Anna, nearly falling into her curtsy. She pressed Anna's hand to her face.

"Majesty," she said, breathless, "you honored me in bringing forth my John to life, and now you will bring him life again."

The old, familiar buzz crept under Anna's skin, a blend of fear and grim determination. Oh, how she missed this.

"Lady Jane, do not tremble so." She helped Jane to rise. "The resources of the whole realm are at our disposal. With the grace of God, we shall see what we can do."

Lady Jane bobbed another curtsy, cheeks pink, and led the way into the manor. Once inside, Anna addressed Bernard.

"Please see to the unpacking in the apartments. I shall attend upon the young Lord John now."

"Surely, Madam, you would prefer to refresh after the day's journey?"

"I thank you for your concern, but I have come to help the lad if I can, not to be a strain on milady's household."

Bernard exhaled and stared at the ceiling. "As you wish, Majesty."

Passing him by, she touched his arm. The corners of his mouth twitched.

Anna, Yvette, and Mary followed Jane through the Great Hall to the private family rooms. The manor's stonework was exquisite, but the décor was decidedly subdued. There were but few tapestries, all depicting stern Bible scenes—the banishment from the Garden, Lot's wife turning into a pillar of salt, and what Anna assumed must be a scene from the Book of Revelation, complete with devils chewing off appendages of the damned. Certainly Jane would not miss the arms of a man who preferred such art as this.

When they finally arrived at the nursery, Lady Jane gave Anna a sheepish look and opened the door to a paneled room. Even this was Spartan, with only a wooden rocking horse with real hair, some brightly painted wood blocks, and a stuffed dog that looked well loved.

As the women entered, John came toward them with a grin to blind the angels and eyes only for his mama. Anna's heart leapt. Wanting a child for William's sake and for the realm, she was surprised how her heart could ache for such unconditional affection.

John toddled over to his mother, arms uplifted. "Up, mama, up, up!"

Jane flicked her eyes to John's nurse, who was glaring at Yvette and Mary, then to Anna. She bent to pick up her son, who promptly gave her a wet kiss and began to play with her simple pearl necklace.

"Begging your pardon, Majesty," she said, "my lord does not like me to indulge John so, but I cannot help it at times." She beamed at his blond head and curling lashes.

"Indulge him?" Anna said, taking in the happy scene. "Why, cuddling one's child is not only proper, 'tis a mother's duty and dearest pleasure."

This statement met with a grunt from the nurse, covered quickly by a cough. Lady Jane nuzzled John's hair. She set him down and off he scampered to his dog, hugging it under his arm, then proceeded to his blocks. He was much slighter than a typical boy of two and a half years and fairer than he should have been, especially living in the south.

"My Lady," Anna said, motioning for Mary and Yvette to set up their supplies, "does Lord John see the out of doors?"

"Oh no, Highness." She clutched her chest. "The doctor said he might catch chill."

A cough roused the room. It was deep and wet, John's face flushing red with the strain of it. When it stopped, he continued building his tower.

"So this is the cough you speak of?" Anna went to him, bending down and placing a hand on his back, feeling the bony bump of his spine.

"Yes, Majesty, and that's not the worst of it." Jane came beside Anna and sat gracelessly on the floor by her son. "About once or twice a day, he coughs up mucus, or on rare occasions, blood." She stroked his hair. "And you can see how thin and frail he is."

"Has he had any fevers?" Anna handed him a yellow block, which he snatched.

"None of late."

"He had the one at Eastertide, mum," the nurse said.

"Yes," Jane said, looking back at her boy with a devotion that stopped Anna's breath. "And when he was a baby, he had those two terrible fevers. Since then it's been nothing but coughs. He seems to be on the mend, then they start again."

Mary bustled over, face creased in concern. "He's skin and bones he is," she said, wrapping her thumb and forefinger around the boy's arm.

"We feed him plenty, thank ye very much," his nurse said, looking down her nose at Mary.

Mary cocked a brow at the woman. "I didn't say ye didn't feed him, said he was skinny. There's a difference." The boy's nurse huffed and crossed her arms.

Anna tousled John's hair, then went to the nurse.

"Good nurse," she said, "it's a wonder he has such energy and life about him. It must be due to your earnest care." The woman gave Anna a measuring look, clearly trying to decide what to make of her. "Tell me," Anna said, leading her toward the boy and his mother, "what remedies have you sought that have given him such help as this?"

The nurse bobbed her head at the playful scene below. "Well, the leeches, of course. Least once a week." Anna nodded. "And he seems to like the tea with honey. 'Specially at night."

"I see," Anna said. "Do you hear that, Mary? Tea with honey at night." She heard Mary mutter and held back a laugh.

"That's right," the nurse said, finally unclenching her jaw. She raised her voice, looking over Anna's shoulder. "Mullein tea! Two teaspoons of honey, no more nor less."

"I thank you, lady nurse," Anna patted the nurse's hand. "You've helped me, and Lord John, a great deal."

The nurse gave a stiff curtsy. Anna hoped she had melted her a little.

"Lady Jane?" Anna moved to where Jane sat in a stiff-backed chair, John in her lap, reading him a book. Jane gave Anna one of the most natural looks she had ever seen on her lady. "Does the manor keep goats?"

"Yes, Majesty, our tenants specialize in tending goats, and the manor keeps chickens, sheep, and pigs as well."

"Your nurse has given me a thought," she said with a side-long glance at Mary, who rolled her eyes. "Keep giving John his tea every night, and make sure he spends ten minutes breathing in the vapors. But also, three times a day, give him warm goat milk with honey."

"And some milk toast for breakfast," Mary added.

"And what of the leeches?" The nurse asked.

Anna looked to Mary, who shrugged.

"For now, let's leave them off." Jane visibly relaxed, but Anna feared any headway she had made with the nurse might be lost. Why did everyone always leap to leeches? They were good for clearing wounds and pus, sometimes relieving pressure, but she did not understand why people thought them a cure-all.

"In the meantime, make sure he has plenty of rest, especially after meals. We'll observe him again this evening and hopefully know more."

"Oh, thank you, Majesty," Jane said, rocking John in her tight embrace, "this means ever so much to me."

"Well, Lady Jane," Anna said, "as you say, I helped him come into the world, I'm not going to see him out of it any time soon."

Anna returned to her rooms that evening fairly certain that what Mary had told her before supper was true: the boy had consumption. Yet it was curious he wasn't more ill, and even more curious that no one else in the household had caught it in the first year. She grimaced, thinking on what Daniel would say if he knew she was exposed to this.

Yvette leaned over the copper bath, adding drops of lavender and rose oil, and stirred the steaming water. "Come, my queen."

Anna needed no prodding. She felt sticky and worn. Easing into the bath, she breathed deep and closed her eyes. Yvette washed her arms with care. Mary joined them, starting in on Anna's hair.

"You know we can't stay," Mary said.

Anna reluctantly opened her eyes, staring at the flames in the stone hearth.

"And why not? Daniel rarely lets me make decisions," she said. "I doubt my presence at court will be missed."

She felt so low. There was nothing back at the palace for her but anxious waiting laced with boredom. At least here she had a purpose, could do something of use, even if it was simply comforting Lady Jane.

"'Tis not what I mean," Mary said, dumping a pitcher of water over her head. Anna wiped her face, spitting into her hands, the oils pungent on her tongue.

"Well?"

"Have you not been lookin' around, milady?" Mary lowered her voice, even though there was no one else to hear.

"Be plain, Mary, for my head smarts." Anna splashed water on her shoulders as Yvette cleaned her mistress's toes.

"The baron and his lady be Lutherans."

Yvette froze, then cleared her throat and continued to dig at Anna's toenails.

"And how have you deduced this?" Anna couldn't help lowering her own voice.

"The baron is a wealthy man, yet there's no wealth about."

"That's hardly heresy." Yvette gave a deep sigh. "Many men—especially men married later in life, like Baron Burn—keep a sparse home."

"But that's not all," Mary said, stopping her work. "They've no priest, no almoner, and that nurse of theirs—"

"Mary, I know you've my best interests at heart, but let's not jump to conclusions. We told Lady Jane we'd stay. It is an honor for her house—"

"Honor be damned when sickness of body and spirit be about!"

Anna looked up, surprised. Mary's jowls trembled, her face gone white. Mary of Beaubourg was scared of nothing.

"Mistress Mary," Yvette said, "if it eases your mind, let me investigate further." She gave Anna a grim look. "In my former life, I was, shall we say, adept at discovering hidden truths."

"Thank you, Lady Yvette," Anna said, still contemplating her matron. "Please keep us informed."

Mary gave a curt nod, then dumped another pitcher over Anna's head.

Late that night Anna woke drenched in sweat, sheets a tangle at her feet, a frowning Mary hovering over her. She'd dreamed she was flying over the battlefield, watching the clash of metal and men below. She saw a flash of golden hair and swooped down, willing herself not to fall. She cast about the battle, and for a split second she saw him. He looked up to the sky, and she into the bearded face of her beloved, smeared with blood, his eyes piercing hers. Then a sword came crashing toward him—

Mary pressed a damp cloth to her sweaty forehead. She closed her eyes and moaned. She heard clinking glass and low muttering. Yvette appeared at her other side, holding a goblet.

"If it's a fever, we can't away now," Yvette whispered.

"And yet we must away from this place, this den of vipers!" Mary whispered back.

Anna could feel Yvette tense at her side as Mary continued to wipe Anna down, the coolness of the cloth calming her skin and mind.

"I care not where your sympathies lie at other times, milady," Mary said to Yvette, "but right now, they must lie with Her Majesty!"

Anna felt the softness of silk bending over her, could smell almonds and jasmine.

"Do you accuse me of—"

Anna moaned again. "Don't . . ." she said, trying to lift an arm to stop their quarreling. "Please."

"Lay still, dearie." Mary gently placed Anna's forearm by her side. Anna opened her eyes to see Yvette leave her in a cloud of indigo silk. She faded into the darkness of the chamber, leaving only her scent behind, as Anna fell into a fitful sleep.

The next morning Anna's head felt like an anvil, heavy and hit upon. She was still sweating profusely despite the windows open to a dreary October day. Her hands leapt to her belly, pressing, feeling for movement. Though the babe's kicks were intermittent this late in her pregnancy, she prayed to God that she would feel the baby move now.

It didn't.

She flung back her sheets, looking between her legs for any sign of blood or fluid. Thank God, nothing. She glanced to her bedside table hoping to quench her thirst and felt a tickle by her right hip. Could it be? She pressed the spot, stilling the rest of her body.

Mary bustled over, picking up the mug Anna had been after. Anna put up a hand to still her.

"Babies kick of their own accord," Mary said. "Not when their mamas want them to—even royal mamas."

She wanted one more kick, anything to let her know the babe was still alive. Tears gathered in her eyes. *Please* . . . She fell back against her pillow. And then she felt it. This time, right in the bladder, a kick so strong it made her jump. "Oh thank you, thank you!" She laughed, hugging her belly. "Hello, little one!"

"I told ye the babe's fine." Mary handed her the mug filled with tea. "But *you*, on the other hand—"

A knock at the door revealed Bernard performing a much abbreviated bow, a thin book in his hand, face gray.

"Majesty," he said, approaching the bed, "we can tarry here no longer. It would be injurious to your reputation."

"Her Majesty's still feverish and mustn't be moved, sadly," Mary said.

Bernard scuttled toward the bed. "I happened upon this while ascertaining the child's health this morning. His cough, by the way, is near gone—more reason to away."

"Give it here, Bernard." Anna opened to the first page of the book. "I hardly think any children's stories . . ."

Der Kleine Catechismus . . . Mart. Luther. Wittenberg. She was holding Martin Luther's *Small Catechism.* A book for children, but a book of treason and of heresy. She nearly threw it across the room, but instead gripped it hard.

Dear God. The baron was a heretic, and so was his wife, her beloved lady-in-waiting. It all snapped into focus—Jane's blushing when Anna read scripture, the knowing glances she gave when Anna expounded on theology. Not only was Jane a Lutheran, she must think Anna was as well. Her face flushed.

Lady Yvette hurried forward with a fresh pitcher of water.

"But the baron fights on the king's behalf," Anna said, as if to convince herself.

"Quite so," Bernard said, "and hopefully he stays on the king's side. He is, after all, fighting with Norwick's men."

Yvette's pitcher crashed to the floor.

"Don't, Bernard," Yvette said. "Don't you dare accuse the duke, or the baron—"

"I did not accuse, milady." Bernard swallowed. "Only pointing out the facts."

"It's not the facts I dispute," Yvette said, "but the way you knit them together."

"And the queen in the bosom of the beast!" Mary said, her eyes wild. "Yet we can't move her in this condition."

"Send for Lady Jane," Anna said. "I will speak to her and put this matter to rest."

Bernard twitched, Mary clucked, and Yvette looked liked she's swallowed moldy bread. Well, if no one had a better idea . . .

"Very good, Majesty." Bernard reached for the offending catechism.

"Nay, Bernard," Anna said, "I may need evidence."

Anna managed to convince Mary to help her be dressed and seated in a chair for her audience with Jane. Her thoughts were in knots. If she dismissed Jane, people would wonder why, though she could say it was so Jane could tend her son. If she kept Jane on, Anna could keep an eye on her. And more to the point, Jane was one of her favorite ladies, always quick with a tender word, a soft touch, a pleasing demeanor.

But there was something more about Jane. Maybe it was the nurturing she saw and felt watching Jane and John together. That if Jane were at the palace, near to Anna, perhaps Anna would feel that same motherly sentiment for her own child. For she deeply feared she was too selfish, too interested in adult matters to truly embrace mothering. She so wanted to be the mother William wanted for their child. But how could she be sure? She had never played with baby dolls as a child, never played "lord and lady of the castle" with Bryan. She assumed she'd have children, as that's what women did, and indeed, since becoming queen, was desperate to do for all their sakes. But she was not convinced she would love her child, not the way her mother loved her own children. Not the way Jane loved hers. Anna's heart sank further at the thought of sending Jane away. Yet the taint of heresy endangered them all.

And what if Bernard's hints were truth? She did not suspect Jane to be complicit in any deceit. It wasn't in her nature. But what of the baron? Was he even then turning traitor and riding against William under Robert's flag? Would Jane have the strength to stand with the crown against her husband? Not if her son were threatened. And yet, had not Anna helped make her son well again? The questions and doubts were endless. *Wills, where are you when I need you most?*

Lady Jane entered and curtsied.

"Lady Jane," Anna said, "I dearly hope you will be forthright with me."

"But of course, Majesty. You have yet again done me such honor, such service, if there is any way I can be of help to you . . ." Her eyes slipped to the book in Anna's lap. Jane dropped to her knees. "Majesty, I—"

"So it's true?" Anna's face fell. Lady Jane kept her eyes on the floor. "You shall not come to harm by my hand, I promise you."

At this, Jane looked up, her brown eyes wet. "I thought I had hidden everything away."

"I must ask you," Anna said, more stern than she wished, "have you been a scout, planted in my service to aid the enemy?" The look on Jane's face told Anna all she needed to know. It was as if Anna had slapped her. No, worse—as if she'd slapped John.

"Majesty, never—oh, no!" She buried her head in her hands, trembling. "I thought perhaps . . . perhaps you tended this way, what with your reading of scripture, your favor of Multman. But never, ever would I betray you so!"

"I thought not." Anna took a deep breath. "But understand that I had to be sure. Lives are at stake, not the least of which our husbands'." She handed the book back to Jane's still shaking hands. "I have turned this many times in my head and come to a decision. Lady Jane, I must relieve you of your service to me."

"Majesty—"

"So that you may tend more fully to your son." Jane's eyes searched Anna's face. "I have never seen you more full of life than I have these past days." Anna paused to cough, wincing.

Jane's face went white. "You've taken ill, Highness? God in heaven!"

"Worry not, milady, 'tis only a cold I surely caught at court." Jane frowned as Anna continued. "As I was saying, your duties will be best served in caring for your son. I have ten other ladies to swirl about me. He only has one mother."

"But—"

"You may come to court at will and be welcomed, but no longer into my service."

"Yes, Majesty." Jane bowed her head.

"Upon my honor, I will breathe nothing of what I have found here to another soul. But if you, or your husband, become more bold in your beliefs, I will have no choice but to censure you in the harshest way."

"You have my word, Highness."

To be so formal with her didn't seem right. "Jane, dear." Anna sighed. "You must know that I've treasured you as my favorite these short years. I will miss you most heartily."

A tear rolled down Jane's reddened cheeks. "And I you, my dearest queen."

Jane gave a tearful leave, and Anna sank back in her chair, all her energy spent. She felt her head, damp with sweat. Mary bustled in to relieve her of her clothes and get her safely ensconced in bed. Anna hacked out a cough, her head pounding. She lay back, desperate to sleep it off. She felt another kick, this time by her left hip. She brought her hand to rest on her belly.

"Let's rest now, little one." She pulled the sheets to her chin rolling onto her side when she felt it—a pain like a dagger to her gut, her womb contracting into a hard ball.

"Mary!" she screamed.

Anna woke coughing, confused, but no longer sweating. Her first thought was for the baby. She searched the room, eyes landing on a snoring Mary, slumped in a chair in a ray of sunlight. Then she saw Yvette in the corner, making up a tray.

"Lady Yvette," she said, "what of the babe?"

Yvette set the tray down at Anna's bedside, took one of Anna's hands, and looked into her eyes.

"You still hold him," she said. "The pain you felt was the start of your false contractions, as you well know from your midwifery. They start quite early on in a second pregnancy."

Anna hadn't realized she was holding her breath until she let it go, her body sinking into the pillows. It was odd to now be feeling what she'd only heard, and counseled others, about.

"More to the point," Yvette said, "your fever has broken. But whether or not you've caught the consumption, we've yet to know for certain."

Anna shook her head. "It's only a cold, I can feel it."

"Just as you could feel you were about to lose the babe?" Yvette said, and Anna scowled. "I beg your pardon, Majesty. I should not presume to be so informal."

"'Tis not your informality but your implication," Anna said.

"I apologize. You of all people have a right to worry about your womb." She went to fix Anna's drink and tincture on the tray. "But you must remember that we all worry, for the babe and for you."

She handed Anna the same concoction they'd prescribed for John, goat's milk with honey. Anna inhaled the steam, letting it soak into her pounding head. She felt her womb cramp again, and she yelped.

"You're sure it's normal strains?" she said.

"As I am not in your body, I cannot say, but Mary certainly seems to think so."

Another cramp hit her and she moaned, causing Mary to wake with a start.

"Dearie! You're awake!" Mary shoved herself up and out of the chair to a chorus of creaking joints.

"Yes," Anna said, "and I'm wondering when I can leave this place."

Yvette and Mary shared a worried look. A knock at the door saved them. In strode Bernard.

"A message from the battlefield." He came to her bed and handed her a note written in Daniel's precise hand.

Majesty,

Our men have reached the rebels. The battle has more than likely begun by the time I received this last word. Please continue to pray, as I know you do without ceasing.

Your Humble Servant,
D. Cecile

"I don't care how sick I am!" Anna coughed again. "The battle's begun. Quarantine me if you must, but I and the heir must be at Palace Havenside."

Bernard had already gone to see about the carriage. Yvette began packing, while Mary stood in the center of the room with her arms crossed, giving Anna that "I used to wipe your bottom" look that only mothers and nurses have perfected.

"Court will exhaust you," Mary said. "As much as I wish to be out of this heretic house, I don't wish you sicker, dearie."

"I appreciate your concern," Anna said as Yvette draped a mink cape on her shoulders. She hugged it about her, wishing it were William's arms. "But my place is at the palace. It gives the people a sense of normalcy, a sense of stability."

"Not if the queen's locked up in her rooms and coughing all over the place."

"I am a symbol," she said, flipping up her hood, "of William's right, of his divine appointment to the throne. And I will not disappoint him or our people, cold or no."

Mary clucked but returned to packing her kit.

Anna had left unspoken the fear that clenched her gut. If William died and she was not at the palace to press their child's precedence, Robert would surely try to claim the throne. Then where would Daniel's loyalty lie? With his half-brother's unborn child, or with his friend and half-cousin?

She must to Havenside at once.

CHAPTER 12

Into the Breach

William and his men had been encamped on top of a forested hill at the eastern edge of Laureland for a week. Against the judgment of Robert and the master general, he refused to attack without direct cause. If he saw a flag of one of the German states, that would be cause, but at that time, all he could see were plumes of smoke rising from the enemy camp, which spread out in the valley at the foot of the long-deserted castle.

He picked up Anna's last letter. It seemed odd, disjointed, as if continuing some conversation he hadn't been privy to. And why was her language so formal, the content so frivolous? Had she been warned against sharing anything vital?

He reread the only line that gave him comfort, the line that convinced him it was from her: *Return to me dearest, for I have your heart, and it's missing its owner, but not more than I. For I am at a loss without your smile.*

Robert burst into William's tent, dragging Bryan with him. They bowed.

"Well, is it time so soon to be off with his head?" William cocked a brow.

"Sadly not," Robert said. He released Bryan's arm and the lad stumbled forward. "Tell the king what you just told me."

Bryan frowned at the ground. "Majesty, I—"

"Speak up, lad!" Robert smacked him in the back, and Bryan shot him a look that would send lesser men scurrying. Bryan then cleared his throat, raised his head, and puffed out his considerable chest.

"Majesty." He bowed again. "As I told His Grace, we near the squall season in the north. In another week or so there may be so much rain that the stream in the valley will overflow its banks to the point of flooding the battlefield."

"The Laurelanders surely know this as well," William said, "so why do they camp on a flood plain?"

"It is my belief, Highness," Bryan said, "that they plan to wait us out, hoping to draw us into the fray amidst a storm, from which they will retreat to the castle ruins, and we will be, well, stuck in the mud, Majesty."

"So you see, my liege," Robert said, "we must form an attack, else we're caught here waiting out storms until winter."

William scratched his stubble. The supplies wouldn't last that long without replenishments. And from what Bryan said, it sounded as if the whole valley would be impassable for miles, making those supplies hard to come by.

"Are the men ready?" He placed Anna's letter on the desk.

"They've been ready since we left the palace, Highness."

"Send me the general." He rose and strode out of his tent into the overcast day. In the distance he saw two horsemen heading toward them double-speed, white flag snapping in the wind. For a moment, his heart lightened. Perhaps they had come to surrender.

By the time the two riders were stopped, searched, and led to the king, the grand master general had joined William in his tent, along with Ridgeland and Gregory of Duven.

A muscular man, nearly as tall as William and dressed finely, stepped forward, bowed, and held out a rolled parchment.

"Majesty, I am Lord Joesph of Westerville, sent here with our conditions for peace."

"Conditions for peace?" William unsheathed the dagger on his belt, cutting through the wax seal. "So you wish to surrender?"

Westerville let out a booming laugh.

"Begging your Majesty's pardon," he said. "These are so you may return to the palace with dignity rather than defeat upon you."

"How dare you, sir!" Ridgeland started toward Westerville, hand on his sword hilt.

William stayed him while he read the conditions. He flicked his eyes up to meet Westerville's.

"Were they drunk when they penned these?" William said. "Break with Rome? Abdicate the throne? Not to mention the rest of these ridiculous, convoluted demands."

Westerville stuck his thumbs in his pockets, looking like a butcher debating the price of a prized pig.

"How else can we be assured that we'll be left to worship in peace?"

"You *have* worshiped in peace under our rule."

"Tell that to the mason you set flame to—"

"Enough!" William strode to Westerville, inches from the man's face. "You come here with lies as proofs and demand we throw the faith of our people in the dirt, so you may flirt with Germans?" He held up the parchment, ripped it in half, and threw it in Westerville's face. "This is what we think of your 'conditions,' sir."

Westerville's mouth curled up at the edges. "I thought as much myself, Majesty." He had the audacity to wink at William. "Alas, I am only the messenger."

"Your loyalty is astounding." William turned away.

"My loyalty is to the wind, Majesty, and she doth blow east around these parts."

William was glad the man couldn't see his smile. If these lesser lords simply fought alongside the largest dog, there was hope. Surely they would desert and come to William's side when the pope's promised troops arrived.

He swung around, smile gone. He studied Westerville.

"The winds do blow, Westerville. And the wind of our sword blows quick and without mercy."

Westerville bowed. "So, Majesty, no message then?"

"My message is this: I shall see you all in chains or in hell."

Later that night, to the sounds of men grunting and iron clanging, he received another letter from Anna:

Wills –

I care not whose eyes find this. I am at my wits' end with the deafening silence from the battlefield. Tell me you are well, tell me you are safe, and I will be content. Your son grows daily in vigor, and in his will to live. I hold tight to the belief that you too are triumphant. May the God who is my hope and strength, a fortress not to be moved, protect you with all his angels and bring you back to me, my love. You are William, King of Troixden, man of honor, placed upon the throne by God himself. Forget it not. And return to me victorious in all haste. I bind you to my heart yet again . . .

xx - A

It gave him courage. It gave him hope. And with it tucked in his breast he would ride into battle, heart and mind bent to a singular task: getting home alive.

Before dawn, William and his army charged into battle. The crown's archers laid their siege on the enemy fighters, picking holes in their pike formations, creating leeway for the cavalry. The Laurelanders were vastly outnumbered in horses, but their foot soldiers were scrappy, hungry, and stubborn. William's cavalry tramped easily through their lines, but behind the pikes, the men swarmed like hornets and stung like them too, with bows and poleaxes more numerous than William's war council had anticipated. He would be less of a target on the ground. Robert also had dismounted and was pushing through a hole in the hive of Laurelanders, aiming for their center. Robert's men would take the middle and spin out, widening his circle further and further, while the rest of the troops under Ridgeland, Duven, the grand master, and the king would attack those retreating from Robert's expanding domain. That was the plan, at least.

William pushed his men along Laureland's left flank, trying to herd and thin the rebels up against Robert's men, maneuvering more than fighting. He wore nondescript armor to avoid recognition, but his height was not disguisable. Whenever he heard a call of "the king," the Laurelanders would bunch up and attempt to kill him, undoing all the steering his men had accomplished.

By midday, he finally met up with Ridgeland's forces, completing the battle circle. But leaks in their defensive walls allowed enemies to escape their trap and move to fight behind the crown's lines.

Sir Bryan fought under Ridgeland, and William could see his steady and lethal progress, his strikes almost graceful in their bloody precision. He bore two short-swords and fought with ease, twisting and twining like a dancer. Robert too was in sight, plowing through the fighters like an ox, shouting orders to his men as if he were a foreman harvesting wheat, not a soldier risking life and limb. Once again, William was glad to have Robert on his side.

Another shout of "the king" had William facing one more skirmish. Three men, one of whom William recognized as the butcher who brought sausage to William's first Festival of Harvest, came against him. His heart sank again, knowing these were his countrymen he fought.

Despite his size, William was light on his feet and easily dodged the incoming clumsy blows of the mace, stabbing a man in his kidney as he stumbled past. He sliced his sword easily through the paltry leather armor of the next man, his entrails spilling forth in a gush of blood and excrement, the man too stunned to scream.

William turned back toward Ridgeland's men to hold the outer circle when he heard someone shout, "Majesty, watch out!" He whirled to find none other than Sir Bryan, sword clashed against Robert's, restraining it from delivering a death blow aimed at William's head.

"Get off, damn you!" Robert yelled, swinging back his sword.

The butcher, whom William thought had fled, ran out from behind the king, heading back toward the ruined castle. In a flash, Robert unsheathed his dagger and flung it into the retreating man's back, bringing him to the ground like a felled boar.

Robert spun around. "You almost got the king killed!"

"I was protecting him from *your* blow!"

"I was after the fat man, you idiot!" Robert spat blood. "He almost had a sword in the king's back!" Robert strode to the butcher, retrieving his dagger and the man's short sword.

"Majesty, that blow, it would have hit you—" Bryan argued.

"Enough," William said, swallowing a twinge of unease while remembering the queer look on Robert's face. "You of all people shouldn't be pointing fingers of regicide."

"The king!" Came another shout.

"Oh dammit, not again." William swore under his breath.

No less than eight men were upon them. William, Robert, and Bryan put their backs to each other and began striking out against all comers. If it weren't for the death and gore, it would have been beautiful to watch, as if the whole of it had been staged, each man honed to the other's movements, their enemies jumping back at each advance.

Robert cut off one man's ear, sending him to the ground, and finished him off with a blow to the head. Bryan, in his turn, was slicing off heads like an executioner. William struck home with blows to another man's shoulder, finding the tender exposure where his armor was tied on. The man sank, falling on his own dagger.

William relaxed, thinking this skirmish was done. But in stepping back, he tripped over a body, landing hard, the wind nearly knocked out of him.

"My liege!" Bryan cried.

William opened his eyes to see a Laurelander poised above him, sword aloft, face twisted in anticipation of victory. William tried to roll but was hemmed in by bodies. All he could do was grab his dagger, shield his face, and pray the blow didn't end him.

But it didn't come. Opening his eyes, he saw the man, eyes wide, a river of blood spurting from his mouth, the tip of a sword sticking out of his belly. He tilted, like a timbered tree, sword falling from his hands with a clang. Standing right behind him was Robert, self-satisfied grin on his face. He gave William his hand, helping him up.

"Thank you, cuz," William said, clasping him on the back.

"All part of my services," he said, and charged back into the fray with a roar to cower a lion.

The battle eventually ended for the evening, with heavy casualties on the rebels' side, but the king's troops remained unable to capture a strategic hill that protected the castle serving as the Laurelander's refuge. If only the pope's promised forces would arrive, this war would be nothing but a tale to tell by week's end.

And by noon the next day, as Sir Bryan predicted, the rains commenced. In a matter of minutes the heavens opened, and sheets of water lashed them, soon turning the entire battlefield to mud thick as porridge, the hills into slick mounds. Then, as if God himself wished to join in the fight, lighting rent the sky. Both sides stopped, for barely a breath, swords in midswing, thunder shaking their bones.

Then a great cry swelled from the Laurelanders as they plowed once more into the fray. This was their land, and they knew how to fight in its weather. But the storm gave William some advantage. A contingent of his men had finally won the top of the hill separating the Laurelanders from the castle ruin, and the enemy fighters struggled to keep their feet on the hill's slopes, sliding back again and again into a trench of blood and mud and vomit. The Laurelanders finally left the hill to attack the rear of Robert's right flank.

"This can't be borne," William said to the general, twisting in his saddle. "We must assist."

"Begging your pardon, Majesty," the general said, "but don't let your loyalties obstruct your goals. We must keep the hill."

"The hill is damned kept!" William shouted over another blast of thunder. "The entire army will be defeated if we don't close in behind."

"And we will be defeated if we do!" the general shouted. "Norwick will surely split off a flank to surround them from behind. They may know the terrain and welcome the weather, but we have them outnumbered and out-trained. They'll be finished so long as we keep this hill!"

"Norwick makes no move to do anything of the sort. You may stay here with your five hundred, General, but I will not stand and watch my best men be slaughtered."

"And I'll not allow both king and heir to be slaughtered—"

"Then it's a good thing I have the final word."

With that William raised his sword, slammed his helmet shut, and charged down the hill, a stream of men following. They slashed through a good three rows of rebels before the Laurelanders noticed. As William had hoped, the enemy split their attack, and William's troops, forming an inverted arrow, worked their way toward Robert's men. The enemy line would have to break in two or drive through Robert's center. And Robert would never let his center break.

Hail big as robin's eggs pelted them, the din of ice on metal as loud as the screams of victory and death. Thunder clashed and the rebels, be they field hands, merchants, or lords, were trampled like the sodden grass beneath their feet.

As the hail stopped and the rain began again, the Laureland line finally broke in two. William saw Sir Bryan among Ridgeland's men, slicing down attackers as he rode. But the distraction cost William. His steed buckled beneath him. Someone had sliced its hamstrings. He fought to get his feet out of the stirrups as the horse fell.

"The king!" a rebel shouted.

The horse had folded to the ground, and William found his feet. Though the rebels nearest him cheered, none moved to harm him.

"We've no wish to see more of our people dead," William shouted to them. "All who surrender their arms to us now shall be pardoned. You have the word of your king!"

The circle tightened around him, cutting William off from Robert or any of his men. One of the rebels stepped forward.

"And what be that, the word of a king?" The troll-like man spat into the mud and raised a fist to his brothers in arms. "Why do you all stand lolling about!" He hoisted his mace in the air.

Have it your way, good man. William unsheathed his sword.

The man's eyes grew ferocious, but he was slow. Before the mace met its target, William sliced off the man's arm. And all was chaos. The rebels charged from all sides, and he saw flashes of his own men swarming in. The spewing blood, the severed limbs, the desperate wails, the crunch of bones—all this was out of mind as he cut down any who came in his path. He knew no mercy.

At some point he realized he should fight his way toward

Robert, who was about fifty yards away and still mounted. But when William looked at the man directly in front of him, he beheld the hulking frame of Sir Joesph of Westerville, visor lifted, one brow raised.

"We meet again, Your Majesty," he said.

"You can see you are defeated, Westerville. Come join our forces and be spared."

Westerville squinted at William as if sizing him up. "I wouldn't count your chickens just yet, Highness."

Then all was black.

Robert managed to maneuver his horse around toward the sound of cheers. He'd seen William ride down from the hillside into battle but hadn't been able to spot him since. "The king is dead!" Someone shouted. "Long live the king!"

Robert sat stunned in his saddle. It wasn't true. It couldn't be. A small mass of Laurelanders surged toward Robert, holding William's sword aloft.

"Long live the king!"

Robert's own men milled about in confusion as word spread, and the fighting slowly ceased. One by one, the soldiers around him took to their knees.

"Lay down your arms!" His loud voice cracked. "The battle for today has ended!" He spied a pair of bright blue eyes staring up at him.

"Stay near me, Sir Bryan," he said, "for I will soon have need of you." Robert then called out to the rest. "We shall both sides retreat to our camps to mourn our dead." Mumbles of ascent followed. "Tomorrow we shall receive the envoys of Laureland to discuss new conditions."

Slowly the men started to disperse, some carrying friends and fallen, some trudging back to their camp alone. Robert turned to Bryan. Certainly the boy had fought bravely and proved himself loyal. And right then Robert needed someone loyal. Something simply wasn't right.

"Sir Bryan, I require a service."

"My liege?"

"Find the king's body," Robert said as he stared out at the expanse of corpses littering the field. "And don't come back to me without it."

Robert paced the darkened tent—William's tent—for what seemed like the hundredth time. The queen had once called him an eel. Slippery. Yes, he was shrewd, playing many roles for many people, all the while putting himself in the best position. And yes, he'd given great thought to being king. But he hadn't planned it this way. He took his head in his hands. William was as much a part of him as his own sword arm. His goodness, his joviality, tempered Robert's wilder impulses.

Oh God—Wills . . . He closed his eyes and gathered his thoughts.

By all rights, Daniel and the queen should rule as regents until William's child was of age, if the child was a boy. If not . . . if not, then he could finally wrest the country away from the pope, and watch the Protestant fire sweep through Troixden and into France. He threw himself into Will's chair. For once he had no energy for plotting.

"Sir Bryan, my liege," a guard said.

"For God's sake let him in." Robert rolled his head back against the chair.

Bryan hastened in, taking a knee before him. "Your Grace—I mean, Majesty . . ."

"Get on with it!" Robert said. "Where's the king's body?"

"I didn't—"

Robert dove out of his chair and seized Bryan's neck. "I told you not to come back without his body!" His spittle rained down on Bryan's reddening face. He started to choke. Robert gave his neck one last squeeze, then released him. Bryan gasped for air and steadied himself with his hands on the ground.

"It's . . . not . . . anywhere," he said between gulps. "There's no body."

Robert's stomach lurched, with hope or dread he couldn't tell.

"What do you mean? Did you search everywhere?"

"I searched the battlefield entire, waved the white flag to gain entry to the castle, bribed I don't know how many soldiers and servants, but there is no body. The king has simply vanished."

"And were you looking for a body intact?" Robert felt bile surge in his throat but had to ask. "What of a headless body, or simply a head?"

"Every part of him—his body, his armor, his clothes. There's no trace."

"That's not possible." Robert kicked over a footstool. Surely the Laurelanders would have William's head on a spike by then.

Or they'd have tossed his body to the foot of the hill. They wouldn't have buried him outright. Oh God . . . were they desecrating Will's body, slicing it up to send to the four corners of the kingdom? To the queen? He shuddered. He didn't like her, but right then he pitied her.

"Lord Joesph of Westerville!" Robert's guard called. He looked to the opening of the tent but saw only torchlight and darkness beyond.

"Send him in. Unarmed."

Robert heard some jostling and Westerville's low chuckle.

"That be not a sword, man," Westerville said, "at least not one made of metal." At this Westerville stumbled in, likely having been shoved. He doffed his cap in an awkward bow.

"Your servant, my liege," he said.

"I didn't ask for terms until the morrow." Robert strode to the back of the desk. Maps and miniature knights scattered the expanse, along with a half-drunk goblet of wine. William's last glass. Robert looked away.

"If you come here to play on my mercy," Robert said, "know that I have none."

Westerville swiveled his flat cap on his finger. "I'm in no need of mercy, my liege. Rather, you're in need of it from me."

"How dare you?" Bryan said, coming to stand beside the desk. "How dare you speak to your king so?"

"Who is or isn't my king is debatable."

"So you wish to join the German states?" Robert said.

"I didn't say that."

"King William," Bryan said, face red with anger, "God rest his soul—"

"King William's soul?" Westerville fixed his eyes on Robert. "It's quite safe for the moment, since I have him, Majesty." He grinned. "Or is it still just 'Your Grace'?"

"Prove it!" Robert slammed his fists on the desk. William's wine spilled, bloodying the battle maps.

"I thought you might say that." Westerville drew a parchment from under his cloak. "From the king's own hand."

Bryan snatched it from Westerville and handed it to Robert, who unfolded the wrinkled paper.

> *Robert, I'm here, alive, though I could not say well. Take heed, my friend.*
>
> ~ WR.

Robert flicked his eyes to Westerville's and threw the parchment on the desk.

"Anyone could have penned this." The handwriting looked to be William's, but the letters were not well formed.

"I suppose I could have, but why? You're more in line with my interests than the king."

"Then why in God's name are you here?"

Westerville sat in a chair in front of the desk.

"To negotiate."

Having finally sent Westerville off, Robert gave Bryan his instructions. The knight was to venture out dressed as a stable hand and find William in the ruined castle, if they had him at all. Bryan had been there and could find his way around, hopefully unnoticed. Despite a nagging feeling hovering about him like a shadow, Robert didn't believe Westerville and would be damned if he was made a fool of.

Westerville said he wanted Laureland made into a dukedom, and he would be the duke. He wanted to be Master of the Horse at Council Table. He wanted two manors and one castle. And he also wanted Beaubourg. "Access to the sea and ports" he had said.

"This could go one of three ways," Westerville had explained, counting out options on his sausage-like fingers. "One, you do as I demand, I restore the king to you, and you go your merry way. Two, you do as I demand, *you* remain king, and no one need know about my 'house guest.' Or three, you don't do as I demand, and I reveal that you knew the king to be alive and allowed him to be put to death to further your own ambition."

It took every ounce of strength for Robert not to kill the man on the spot. Robert flashed Westerville a smile.

"You shall have my answer tomorrow."

And now, all Robert's hopes were pinned on this knave at his side.

"Go change and be on your way," Robert said. "And on your guard."

"Yes, milord." Bryan bowed.

"And this time, find the king—dead or alive."

CHAPTER 13

The Captive
& the Free

Anna's fears were all for naught. In her absence, Daniel hadn't wrested all control of court matters, nor had he shown anything but doting concern for her unborn child, already seeking recommendations for tutors and drawing up lists of godparents. He inquired only briefly about Lady Jane's absence and moved on.

Daniel insisted on a pause in privy court. Her headaches had passed, but her cough lingered, and she could see the worry in his face every time she brought her kerchief to her mouth.

"Majesty," he said, rising to serve her more tea on the dais, "we can call off the rest of court today. You should have your rest."

"Thank you, Daniel, but I get plenty of rest." She drank in the warmth, herbs soothing her throat. "What I need is the distraction of news. Otherwise I worry, which can't be good for my health."

"I worry too, Majesty, but surely we'll hear something soon. Besides, I doubt they fight in a deluge. Our messengers say the rain is torrential."

Anna set her mug on the arm of her throne and waved her hand for the proceedings to start again as Charity burst into the throne room, stopped short, dropped a quick curtsy, then seated herself among the ladies.

"And has your new lady indeed been the comfort you hoped?" Daniel said, watching Charity settle herself.

"She's finding her way, though still new to the subtleties of court." Anna looked at him. His eyes lingered on Charity for a moment longer, then flicked back to Anna.

"I seem to remember a woman new to court who found her way quite well." He gave her a warm smile that she returned.

"Majesty," Brigitte said, "are we to have dancing tonight?"

"Oh please, Majesty!" Charity held pleading hands out to Daniel. "Your Grace, it's been so long since we had any festivities." Daniel blanched.

"It is barely past a fortnight since the last," Anna said. "Besides, we are at war, ladies. There is nothing festive about it."

"Although," Daniel said, clearing his throat, "a small event might show we have every confidence that the battle goes well."

"Oh yes, Your Grace!" Charity clapped. Daniel's ears reddened.

"We don't know that." Anna frowned. She couldn't stand the thought of merriment without William at her side. Daniel studied his fingernails.

"I suppose we could have a bit of music and dance," she said. "And if that be so, I should, as Your Grace suggested, take my rest." She rose and left the throne room, her ladies trailing behind, giggling and gossiping.

Back in her chambers, she inspected the post. Though she knew there'd be nothing from William, she still hoped. He had come to her last night in a dream again. He wrapped her in his arms, then his lips—

"Majesty." Anna looked up and saw Yvette, who curtsied. "I have word."

Anna guided her toward the hearth, away from the other ladies, her breath quickening. She didn't like the look on Yvette's face.

"Normally I would go straight to His Grace of Norwick, Majesty. But in his absence—"

"Yvette, please. Just tell me."

Yvette looked at the floor. "I've learned that the forces the pope promised won't be coming."

"What do you mean?" Not coming? William had been counting on reinforcements.

"Apparently they never left their posts from France."

"His Holiness would not betray us so."

Yvette reached into her bodice, produced a piece of

parchment, and handed it to Anna. The top portion was ripped, words scratched out here and there, but the final sentences were legible.

> troops are not needed ~~unneeded~~ and we ~~I~~ thank Your Holiness for your blessed ~~blessed~~ gracious generosity. I am sure in short order to inform Your Holiness in person of our ~~swift~~ glorious victory against these heathen heretics.

> Forever your most humble, ~~grateful~~ and devoted servant in the Lord

> A. Bartmore

"This is treason!" Anna clenched the note in her hand.

"Majesty, we still don't know—"

Anna grabbed Yvette's wrist and stormed through her chamber, ladies scattering in her wake, nearly running over Bernard.

"Where is Lord Cecile?" She said to the hallway in general. Bernard hopped forward.

"I believe His Grace is in his chambers, taking leisure—"

"'Leisure' is not in his vocabulary." She set off again down the hall, Yvette and Bernard behind her. Bartmore! The grasping, selfish man had put the king—nay, the entire country—in peril. But how on earth would hurting William further Bartmore's cause? And how could he think such a thing would go undiscovered?

She burst through Daniel's doors, ignoring a flurry of protest. But what she saw made her stop short. Daniel, in his thin white, nakedness, was rising out of his bath before the fire. A faint, acrid smell filled the air, the bed mussed. Surely Daniel hadn't been, well, taking his leisure?

"Oh! Your Grace, I'm sorry." Her face grew hot. She shielded her eyes and turned away as he stammered, "Majesty."

She was too embarrassed to speak, yet she couldn't leave, so she stood there, dumbly, listening to his dressers dart about and watching Bernard's face go through various phases of astonishment. She finally heard Daniel clear his throat.

"Majesty. I am better able to receive you now."

She faced him. His hair was still wet, combed forward in the current style, his face impassive. He took her hand, kissed her ring, then gestured toward his desk. She could not help but glance again at the rumpled sheets. He cleared his throat.

"I take it, Majesty, your errand is of import?"

"Your Grace," she said, "the most grievous news has come to my attention. We have been betrayed, by none other than our own churchman."

She thrust the offending parchment at him. He smoothed it with his hands on his desk and read, brow creased. His eyes widened.

"Where did you obtain this, Majesty?"

"Your Grace," Yvette said, stepping forward with a curtsy, "it came to me secreted in a snuff box. I don't know who the informant is."

Daniel raised a brow at this, then motioned to his page. "Send for the archbishop's clerk."

"Why not the archbishop himself?" Anna said. "For he should answer to this now."

"The archbishop is gone." Daniel sank into his chair. "He took leave to Rome when Your Majesty was attending upon Lady Jane."

"He must be ordered back immediately, arrested!"

"He will be sent for, but if he's made it to Rome, and if this is indeed his treachery, we may find it hard to acquire him."

It took ten minutes, but it felt like an hour standing there in Daniel's chamber, waiting for Bartmore's chief clerk. He finally arrived and read the offending slip of paper.

"Your Majesty, Your Grace," he said, "I know nothing of this." He handed the paper back to Daniel. "And it is certainly not the archbishop's handwriting. Nor is it mine."

"You claim it a forgery?" Anna scoffed.

"Majesty," the man said, "His Grace does not make copies or drafts. This cannot be his doing."

Daniel called to his secretary with a flick of the wrist. "Go to the archbishop's rooms. Obtain any papers he or any of his scribes and clerks have written upon and bring them back with you."

"Your Grace," Bartmore's man said, "those are his private papers—"

Anna turned on him, patience gone. "Nothing in this court is private, sir, least of all treasonous writings!" The clerk's mouth opened and shut. "Your Grace," Anna pressed her hand to her pounding forehead, "do you have any refreshment?"

Daniel motioned to his page. Anna rested her weight on the back of the chair that faced his desk.

"Majesty, please sit," Daniel said, extending the freshly poured cup. "You look pale."

She slumped into his chair. A page brought a footstool, and she let the man place her aching feet on it. She glanced at her ankles, swelling near out of her shoes. All the stress, the cold air of the castle . . . she heard scuffling and mumbling behind her, but her head hurt too much to turn.

"Majesty?"

Anna looked up to find Mary wringing her hands, with a wide-eyed Charity beside her. "'Tis Lady Margaux—'tis her time."

"She's not even due to go into seclusion for another week," Anna said.

Charity could contain herself no longer. "Her water broke all over the floor!"

"Then this is no ploy." Anna swung her feet off the stool and hoisted herself up. "We mustn't waste time."

"Please don't trouble yourself." Mary laid a hand on Anna's arm and lowered her voice. "She doesn't wish you to be present."

While there was no love lost between her and Margaux, surely the woman would want a skilled midwife. Besides, she'd want to show off her babe, the rumored bastard heir. She pushed it from her mind. William would never, could never. She sat back down with a thump.

"She didn't want me either," Mary said, "but Brigitte is there, and Margaux did ask for Lady Yvette's assistance."

So it was mere pride. Margaux didn't want any part of her birth tainted by Anna or the queen's favorite.

Yvette came forward to take her leave.

"May I go too, Majesty?" Charity asked, bouncing on her toes.

"The lady has not called for you, Mistress Charity." Anna sipped more wine and closed her eyes. "You may instead attend upon me with Mistress Mary, for I feel I must take my rest."

Charity's frown irked Anna. She rose again from the chair and placed her cup on Daniel's desk.

"Your Grace," Anna said, "please see that I'm informed immediately of any further information you gather, regardless of my state."

"Of course, Highness."

"And in the meantime," she said, "you'd best look into revoking Bartmore's investiture as archbishop and bestowing it instead upon Bishop Multman."

"As you wish, Majesty."

CHAPTER 14

Hobbled

William's head throbbed. He bent it down so he could touch the gash across his brow, then looked at his hand. His fingers were dark and glistening in the moonlight. Thankfully the blood was no longer dripping down his face.

He adjusted his hips, trying to ease his aching muscles. His hands and feet were shackled, the chain running through an iron ring bolted to the wall. He'd tried to shake the ring loose—it was lodged in decaying wood—but his waning strength and awkward position made that impossible.

Why Westerville chained him in the back stall of an old stable was beyond him. Certainly the ruined castle's dungeon would have been more appropriate, not to mention more secure. Though he had to admit, the stable felt as desolate as any dungeon. He'd seen and heard no one but Westerville and a single guard who paced outside the stable window and occasionally dumped fresh hay in, not caring if it hit William in the face. His only other companion was Westerville's horse, four stalls away and so gassy he'd probably been left there as some sort of olfactory torture.

Was this really what his countrymen thought of him? Hadn't he allowed them to worship in peace? Hadn't his reforms brought more trade, more money in their pockets, more food in their bellies? Why could they not see sense?

He didn't give a damn who worshiped what or how, but the vast majority of Troixden was staunchly Catholic. To tear them from the church would be cruel and politically idiotic. Much better to allow the Laurelanders to go on quietly worshipping as they pleased, he'd assumed. But look where that had gotten him.

The last thing William remembered was trying to reason with Westerville on the battlefield. Then he woke up in the stables, bleeding and sore and dressed in only his shirttails, trunks, hose, and boots, a lump of moldy bread by his feet. Whatever Westerville's purpose, he wanted William alive, for the time being. And so, for the time being, William would try to escape.

He scooted on his bottom until his feet could touch the stall's back corner. Bracing himself against both walls, he pulled against his shackles, trying to force himself up, and in doing so further loosen the ring. He fell back after a minute's hard effort. The chains clanged, and the guard pounded on the side of the stable.

Dammit! William leaned his head against the wall and groaned. Here he was, powerless, cast away again from his rightful place, when all he wanted to do was help his people. What a waste it all was.

The horse stamped and whinnied.

"Exactly," William said.

The horse pawed the ground again and shook its head. It should be resting. Perhaps it didn't care for the company of kings. The beast looked toward the stable door, flattened its ears, and neighed. This was more than mere annoyance. William strained to listen, but he only heard trees rustling and his guard's heavy breathing.

"Fine evening after all that rain," he heard a voice say.

"What d'ya think yer . . .? Halt!" That was the guard.

William heard a muffled thump, a long groan, a thud, like a body hitting dirt, the scuffle of feet, then metal hitting metal. He strained to see what he could through the window, but all he could discern was the side of a stone outbuilding.

Then up popped a handsome face covered with grime, blond hair wild, blue eyes blinking. Never would William have thought he'd be glad to see Sir Bryan.

"Highness," Bryan said, "I've come to rescue you."

William couldn't help smiling. "Only you? I'm sure I had an army not that long ago."

"No, my liege. I mean yes, you do, but they couldn't come." Bryan ducked out of sight then popped back into view, taller this time, and started to clamber through the window.

"We all thought you dead, begging your pardon, Majesty. And if you were, we thought it might be a trap—"

"Has anyone sent word to the palace?" If Anna thought he were dead . . . Bryan knelt over William's wrists with a key. He looked up.

"I don't know, Majesty. That would've been up to Norwick."

William's heart unclenched. Robert must know he was alive, or he wouldn't have sent Bryan to free him. "Thank God." William sank against the wall.

"He sent me to see if what Westerville said was true."

"So Westerville did meet with him?" Things were looking up indeed.

"Norwick sent me on strict orders to find you out and report back. But, well, I thought it best to release you."

"I'm grateful, but you do realize that flaunting hierarchy is what got you in prison?"

"No, Majesty." Bryan gave him a droll look. "What got me in prison was my stupid heart."

"And still you would save me?"

Having no success with the wrist irons, Bryan moved to William's feet. "You are my king, sire," Bryan said. "I've sworn to follow you to the grave if I must."

"You're a better man than I gave you credit for."

Bryan's hair obscured his face. "'Tis not all honor, I admit." He looked up again, his eyes sad. "For she would never love me as she loves you. I know that now."

They heard a low moan from outside the stable.

"You'd better see to him," William said.

"He's tied up—he won't be a problem."

"His mouth will be."

Bryan shrugged, climbed out the window, and after another thump came bounding back in.

"These keys aren't working. I need more light."

William squinted at the manacles. "Try the hands again."

As Bryan whipped his hair out of his face, they heard someone at the barn door.

"Hide!" William whispered, jutting his chin toward the opposite stall. But before Bryan could move, the stable door flew open, a bulky silhouette blocking the moon's light.

"You didn't think I'd be stupid enough to leave the keys with that soppy guard, did you?" Westerville chuckled and lumbered in, swinging a cudgel. "Now isn't this a pretty picture, young knight in the service of his king?" He clucked his tongue and thumped his hand on his horse's rump.

William flicked his eyes to Bryan, who'd unsheathed his dagger.

"Here I've got two pieces to play, knight and king," Westerville said, propping himself on a post. "How shall I checkmate Norwick? Perhaps I should counter-negotiate with you, Majesty?" He bowed his head in mock obeisance.

Bryan flung a handful of hay in Westerville's face and dove forward, dagger aloft, aiming for the chest. But Westerville was faster. He sidestepped, grabbed Bryan's wrist and cudgeled Bryan's right arm. William heard a gruesome crack, followed by a wail.

"You think I'm no better than a stable boy?" He spat at the fallen Bryan, then kicked him in the gut. William glared at Westerville.

"Your gaze might make others weak," Westerville said, "but it only makes me all warm inside."

"Is that how you usually open negotiations?" William said.

"You're in no position to negotiate." Westerville twirled his club.

"I am if you want to play me against Norwick."

Westerville nodded. William could see the key ring bulging out of his right pocket. If he could scoot forward, maybe kick him in the groin . . .

"Norwick, now there's a good lad." Westerville glanced at Bryan, and William inched forward. "He heard I had you, and all he did was send this pup. Seems to me your absence suits him fine."

"His Grace has cunning, true." William kept his voice steady, though his heart raced. He moved forward another inch, his eyes trained on Westerville's. "But his loyalty has never wavered."

Westerville laughed. "Ask your little knave here," he said. "He was there when I gave Norwick my demands. Told him I'd trot you out headless if he didn't play nice, but he didn't even flinch. Actually smiled at me."

"Then why is Sir Bryan here?" William said.

"He simply wants to make sure I really have you." Westerville waved his hand. "What I do with you is up to Norwick."

William's heart clenched. He remembered Robert's fury over the line of succession, knew Robert wanted to break with Rome. Had Anna been right? Had he simply not seen it?

"Until then," Westerville said, "what shall we do with your gallant?" He cocked a mocking brow at William, who stared back.

There was sudden movement near the ground, and Westerville screamed, clutching his calf, his tendon sliced. Bryan's knife clattered to the ground. Still yowling, Westerville bent to grab the weapon.

William thrust his foot toward Westerville's pocket. He made contact, but the keys didn't budge. Westerville stopped grappling for the knife, hand flying to his pocket, but the movement unbalanced him on his wounded leg. He fell forward, on top of the key pocket, and yelled again.

"Bryan, the keys—his other pocket!"

Westerville twisted on the floor, trying to get up. Bryan knelt and drove a knee into Westerville's groin. Westerville coiled in on himself like a woodlouse. Bryan rolled him over and extracted the keys with his good arm. But Westerville lurched up, knocking the keys to the hay-covered floor. William reached out with one foot. Finally, he caught the key ring with his heel, dragged it over, and unlocked his feet. Bryan and Westerville struggled on the ground, the horse frenzied behind them.

The key was too long to insert into his wrist manacles, but unshackling his feet had given him more leverage and more chain length. Bryan was underneath Westerville, shielding his face from blows. William scrambled to his feet and lunged for the club, grabbing it in both hands. Wrists still bound, he couldn't trust his aim on Westerville's head. He might club Bryan in the face. Instead he cudgeled Westerville's bloodied calf.

Westerville arched with a scream, and William swung with all the force left in him, the club connecting with Westerville's face. The man's hands flew up, then he crumpled on top of Bryan, moaning.

"That's for insulting your betters." William slammed the cudgel on Westerville's calf again, exposing muscle and tendon, blood black in the faint light. Westerville rolled to the side, giving Bryan enough room to shimmy out from under him.

"My wrists." William tossed the key to Bryan and extended his hands. Westerville writhed on the floor, covered in blood and hay, cursing them both.

Bryan unlocked William and slumped back on his haunches, dazed. William picked up Bryan's blade, tucked it in his trunks, and strode toward the panicked horse. He tried to calm it. There'd be no time for a saddle. He returned to Bryan.

"Can you ride?"

Bryan squinted at William and stumbled to his feet, swaying. William wrapped Bryan's good arm around his shoulder. He could hear men shouting, running, nearing the stable.

He propped Bryan against the stall. He grabbed a groom's stool, helped Bryan onto it and then the horse. William heard the ringing of metal and whirled around. Westerville held himself up, a sword in his hand.

"Not so fast, Majesty," he said. "Your head is worth a lot of money to me."

William narrowed his eyes. Westerville had more reach and mass, but he was wounded. William sliced the horse's ties loose from the wall. At least Bryan could get away, bring back help . . .

"If you kill me, you'll be killed," William said, edging his way out of the stall.

Westerville's lips curled. "The only other person who knows you're alive is Norwick. And he's not telling."

William lunged forward, ducking Westerville's sword

thrust, the blade just missing his side. The trick would be to force Westerville to use his legs. William stepped to the side. Westerville followed. Another blow came at William's shoulder, and he spun. Westerville stumbled but came back with surprising force, slicing at William's midsection. The sword tip ripped his shirt, drawing blood across his torso. He frowned.

"My wife made me this shirt."

William saw Bryan nudging the horse toward the open door. About thirty yards away he saw torches and the shadows of running men.

William charged. Westerville swung out to meet him. William ducked, letting Westerville's weight carry him forward, as William stepped to the side and thrust the dagger into Westerville's back.

"Highness!" Bryan called. "They come!"

William let Westerville fall to the ground. He wasn't dead but surely would be soon. William grabbed the fallen sword and ran to the horse. Clutching a fistful of mane, he swung himself up behind Bryan as several half-dressed men arrived.

"Drop your weapons!" William said. "Or feel the smite of your sovereign!"

"The king!" a man yelled. "Don't let him get away!"

William kicked the horse, which reared then set off at a desperate gallop. He steered it toward the woods behind the stable.

Calls of "After them!" and "Get the horses!" followed, but they soon left the stable far behind. Bryan slumped over the horse's neck and William held him up at the waist. All he could hear was his own breath and the thud of hooves as the woods enfolded them in a dark embrace.

CHAPTER 15

Life Springs Eternal

Anna loathed waiting. And it seemed the last few months had been nothing but waiting, for word of William, for movement in her womb, for Daniel to stop cosseting her. And now she was waiting again.

It had been more than twenty-four hours since Margaux went into labor, and all the word she'd had was from a grim-faced Bernard who rushed back and forth, being fed information through the door by Yvette.

Mary grew more anxious with each hour. She'd readied her birthing kit just in case, mixing salves, preparing tinctures and cloth. Anna sat sewing, continuing the unicorn tapestry, the rest of her ladies stitching as well, all except Brigitte and Yvette. And, of course, Margaux. Anna was surprised how subdued the mood was without them. Lady Cariline, well into her forties yet still fit as a spring foal, read to them from the Psalms. Anna only half listened. She had to admit that her worry was not only for Margaux. If the baby looked like William . . .

Margaux was William's cousin, so the baby was bound to have some resemblance. Yet no one, including Anna, believed the baby was Margaux's husband's. So whose was it?

Her chamber doors opened. Yvette hurried in, her hair disheveled, face red and damp.

"Highness, I've come to fetch you, you and Mistress Mary."

Anna stood, still clenching the tapestry. "She calls for us?"

"She's delirious, Highness. The baby won't budge. I fear it's already dead. You have to come, or we may lose them both."

"She doesn't want me then." Anna sat back down.

"Who cares what she wants?" Yvette said. "You're the queen."

Anna picked up her needle again, fingers shaking. Even in the face of death Margaux would not ask for her. Fine. She wouldn't go.

"My lady." Yvette came closer. All eyes were on them. "Have pity."

"If she does not want me at her baby's birth, she certainly doesn't want me at her death. I will come when she calls."

"*I* am calling, Majesty." Yvette fell to her knees. "You know I have no love for the countess, but even I do not wish her dead."

"God above, Highness." Mary grabbed her kit and stood. "You aren't the sort to abandon a woman in such straits. Come to yer senses."

Anna startled. What had she been thinking? The babe was innocent and would die along with its mother. Anna stood again.

"We must make haste," she said, and in her heart, asked God to forgive her lapse.

Anna had never been to Margaux's rooms, which were not hard to find with the shrill screams echoing down the halls. And when Margaux saw Anna, she screeched all the louder.

"No, not her! Who called her?" She writhed, her voice ragged. "He's *my* baby! Mine!"

Mary frowned, set her box down, and pulled out a serum that Anna knew was made with poppies, alcohol, and honey. The other women draped an apron on Anna and helped her remove her headdress and sleeves.

"How long has she been like this?" Anna said.

"About four hours," Yvette said. "She's been in and out of consciousness."

Anna walked toward the bed. Mary had managed to calm Margaux, who whimpered, her beautiful face puffy, pasty, soaked with sweat. Her eyes were wild. Her hair had come loose from her braid and stuck to her face and neck in clumps. Her body contorted, and she shrieked again.

"She's fighting it," Mary said. "She's got to lean into it, push."

"She doesn't understand," Yvette said. "She's half mad."

"Then we'll have to do it for her."

Mary managed to force the serum down Margaux's throat,

despite Margaux thrashing her head and batting the vial away. Anna went to the foot of the bed, where Margaux's feet were braced on the birthing chair's arms. She covered her hand in salve and slipped her fingers inside. The baby's head was close to crowning, but the child wasn't moving.

"I can feel him," Anna said, "but I can't tell if he yet lives."

Mary frowned and reached in herself. She nodded, then withdrew her hand and wiped it on her apron. She bent over Margaux's womb and pushed hard.

Margaux yowled and went straight into another contraction.

"Relax, milady!" Mary said. "You've got to relax to let the baby out!" She looked at Anna. "There's some movement, but I can't tell if it's her or the babe."

"He's dead! He's dead!" Margaux cried. "I know he's dead!"

Anna reached in again, wriggling her forefinger around the baby's head to its neck. Her blood went cold.

"Mary," she whispered, "the cord. It's around the babe's neck. We must get him out immediately."

"We can't risk her life if he's dead . . ."

"He's not."

"How do you know?"

"I just . . . he just can't be," Anna said. "He's the king's baby cousin."

Mary clucked her tongue and went back to her box.

"Let's give it a try. But if it looks like she's failing—"

"We'll save them both." Anna turned to Brigitte. "I'll need your help. You need to keep the countess calm, and when she feels a contraction, you have to help her push." Brigitte screwed up her face, looking lost. "Here, watch." Anna grabbed Brigitte's hand and led her to Margaux's side. Another contraction hit. Anna squeezed Margaux's hand.

"Push down, Countess," Anna said, "like—like you have to go to the garter robe very, very badly." Margaux looked horrified. "Your babe's life depends on it."

Margaux furrowed her brow and pushed, Anna squeezing her hand until the contraction passed.

"Perfect, Countess! Keep at it." Anna said. "Brigitte, did you watch, did you hear?" Brigitte fiddled with her hair, eyes wide. Anna bit her lips to hold back from screaming at the woman and returned to the foot of the bed.

She put four fingers inside Margaux, feeling for the baby. Its head was tilted up, as if its chin was raised. Another contraction came. Mary leaned across Margaux and pressed on her womb.

"Push, push, push!" she said. Margaux howled.

"The baby's crowning!" Anna said. "You're doing it, countess. He's almost here!"

One more contraction, one more push. The baby's head was close to out, hair wet with blood and fluid. Another contraction. Mary pressed again, as if to squirt the baby out like a lemon pip. Anna scooped up more salve in both her hands and slid her fingers gingerly around the baby's head, hooking them under its skull, her thumbs pressed to Margaux's pubic bone. She nodded to Mary. When the next contraction hit, Margaux wailed to break down doors. She was pulling back again, fighting against the contraction.

"Push, Margaux!" Yvette and Mary yelled.

Anna knew she had to act. She dug her fingertips into the soft flesh, curving them around the skull bone, the jaw. If she pulled too hard she'd break the baby's neck, but if she didn't pull hard enough, the baby would suffocate. A contraction took hold. She rocked her fingers and pulled.

"Push!" Anna yelled. She could feel the babe moving. Here came the head. Mary scrambled to Anna's side. The baby's face was blue, the cord tight around its neck.

"Get your hands off my baby!" Margaux screamed. "He's mine! Mine! Don't touch him!"

Anna slid her fingers deeper, feeling the cord down his back.

"The scissors, a knife, anything!" Anna shouted as she pulled out the rest of the baby.

"Don't you hurt him! Get away from him!"

She looped her forefinger around the cord and pulled it over his head. Grabbing him by his feet, she held him upside down and slapped his bottom.

"She's killing him!" Brigitte screamed.

The baby coughed and howled. Anna swooped her arm up his back, cradling him to her chest, his face growing red, his arms and legs thrashing. His eyes opened for a second, and upon seeing them Anna's heart grew light. They were the brightest of blues, like Margaux's. And his hair was the orange of an autumn squash. He wasn't William's. That much was certain.

Mary cut the cord, and Yvette came to Anna's side with a cloth, Margaux screaming vitriol all the while. Anna handed the baby to Yvette and walked to the washbasin. Gripping its sides, she steadied herself. Had she sat stubbornly in her chambers a minute longer . . . How could she have been so cruel? She washed her hands and headed for the door.

"You owe her your son's life—and your own," Anna heard

Yvette say. Anna paused, one hand on her belly, the other on the door.

"I owe her nothing," Margaux said. "She should never have come."

Anna left, feeling as lonely as she'd ever felt in her life.

The night was still deep when William rode into camp. By the time the startled guard realized who he was, he'd dismounted and was struggling to get the semiconscious Bryan off the horse. The guard and his partner genuflected and stammered their surprise.

"Good sirs," William said with a harder glare than he intended, "a little help?"

"Yes! Yes, Your Majesty, of course!" They set down their pikes and got Bryan off the horse, one holding him under the arms, the other by the legs. Bryan moaned.

"Be careful with him, especially his right arm," William said. "This is Sir Bryan. Take him to his tent." The guards whispered to each other, looking about, pointing in opposite directions. Bryan groaned again.

"Majesty," he said as they finally carried him toward the bowels of the camp, William keeping pace despite his bone-weary legs. "Norwick . . . you must stop . . ."

"Stop what?" William said.

"The heretics . . ." He shook his head, eyes shut tight as if having a bad dream. "You're supposed to be dead."

They reached Bryan's tent. The guards shuffled him inside,

trying not to stumble over a snoring Sir Marcus. After they laid Bryan on his pallet, William grabbed one of the guard's arms.

"The physician, quick!" The makeshift bandage William had made out of strips torn from his dirty shirt were soaked through with blood. As William started to unwrap the tangled mess, Bryan sat straight up and grabbed William's arm.

"He's not your friend," Bryan said, his voice shaky. "And he'll kill me."

With that, the knight passed out.

After William saw Bryan safely into the physician's care, he headed to his own tent, wanting nothing more than a tankard of mead and to fall into bed. But his mind spun with the queer things Bryan and Westerville had said. William arrived at his tent to find the king's guard at attention, all six of them. Their faces registered the same shock as the sentries'. Did everyone truly think he had died? *Dear God, don't let anyone have written to court.*

The men all knelt, doffing their helmets. "Majesty."

William acknowledged them and strode into his tent, straight to his sideboard and the jug he remembered being there. Not caring to search for a proper glass, he raised the entire vessel to his mouth. Then he smelled its contents.

"Ugh." He didn't mind wine, often preferred it, but that night he needed mead to quench his thirst and clear his brain. He put the jug down with a thump and searched for something to eat. His hand found an apple. Grabbing it, he sank his teeth in, the juice dripping down his chin. But before he could finish his bite, he felt a prick of cold metal pressure at the back of his neck.

"Don't move, or I'll slit your throat."

"Rabt, iz me," William said through the apple.

"Turn around. Keep your hands up."

William raised his hands and rotated to face his cousin.

"Fr Gwds sk, Rawbt . . ." William bit through the apple, sending it rolling to the muddied rugs. "Put your sword down and give me something to eat."

Robert stared. "Wills?" He stepped closer, eyes wide in the moonlight. With his free hand he touched Will's shoulder. "You're . . . you're alive."

"Try to contain your excitement," William said.

"But how did you . . .? We thought you were . . ." William thought he saw a flash of disappointment, which swiftly changed to relief, in Robert's dark eyes. He dropped his dagger with a clang. "You're bleeding."

"Also aching, thirsty, and exhausted."

"You're back," Robert said, almost to himself. Suddenly he lunged forward, squeezing William against his chest in a rib-crushing embrace.

"Thank God," he murmured. "Thank God."

A page shuffled in, wiping bleary eyes. He lit candles and freshened up the tent. Robert's arms didn't loosen their grip.

"Will we stand like this all night?" William asked.

Grinning, Robert finally released him, then took William's hand and kissed his ring of office.

"Thank God you're back," he said, slapping William's back. "I've been keeping your bed warm."

"So you knew I was alive?"

Robert grabbed a bunch of grapes and collapsed in a chair. "Yes and no. They said you were dead, but there was no body, no armor, just your sword. Then Westerville came here, claiming he had you."

William tore off a chunk of bread from a platter, ordered mead from the page, and slumped on the foot of his bed.

"And you sent Sir Bryan to fetch me?"

Robert's face froze for a moment. He nodded.

"Why our favorite knave?" William extricated his boots from his sore feet, flinging them toward the wardrobe.

Robert shrugged. "He was here when Westerville came. And I'd sent him earlier to find your body." Robert glanced at William. "I had to know for sure before . . ."

"Before you made yourself king."

Robert threw up his arms. "What did you want me to do? Send our men into a trap and have them slaughtered? Or worse, have them see us coming and cut your throat?" Robert shook his head. "Where is the knave, anyway?"

"He's in his tent, with the physician." William jabbed his thumb over his shoulder. "I doubt he'll ever use his sword arm again."

"'Tis a pity. Much as I hate to admit it, the boy fought brave and fierce." Robert sighed. It struck William that he'd never seen his friend so weary.

"We'll tell each other all in the morning," William said, "but what I want to know at the moment is whether or not word of my death has been sent to Havenside."

"The queen will not have heard of it from my pen. I cannot say what others may have done."

William sprang to his feet and to his desk. He scribbled lines on a torn piece of map: *No matter what you hear or who you hear it from, I am alive and coming home to you, my Anna. Take heart and have hope. X - Wills*

He dated it, blotted and sealed it, then handed it to a guard to be sent to the palace with all haste.

"Westerville is most likely dead. The weather keeps against us. If we wait out the storms, our supplies will run dangerously low. With no sign of the pope's enforcements, I fear this war is at a stalemate. But we'll see where we stand on the morrow."

Robert walked to William and placed a hand on his chest. If William didn't know better, he'd have thought his cousin near tears.

"Regardless of what you or others might think," he said, "I'm damn glad to see you again."

He then left William to finally fall into bed and an aching sleep.

The sounds of shouting woke William at dawn. He rolled over with a grimace, flopping his pillow over his head to block out the light and noise. He felt as if a handful of hounds had trampled him. Not to mention the stings and throbs of his various lacerations. For once, couldn't he lie there in bed and not be bothered?

"Cuz!" Robert sounded chipper, damn him. "Still sleeping?" William groaned. "Come now." Robert flopped on the end of the bed. "The men wish to see you in the flesh. And besides, we have much negotiating to do. Your favorite pastime, no?"

William opened one eye. Robert was grinning like a satiated wolf. What on earth was he so happy about?

"I brought you some salve for your muscles. Would you like me to find you a wench to spread it on you?" William threw his pillow, hitting Robert in the face. "Suit yourself." Robert clapped, and William's dressers entered.

"It seems being in charge suits you, cuz," William said, pushing himself up.

Robert's eyebrows bounced. "A contingent from Laureland has been here for about an hour."

Wincing, William raised his arms to allow his dressers better access with the salve. "Why didn't you wake me?"

"Why should the king be disturbed by such rabble? I left them out in the rain for a while."

William chuckled, but it was painful. "We treat our horses better than that."

"Perhaps you'll change your tune when you speak to them," Robert said with a crooked smile.

After William had breakfast, appeared to his men, and gave a short speech, the Laurelanders were invited into the royal tent under heavy guard. Robert, Ridgeland, the grand master general, and Duven flanked William, who sat on his makeshift throne. The Laurelanders made uncertain bows.

"By rights your entire company should be hanged for treason, attempted regicide, and abduction," William said.

"We had no part in the kidnapping," the earl said. "That was all Westerville's doing."

"And yet, as the head of this unruly mob," William said, "you are responsible for their actions."

"I'm not the head of anything, sire."

William rose, his considerable height cowing the man.

"If you do not speak for Laureland, then why are you here?"

The earl looked over William's shoulder. "Majesty, the weather makes the fighting untenable."

"You find the rain a bother, do you?" William returned to his chair. "Then surrender. You are duly routed."

"Begging Your Majesty's pardon, but I think not." The earl glanced obliquely at his men. "Your stores run low, and your men will not survive the winter here, not without access west and south."

"And what is stopping me from sending my entire army down in the muck to slaughter all your men and be done with it?"

"I'd expect that of King James, God rest his soul," the earl said, "but not of you. Not of the king who claims he will leave his people to worship in their own fashion."

"This is not about religion anymore," the grand master general said, his voice all but shaking the tent. "You've taken up arms against your king. And worse, you let us believe he was dead, would have killed him if not for Norwick and Sir Bryan—"

William held up a hand. "I have two papers here." He motioned to Robert, who came forward holding the scrolls. "One is the immediate death warrant of you and the other ten lords of Laureland. I need only sign it." The earl's face turned red, his beady eyes darting about the tent. "The second declares your immediate surrender, the laying down of your arms, and your vow on behalf of Laureland to never again rise against your sovereign." William's gaze lingered on the earl. "We would be well pleased with either outcome."

The silence that followed was broken only by the heavy rain on the tent. The earl swallowed, then looked at his two compatriots. The guards behind the men unsheathed their long swords, resting the tips on the ground.

The shortest of the lords knelt and bowed his head to the king. The other lord followed suit. William watched the earl's throat bob as he swallowed, his hands working his sodden velvet cap. He looked at the ground as if vomit lay there, then knelt.

"Your Majesty is too magnanimous."

"Enough, milord," William said. "On your feet and sign the surrender. My men will accompany you in rounding up the rest of the lords."

Robert rolled out the parchment for the three men. William knew they would never keep to these terms, but their signing the surrender gave him time. For now, he would take it.

CHAPTER 16

Watch & Wait

Anna brought the letter to her chest. Lady Jane's husband had died in battle, and though her son was to inherit, she feared living in the great home alone, especially given her "circumstances."

"Surely the Duke of Cecile will offer his protection," Yvette said. "She's his countrywoman and of some rank. He can see to her needs."

Anna shook her head. "If she comes under his protection, he'll discover her secret. And with the fervor of the country as it is . . . Lady Jane and her son must come live at court."

"Majesty." Yvette's eyes were filled with concern. "If she

comes to court under your sanction, and if . . ." Yvette looked around to make doubly sure they were out of earshot. "If it comes to light that she's a Lutheran, that implicates you. And the king."

"It will not come to light."

"How can it not? Will she to mass? Will not her maids see her stark rooms? Will—"

"I know that she would do anything to protect her son," Anna said. "If that means attending mass and sending Lord John to priestly tutors, she'll do it."

"But why entangle yourself? I'm sure Cecile would see a way for her husband's investments to last until her son is of age."

Anna grimaced. "Her husband left her destitute. He gave all his money to the Lutheran cause. Don't you see? Involving the duke will surely expose her."

"But why must *you* protect her?"

Anna looked away and ran her hand up the carved wood of her bedpost. She did not know what made her heart go out so to Lady Jane and her boy. Perhaps it was because Jane's was the first kind face she saw at court.

"She's a woman alone," Anna said. "And the last thing she needs at the moment is the prying eyes of men."

"You will have to receive her back in your service, then."

"I suppose you're right." Anna exhaled. "Now, how do we get this past the Duke of Cecile?"

That evening, Daniel asked for an audience. He entered her

chamber, eyes downcast, face unreadable. He held a small paper. Anna instinctively grasped the ruby at her chest.

"Majesty," he said with a short bow, "thank you for allowing me to speak with you."

"Of course, Your Grace," Anna said, trying to steady her heart. "You are always welcome."

"I must apologize," he said. "I have this note, and it was for you. I didn't know it until I opened it." He held the paper out to her. "It's the only word I've had in four days' time."

Anna's hand trembled as she accepted the paper, a torn map, haphazardly folded, with Will's words to her scribbled on it: *No matter what you hear or who you hear it from, I am alive and coming home to you, my Anna . . .*

She clutched the letter to her bosom, her eyes closed. Thank God.

"The king lives," she said, smiling to her maids, "but he is in distress, though I know not what kind. We shall have a mass said for His Majesty and all our men tonight. Bernard?" Her chamberman stepped forward. "Please see to the arrangements. We will to chapel at half past the hour."

"I am so glad of this news, Majesty," Daniel said. "But you are correct in deducing ill tidings. I cannot fathom what gave him cause to write such a cryptic note."

"I can fathom very well," Anna said, "and his name is Norwick."

"Majesty, I know you do not think highly of him—"

She lowered her voice and steered Daniel toward the east window.

"He has been after the throne since King James's time.

I wouldn't be surprised at all if he were the cause of James's demise."

"Many wanted James dead," Daniel said, looking past the stables to Stone Yard, scanning its height with his eyes, "but I know for a fact it was not Robert."

"And how do you know this, for a fact?"

"Robert was in Norwick for his son's birth celebrations."

"There is such a thing as slow poison." Anna folded her arms. "I wouldn't put it past—"

"He died of a heart attack," Daniel said, looking into her eyes, "brought on by too much feasting and whoring. And now, it is up to m—to us—to keep the realm in one piece until the king returns."

She broke their stare. "Have you heard any more on the whereabouts of Bartmore?"

"No, Majesty, but I have reason to believe he has made it to the outskirts of Rome."

"Yet one more thing to pray for—justice." She walked back to her seat. "You will join us for mass?" Daniel nodded. "Good. It will be a boon to have the king's closest friend near at hand." She paused, gathering nonchalance. "With all of this news, I nearly forgot. Poor Lady Jane's husband was killed in one of the first skirmishes."

"Yes, I heard," Daniel said. "'Tis sad news indeed."

"What's even sadder is that he left her nothing but their manor, which of course the boy will inherit at age." She picked up her sewing to avoid his eyes.

"I hadn't heard, Majesty."

"And so I've decided to take her back into my service and

to have her and the boy live at court. If your man and Bernard could see to the arrangements, I'd be much obliged."

"You needn't take her in, Majesty. I can certainly provide a house for her, a small allowance."

"That is kind, Your Grace," Anna said, looking up from her needlework to give Daniel her best smile, "but her boy is sickly, and Mary's special tincture seems to be helping. To have them here would be easier."

"Surely the medicines could be delivered—"

"She could have a living here at court. Her son would be mere steps away, and nurses and medicines whenever needed." Daniel was quiet, frowning in thought. Anna raised a brow. "Surely you would wish your countrywoman the very best we can provide."

He snapped his head up at this. "Of course, Your Majesty. I don't know what I was thinking. If that is all?"

"Until mass, Your Grace." She said. "Your prayers will mean the world to me."

He inclined his head in a bow and left.

No one batted an eye when Lady Jane and her son were ensconced at the palace two weeks later. When Anna heard that Daniel had placed them in the rooms adjoining his secretary, she worried, for his eyes were as keen as Daniel's. But Lady Jane behaved as Anna predicted, dutifully attending mass, wearing a rosary, sending her son to lessons with the other court children. At present, she wasn't a concern.

The current problem was Charity.

Anna watched the girl from the throne in the Great Hall, dimples winking in her cheeks, hands clasped behind her back so her bosom popped forward, feet swaying on her toes to make her lush skirts swing. She was widely acknowledged to be the most determined flirt at court. And it didn't help that she played up her sport at Daniel's expense. It would be almost cruel to send her home after giving her a taste of court's trappings, but perhaps it was for the best. Anna certainly didn't need more ladies around her, with Jane back in service and Margaux about to return. She would wait until after the heir was born, then send her home, perhaps with a betrothal, to soften the blow.

Exclamations at the back of court drew her eyes from the girl. A royal messenger, his pantaloons muddied and his eyes bloodshot, marched through the crowd. He pushed to the foot of the throne, doffed his cap, and knelt.

"Majesty," he said, "I bring news of the king's forces." A hush fell as lords, ladies, and servants stilled themselves to hear. Anna steadied herself, clutching the arms of her throne.

"Do tell, sir."

"They are on the move. Homeward." Court collectively sighed. Anna leaned back. "Laureland has surrendered." A great hurrah erupted from the crowd, but Anna kept her face stoic.

"How many dead? How many injured?"

"I only know the king and his men are riding under a banner of victory, Your Majesty. They are two days, at most, from the palace."

Two days! She had to restrain herself from leaping up and

hugging the man. She must remain regal, even though every bit of her screamed with joy.

"We thank you, sir, for bringing us this news." Anna handed Lady Cariline a gold coin to give to the messenger. "While we grieve those we have lost, we nevertheless rejoice in the safe return of our king."

"The honor is mine, Majesty." The man bowed and went to Daniel's secretary to unload his bag of messages.

"Ladies! Bernard!" Anna called. "Let us make ready the palace. We shall show His Majesty a homecoming he shan't soon forget."

Finally, she allowed herself a smile.

By the fourth day, Anna indulged her worry. She had gone to bed the night prior bursting with disappointment, crying without restraint or care for what her ladies thought. That day, she tried to convince herself that inclement weather delayed William and his men.

It was nearing supper when Anna and Daniel emerged from privy court. All she wanted was to retire to her chambers and wallow in self-pity. But it was the night of the feast she'd planned for William's return, and she was required to attend upon the wider court, toasting and receiving good wishes. It was also the last night before her confinement. The next day, after a light supper, Anna would take to her chambers and eschew all male company until her babe's birth. She prayed that she would see William's face before then.

Her cupbearer handed her a goblet of wine as she and her ladies processed into court. She walked to her throne, straining not to look upon William's empty seat. Her ladies, flanking the dais steps, made a tapestry of silver and white against her blue.

"Your Graces, lords and ladies," she said as she raised the goblet high, "tonight is for celebration, to cheer the return of our men and our king. And while we had hoped His Majesty would be here to join us, we implore you to imbibe deeply in merriment. We know not what the morrow brings, so tonight we shall make glad hearts."

"Hear, hear!" the crowd chorused. Hands clapped and glasses clinked as minstrels played and people chattered. Plates of fruits, cheeses, and cold meats, merely a taste of the bounty to come, were devoured. Anna sat, a falsely happy face on, her heart heavy.

She took another bracing gulp of wine, then looked at Daniel. He was squinting at the back of the hall, face white, mouth half open. He stood. She followed his gaze.

The Great Hall doors opened wide. The room quieted as the people gathered at the back of court fell to their knees, melting to the ground in fealty.

She rose, still clenching her goblet, giant stone pillars blocking her view.

Then she saw him.

He laughed that full-bellied laugh of his, clasping the hand of some noble at his feet. He was thinner, with a scruffy beard, but he was here and whole and safe.

Her wine fell to the marbled floor as she ran down the dais, confused courtiers parting way as she moved through the crowd. He hadn't seen her as he still picked his way through the sea of people. Then Robert touched the king's arm, nodding in her direction, and William's eyes found hers. He stopped in his path.

She ran, one hand holding her belly, the other lifting her skirts. She didn't care who thought what or how unseemly she looked. All she wanted was his embrace, his lips, his words. She reached him and flung her arms around his neck, his arms tightening about her waist.

"Wills, Wills, Wills," she whispered in his ear, "you're home."

He grabbed her cheeks, scanned her face, then pulled her back to him, mouth pressing hard against hers. Releasing her, she nearly lost her legs.

"Dear God in heaven, how I've missed you, my queen." His hand traveled down her arm, resting on her belly. "And how you've grown!" He brought her hands to his lips, lingering. She realized how many eyes were on them, some aghast, some amused. She curtsied and kissed both his rings, smiling into his glorious face. He was bruised, dirty, and scratched, but he was home.

"'Tis your victory feast, Highness," she said, holding back tears.

"Then we're just in time." He squeezed her hand.

She escorted him to the throne. Daniel bowed, and the king embraced him. She didn't know whether to laugh or cry. She might do both.

William beckoned Robert up to the dais. Robert flicked his eyes to Anna, gave her a wisp of a smile, and took his place.

"Friends, countrymen," William said, raising his goblet, "in all the years of our banishment, we never dreamed that the sight of Palace Havenside would bring such joy. And tonight, it is the happiest sight to meet our eyes besides our blooming queen."

"Hear, hear!" they shouted.

"While this feast is supposed to be in our honor, we claim it in yours, and in the queen's and the Duke of Cecile's. For you have all done your part to keep the country running smoothly whilst we fought. Sadly, we have lost many a brave soul, but we do not think on it tonight. Tonight we feast, we frolic, we laugh, we embrace. For tonight we are home."

The peopled cheered. William squeezed Anna's hand again and leaned toward her.

"And after that, I want you all to myself."

"My thoughts exactly," she said, stealing another kiss on his cheek, feeling the welcome scratch of his beard beneath her lips.

William steeped in a warm bath next to the fire, his muscles slowly unclenching. Anna fluttered about him in a thin night-dress, sponging away the grime. Every part of him ached for her, but she was right to insist he bathe first.

He had ordered his candles lit and sent everyone else away. He grinned at his wife like a love-struck boy as she moved about him, silently washing away his worries. He knew they'd all come roaring back soon as the sun rose, but that night he would savor their absence.

She cupped his cheek. "I can't believe it's really you. And that tomorrow I must hide away from you."

He pressed his lips to her palm. "I was thinking the same thing." His eyes roved over her. "I'd yank you in here with me, if it weren't for the babe."

She laughed. "And if it weren't for the fact that the water is so thick with dirt I can barely see through it, I'd be in already." She traced the fresh scar from his forehead to his eyebrow. "Will you tell me what happened?"

He brought her wrist to his lips. "All you need to know tonight is that I am here, and we are together."

He stood, feeling the cooled water drip off his bare body. Bringing her cheek in his hand, he bent his mouth to hers, feeling her lips relax beneath his, feeling her body press into him. But he could not have her as he wished, not this far along. With a sigh, he released her. She sat, her keen eyes taking him in, every sinew, every scratch and scar, every hair. She bit her lip.

She stood and went to gather his drying sheet. He stepped out of the bath onto the prickled warmth of his bearskin rug.

"You'll need a shave," she said, wrapping the sheet around him, all business. He held her in place and shook his head.

"You had the advantage of seeing me, and now I wish to see you." He tilted her chin up and pressed his lips to hers, then moved his hands to her shoulders, pushing off her shift. He stepped back. She was so . . . *full*. Her breasts, her belly, her hair, her face. She was filled with life, near bursting with it. Even her nipples had grown.

She turned pink all over with his staring. He looked once more at her belly, wondering if he would see the child move. Then he saw them: great, gruesome, angry scars coming up from the underside of her belly.

"Good Lord, Anna!" He crouched down to examine them. It looked as if tigers had mauled her. "What happened?"

She laughed and patted his head. "They're just signs of my skin stretching." She shook her head at his concerned look. "They don't hurt, and they mostly fade once my belly goes back to normal. Some women's are not as severe."

He wasn't sure he believed this, but the ways of pregnant women's bodies mystified him. He again rubbed his hand across the red and purple marks, feeling the bumps and grooves. Taking her belly in his hands, he kissed each mark with reverence. Then rising, he pulled her into his arms.

"You are beautiful, my love." He ran his hands down her bare back, feeling her flesh goose-bump at his touch.

"I know we cannot couple as you would wish," she said, fingers roaming his torso, "but perhaps . . ."

"Say no more." He led her toward the bed. He leaned against the footboard and brought her between his legs, cupping her soft breasts. He rubbed his thumbs across her nipples, looking into her eyes.

"Tonight, we are Anna and Will," he said. "No kingdom, no wars, no anxious courtiers. Just us."

She gave him that dazzling smile of hers, kissed him long, then went gingerly to her knees.

Robert barely had time to shave before Daniel was at his door. At least the man allowed him a night's rest. The king and queen still hadn't emerged from chamber, and Robert could tell Daniel was eager to get back to business as usual.

But matters were nowhere near usual.

For one, his sister had brought a baby boy into the world, rumor had it, with the queen's unwanted help. It was obvious the child wasn't William's. Not that Robert had ever believed that in the first place. Maybe the boy was Mohrlang's spawn after all, with all that red hair.

And of course, there was Bartmore's alleged betrayal. For Robert, it was one more piece of ammunition against the pope.

"I've received word from my people in Rome," Daniel said, pacing Robert's floor. "Bartmore is definitely there, though not under the official hospitality of His Holiness."

"Serves the bastard right." Robert yawned, stretched his arms, and gazed out his window at the low mist. The sun would burn it away soon. "Where's he holed up?"

"He's staying with Cardinal Marchello at his in-town estate." Daniel walked to the desk and flung himself into Robert's chair. The man was never comfortable unless a desk was nearby. "As luck would have it, one of Marchello's servants is in my employ."

"I doubt luck has anything to do with it." Robert laughed. "You seem to have eyes everywhere."

"Even bastards have to make their way." Daniel's eyes glinted. "Did you not wonder, friend, why I haven't asked about the battle? Of the king's abduction and escape?"

"Do I detect a warning in there, half-cuz?" Robert strolled to the desk.

"How could you?" Robert rocked back, away from the heat in Daniel's voice. "How could you plot against him? How could you even consider letting him die at Westerville's hands, all for some sick notion of revenge?"

Robert slammed his hands on his desk and glared at Daniel. "Don't," he said. "Don't question my fealty to the king."

"I wouldn't have believed it, but after—"

"After what?" Robert shouted. "After your spies misconstrued gossip as fact? You *weren't there!* You were here, warm and cozy in the palace, doing whatever you pleased as we slogged through the filth and fought for our lives!"

Daniel glared right back. "You swore to the queen mother at her deathbed that you'd stand by his side."

"And here he is, back and in one piece."

Daniel stood and walked to the door. He paused before opening it.

"I've done far more for this family than you realize," he said. "And I will never let any harm come to him."

How dare Daniel scold him as if he were an errant child? "You've no need to lecture me on how in love you are with the king."

Daniel blanched. It was a low blow, but many at court thought it. Of course, William was too blinded by affection and loyalty to see it.

"He is my blood," Daniel said, quieter, "and his support saved my life. For that, I am indebted to him in ways a born noble like yourself can never imagine."

"Daniel . . ."

"I am watching, and I am being watched." Daniel rested

his head against the open door. "Both can be misconstrued, as you say."

"I didn't mean—" But Daniel had already shut the door.

CHAPTER 17

Hens & a Rooster

It was her first week of seclusion, and Anna couldn't help but sulk. Her lying-in meant no men, including William, for any reason, save the royal physician, if summoned. Well, she'd finally have this baby born. Being so advanced in late November meant the special torture of all these constricting layers. She longed to have soothing baths and pad around in her shift. And she longed to have William by her side.

Instead she was half listening to Margaux and Charity continue their ceaseless bickering.

"I hardly think we need another report on the weather, Mistress Charity," Margaux said, "for we can look out the window by lifting the tapestry."

Charity's response was a glare. Anna shook her head. Hard to believe she'd be taking sides with Margaux, but Charity talked too much and too often excused herself to flit about court. It wasn't seemly, and it made Anna envious.

She fanned herself with William's latest letter. He sent them to her at least twice a day, sometimes wrapped around dazzling jewels, sometimes hidden in an empty wine goblet, sometimes shoved under their private door with a soft knock serving as his hello. How she wanted to thrust open the door and wrap him in her arms, or allow him in to liven up the dreary, humid room.

"Mistress Charity!" It was Mary this time. Charity had run into a basket of thread, spilling the whole. Not a terrible mess, but they'd all been putting up with each other far too long.

"If you must spoil all, then be off with you," Mary said. "Go fetch us a fresh batch of spiced wine. Just get out from underfoot!"

Charity made a hasty curtsy to Anna, hiding a grin poorly, and left. Not five minutes passed before Margaux batted her lashes at Anna.

"Majesty, might I be allowed leave to attend upon my son? He's been refusing the wet nurse, the little scamp, and I—"

"Go, Countess." Anna waved one hand and pressed the other against her brow. "And give my love to my husband." Margaux hesitated, but Anna arched a brow at her. Everyone knew where Margaux and Charity would be, and it was certainly not in a nursery or the kitchens.

There she was again. Mistress Charity, escaped from the queen's chamber to flit about the court like a colorful finch. William had dreamt of her the previous night and awakened in a sweat, head and groin pounding. And there she was, as if his dreams had conjured her. He didn't normally care for ginger hair, but there was something about her . . . He grimaced, reminding himself that his wife languished in seclusion, ready to bear *his* child. The least he could do was ignore his loins. Turning back to Daniel and Valencia, he found Daniel blushing and averting his eyes from the girl. Apparently, William wasn't the only one tempted.

"Of course, if there is anything My Majesty can do," Valencia said, "we would by all means help to apprehend him." He smiled as if he could tell neither man was paying attention.

"Thank you, Excellency," Daniel said. "The latest word is that Bartmore has yet to receive official welcome and invitation to the Vatican."

"Oh, excuse me!" came Charity's voice, talking to some courtier or other, "'twas my fault entirely." William watched as she bent over, very unladylike, to pick up her fallen fan. She tittered, opened and fluttered the fan, then faced the king. Her eyes met his and . . . Did she just wink at him?

William's blood warmed. He prided himself that he had not taken any of the prostitutes who roamed camp at war, instead taking matters into his own hands. Still, he was king, and kings had needs. By God, it was almost tradition!

"Excellency, you may tell King Philip we appreciate his overture." William put his hand to Daniel's shoulder, leading him away from the ambassador and the sight of Charity. "You'll excuse us."

He made it only three paces before nearly tripping over Margaux. She wore bright green over the fading plumpness from her child bearing, her breasts straining against her corset. With a snap, she covered herself with a fan and fell to the floor in a curtsy.

"Majesty," she said, offering him her hand. He took it, holding her fingers to his lips for longer than was proper. All these women were maddening.

"Fair cousin." William released her. "What brings you out to court? And how fares Her Majesty?"

"Her Majesty sends me to tell you of her love and good tidings, my liege."

A pang of guilt flushed him. He swallowed. "We miss her company—all of us." He opened his arms to include the whole of court. "But most of all we wish her health and a quick delivery."

"But of course." Margaux curtsied. As William moved past her, she placed her hand on his arm and leaned in. "And if my liege is ever bereft of company . . ."

William raised an eyebrow at her. "Was that part of the queen's message?"

But as soon as he'd escaped one Norwick, the other appeared.

"A bit crowded at court today, is it not?" Robert said, falling in step with William and Daniel.

"Entirely," William said.

After a chilled and stilted walk through the gardens, William found himself guiding his friends toward the stable yard.

"Do we ride, then?" Robert asked. William squinted at the castle, then glanced around the yard. "Wills—ah, Majesty?"

William found what he sought—a coin-sized pebble. He stood within twenty feet of the castle walls and looked up at the queen's windows, shrouded in tapestries. He threw, rock hitting the brick. Shaking his head, he canvassed the ground for more.

"Are we playing young suitor then?" Robert grinned. William scowled and picked up another rock. This time it hit the window but only made a plink.

"Oh, cuz, you don't do it that way," Robert said, bending to inspect the dirt, "the power's in numbers." He reached up to tug Daniel's sleeve. "Come give the king his pleasure."

All three scrambled about the stable yard like chickens, servants eyeing them warily. William laughed. There they were, grown men, king and nobles, scrounging about to tease some ladies. It reminded him of an easier time.

He rose, pockets full.

"Ready?" Robert hefted a handful of pebbles. "One, two, three!" Gravel rained on the queen's windows like hail, but the tapestry remained unmoved. They looked at each other. Robert shrugged.

"Again!" William said.

They gathered more stones and threw again, even Daniel laughing at the sport. At last a hand gripped the side of the tapestry, but the fabric stayed in place.

Robert cupped his hands around his mouth. "Queen Annelore!" he shouted. "Your Highness!"

Daniel swatted Robert's arm and threw another handful. Countess Cariline's stern face appeared, then vanished behind the tapestry. The men threw their last volley. Back came Cariline and then Mistress Mary, hands on her hips, a hint of humor beneath her scolding brows.

"Send us Her Majesty!" Robert called again, laughing.

The women again vanished behind the tapestry. William started to whistle. There was a stirring at the window. Yvette this time. She shook her head but opened the window. Soon the tapestry was pulled back, and Jane and Stefania escorted Anna into view. She was beaming.

"It does our heart good to see you, Highness." William blew a kiss up to her.

"And mine you, my liege," she called.

"Any sign?"

She shook her head.

"Cheeky git!"

She laughed, her ladies covering their own smiles.

"I wish you were here," she said.

"And here I am, at your service." He bowed theatrically.

Mary shoved her head halfway out the window.

"The draft's not good for her, Majesty!"

"Come now, Mistress Mary," William said, "'tis not the sight of her fair husband more than medicine enough to combat a breeze?"

He stared up at Anna, unsure what to say.

"I love you," she mouthed.

He smiled, nodded.

"Now go to bed, Majesty," he called. "What are you thinking, putting yourself in a draft!"

She laughed as Yvette shut the window with a bang, Cariline replacing the tapestry with haste.

The men went back toward the Great Hall. A few courtiers, Charity among them, had wandered out to see what all the commotion was. Robert veered off to speak with a clerk and William leaned in to Daniel.

"Your Grace," William said, jutting his chin in Charity's direction, "I ask you to help your brother not to stumble."

Daniel followed William's gaze. "She is very . . . young," Daniel said. He looked toward the shrubbery. "I shall gladly be my brother's keeper."

Charity tittered, drawing William's gaze back to her. He needed all the help he could get.

Council Table was dour that evening. Robert drew his thumbnail along the wood's grain, thoughts still tumbling after his time with Yvette an hour prior. In their almost six years together his eyes had wandered, but not his body—marital duties with his wife excluded. And the war, of course. But what did whores count? And he'd been talking about the king, not himself. So he couldn't understand her anger.

"Don't tell me you promised Margaux to the king?"

Robert scrunched up his face at his normally placid lover. "You didn't see her face when I told her she had to marry Eustace."

"That was forever ago. And since when do you pity anyone, let alone her?" He could feel her wrath like rising steam. "How does this benefit us? The king, distracted right when we're most in need of his devotion to his wife."

"I suppose you have a point . . ."

"It's *your* point, Robert!" She breathed deep and began again. "You're the one who's been waiting for this, and the timing couldn't be better. With Bartmore fled, Laureland biding its time, and the pope's forces abandoning William's case? The queen was incensed. She'll be begging for a break with Rome in no time."

He looked out the window at the gloom hovering over the browned gardens. He could barely admit it to himself, but he rather thought Margaux deserved a bit of fun. Besides, if the king was going to bed someone, it might as well be someone in Robert's pocket.

"Perhaps if I allow Margaux one chance?"

"The king won't have her," Yvette said, crossing her arms. "Besides, what has she done to deserve it?"

Robert knew Yvette found Margaux obnoxious, but he hadn't expected this much resistance. Normally, their quarrels were slight and fuel for their mutual desire, but this one felt different. As if Yvette thought she were in charge, thought they were somehow equals.

It was the queen's influence. All those long talks with the king, him taking her advice . . . The council might think Daniel ruled the roost, but Robert knew better. Perhaps he had given Yvette too much influence, sending her after Valencia, letting her too far into his plans. Time to remind her who was the head in *his* chambers.

"My dear," he said, "what's done is done. If he'll have her—and he must have someone, for the man cannot go so long without satisfaction—let him have my sister. Who am I to stand in the way?"

"Don't patronize me, Robert."

Something inside him snapped. He grabbed her wrists and drove her to the wall.

"And *I* am to be trifled with?"

She wrenched herself from his grasp, shoving him off with strength he didn't know she possessed. She straightened her garments and stared at him.

"If you ever touch me with violence again," she said, "I will leave you completely. And all of your secrets with me."

There was a long pause. Neither of them breathed.

"Yvette . . .," Robert finally said.

She shook her head. "Good afternoon, Your Grace."

Robert worried his hair and returned his attention to council, eyeing the Duke of Beaubourg.

"Sadly," Beaubourg said, "the talk in the fields claims this victory as false."

"Surely idle gossip is not so easily swallowed," the king said.

"Begging your pardon, Majesty," Beaubourg said, "the problem is larger than that." The old man leaned in, as if speaking the words too loudly might bring down the ceiling. "The people remain afraid that Your Majesty, out of excessive desire for peace, will break with Rome."

"As if breaking with Rome would bring the rest of the country peace!" The king grimaced. "But what of the men who returned home from the war to store the harvest? Certainly they have tales to tell of the victories on our side?"

The grand master general, who had been silent the whole time, shook his great head.

"Majesty," the general said, "the men were disheartened to see things ended so abruptly. Certainly they were glad to go home, but they wanted to see Laureland laid to rest once and for all."

"They wanted wholesale slaughter?" William exhaled. The general shrugged. "Your argument is well made, but since we're not breaking from Rome, regardless of what ploys our own archbishop tries—"

"It doesn't matter," Daniel said.

The king looked at him, brow raised. Daniel flushed.

"Your Majesty, please excuse my outburst. I, I merely . . ."

"Continue, Cecile," the king said. "For common courtesy seems forgotten today."

Why was everyone acting like women having their courses? Robert dug a thumbnail further into the table.

"I merely meant that the people need only *believe* we would break from Rome," Daniel said. "The veracity of that belief, in the end, does not matter. As we have seen with Laureland itself, not to mention the riots in Havenside."

"Indeed," the general said. "Your Majesty has been more than gracious to those traitors."

Robert, eyes still on the table, hadn't noticed William move to stand behind him.

"So, what then do you advise?"

Robert startled, the hairs along his neck standing up. Mercifully, the king moved along.

"If the people aren't swayed by the truth," William said, "what is there to do?"

"We must plant rumors of our own," Daniel said. "I suggest we use Sir Bryan."

William had given the knave an honorary re-knighthood— for he'd never wield a sword again—and a parcel of land. Even Robert had to admit he'd earned it, but what possible use could the boy be now?

"Send him out among the people," Daniel said. "Let him tell his fellow northerners of your brave escape, your devotion to your people."

"That could easily be done," the Duke of Beaubourg said. "Sir Bryan is well known throughout the north, not just in Beaubourg."

Robert frowned. Bryan was not smart enough to handle this kind of intrigue.

"So the man who tried to kill me becomes my champion?" William gave a snort.

"Majesty, it makes him the perfect candidate," Halforn said. "The man who once rallied against you has seen the light— your true nature, your goodness, your heart for your people and the faith."

"The knave is as thick as a post," Robert said. "Besides, soon we'll have an heir to boast about. And a stronger line of succession is more unifying than a war hero."

William bent in to Robert's ear and whispered. "As you well know."

Robert's heart clenched. What poison had Daniel or the queen put in his mind?

"We will all rejoice when the prince is born," Robert said. "That will give the harvesters something to crow about, and Laureland will be old news."

William grunted and walked back to his seat. "But 'tis not old news yet," he said. "Your Grace, I send you home to Beaubourg to speak with Sir Bryan on this matter. I will send along a letter. Let us trot our golden horse into the sun and see if he shines."

Robert had once told Bartmore the king did as was his pleasure. That day, the king's pleasure seemed to have turned against *him*.

He'd have to change that.

It had been a long day. William was tired, sore, and out of sorts. The last thing he wanted to do was preside over a night of dancing and small talk. He'd consumed enough wine to sleep the rest of the evening away and was contemplating leaving when Margaux appeared at his side.

"Is it the queen?" He struggled to clear his mind from the haze of drink. "Is she well?"

Margaux's rosy lips curved, cheeks dimpling. He'd forgotten how beautiful she was at close range. She put her hand on his forearm and squeezed.

"The queen is in good health," she said. "Her Majesty has allowed her ladies an evening out in time for the dancing."

"Your mistress is most gracious."

"As highest rank in Her Majesty's chamber," she said, blue eyes sparking, "it is incumbent upon me to make sure Your Majesty has all you desire."

He started to wave her off but thought better of it. A few dances among the ladies would do no harm, for he was sick to death of men. Surely if Anna had allowed her ladies out, it was for his pleasure as well as theirs.

"Actually, I do desire something, Countess."

"Anything, Majesty." Margaux's hand had not left his arm.

"The honor of my fair cousin as my dance partner." The thrill on her face was irresistible. He led her out to the middle of the floor.

"Join us on the floor, friends," he said, "for tonight we dance in the queen's honor."

Still rankled by the day, William let the lively dance carry him away. When the music stopped, he was surprised at how disappointed he was. He brought Margaux's hand to his lips, lingering on her knuckles. Margaux rose, a sultry look in her eyes, and sauntered off to her next partner.

"I should retire," he mumbled to himself. How drunk was he that he would dally with Margaux? He heard a distinct giggle to his left. Rotating, he saw Charity, red and radiant, curls bouncing as she flirted with the Duke of Halforn. He moved toward her.

"The honor of the next dance, milady." William held his hand out to her, swallowing a burp. Halforn's eyes widened, but he regained himself quickly. She being of no rank, the king's bid for her hand in the dance was more forward than was proper.

Daniel passed in front of them as William led Charity to the floor. A raised brow was all he gave him, but William knew what it meant. If the room had been quiet when he escorted Margaux to the floor, it was silent as a monk's cell then.

"A line dance," William called to the musicians. Nothing untoward, just doing his duty to entertain. In fact, why not make this the start of Sir Bryan's show?

"This dance we dedicate to our Honorable Sir Bryan of Beaubourg." Charity flushed at this, light spray of freckles standing out at her bosom. "Indeed, all of our men risked their lives for us, but Sir Bryan not only saved us in battle, he also rode out, in a daring plan hatched by our dear cousin the Duke of Norwick—" William tilted his head toward Robert "—to rescue us from the hands of our captors. Without his help, we might not be standing here today." Gentle applause met this speech. "Now, let us dance."

His thick head pounded with the beat, the wine, Charity's hands on him. She beamed at him, beckoning. He must get away. He did not take her hand as the dance ended but abruptly left her and made for the door.

Robert sidled up to him. The slap on his back made William stumble.

"Off so soon?"

William groaned.

"I'll send you some refreshment, something to . . . ease you into bed." This with one of Robert's wolfish grins. William felt the feast churn in his belly. He rushed past Robert, chambermen following in his wake, barely making it in time to the privy.

Anna tried to rest, but sleep wouldn't come. As sick as she was of her ladies, she worried about what they were up to after she'd sent them away. In her mind's eye she saw all of them, even Cariline, batting their eyes and flaunting their breasts at the king.

When she heard the one o'clock bell, she thrust off her sheets and lumbered out of bed. She needed distraction.

Mary bumbled over, yawning. "Dearie, why are you out of bed?"

"I can't sleep." Anna threw up her arms. "I feel as though I'll burst if I lie there one more minute."

"It'll all be over soon." Mary led her to a chair and rubbed her shoulders. "Then you'll see your king and your baby, and all will be right with the world."

"Where are they all?" Anna leaned her head back to look up at Mary. The nurse looked down, eyebrows raised.

"That husband of yours is a peculiar man. I'd swear on my medicines he won't stray from you."

Her cheeks grew hot. "I'm not worried about that."

"Of course you're not." Mary patted her shoulder.

"I'm not, I . . . I simply wanted them to take a little leisure, not spend all night carousing and return unfit for service in the morning."

"If you say so." Mary went to get a fresh wet cloth. Anna took it, grateful for the small relief it brought from the heat of her chamber. They kept the fires at a constant roar, the tapestried windows shutting out any breeze.

Anna felt an achy twinge across her belly and in her groin. These false contractions had increased in frequency and strength for days, but this felt deeper, hitting her sacrum. She winced and pushed herself out of the chair.

"I have to walk. I'll go to the gardens."

"You can't be gallivanting around the castle in the middle of the night!"

Anna held the damp cloth to her forehead. She must think. And walk. She spied her passage to William's chamber. It was a long, cool hall, and she'd have it to herself. She started toward the door.

"Where do you think yer going?" Mary went after her.

Another pain came, and she braced against the doorframe until it passed.

"I only wish to walk the hall, Mary. Besides, the king won't be in his chamber, and even if he was he'd hardly hear me." Anna wrenched open the door. A cold wave of air splashed her face, and she breathed it in. She walked toward the faint crack of light surrounding William's door. It took all her will not to burst through. But he probably wasn't there. Reaching his door, she placed her hand on the thick wood, feeling the grains, trying to feel him.

Then she heard his laugh. Another wave of pain gripped her, traveling up, clenching her heart.

William's mind was still fuzzy, but his gut had calmed. He splayed on his bed, staring at the red canopy that seemed to keep tilting to the left, mentally creating objects and animals out of the damask design. Robert, Ridgeland, and Gregory sat at his desk playing cards and drinking. He didn't want them there, but he knew if they weren't he'd be headed for trouble. He hoisted himself up on his elbows and spied the ladies—Margaux, Brigitte, Charity, Duven's wife, Stefania, and Ridgeland's Amelia—gossiping in the candlelight. He pushed himself up completely.

"Ladies," he said, doffing an imaginary cap, "should you not be attending upon your mistress?" It was strange, though not wholly unpleasant, to have all these women in his chambers. They curtsied and tittered.

"Her Majesty wishes us away," Charity said, her apple cheeks high and playfully pert, "and we intend to make the night a long one." She bit the tip of her index finger.

"Indeed?" William's mouth tugged up at the corners.

Margaux approached, looking him up and down.

"Majesty, come." She offered her hand. "Join us in some frivolity, for you've had far too much strain these last months." He took her hand, and she guided him to the flock of ladies. They sat him down and petted and cooed at him, pouring him more wine, removing his shoes. He closed his eyes and felt small yet strong hands dig into his shoulders.

"Just relax, Majesty," came a purr at his ear.

He relaxed his head back, letting himself sink into the massage, fingers traveling up his neck, feeling their echo in his groin. Oh, that ache. The room fell away and it was only her fingers, hard and sensuous, tickling his earlobes, her breath shallow behind him. He leaned his head into her caresses, his lips finding her palm.

"Anna," he breathed. Her hands stopped for a moment.

"Don't stop," he said. She slid her thumbs along his jaw. Pushing a thumb into his mouth, he sucked it. She moaned quietly, then bit his ear.

"Shall we send them away?"

The reality of the woman fondling him startled William from his fantasy. He twisted in his seat, heart and groin still throbbing, to find Charity, all innocence gone from her face.

"I got lost in the . . . with all the wine, and the lateness of the hour . . ."

"No need to apologize, Majesty." She continued smiling. "For you must need your bed."

He looked into her soft, adoring eyes and saw something there he hadn't thought she possessed. He squeezed his eyes shut. All he knew was he needed release, in more ways than one. He squinted at the room and all the people it contained.

"I think—"

Then he heard a strange cry, like a hound's yowl mixed with the shriek of a woman. It came from his private hallway.

He was up at the door in an instant, mind suddenly sharp. By the time he opened it, he could see Anna limping back to her chambers, Mary half carrying her.

"Anna! Annelore!" If she'd heard him—if she'd seen . . .

As he started down the hall he stepped in something wet. Picking up his foot, he peered at a puddle about two feet away from the door. He dipped his pinky in and brought a drop of the liquid to his nose. There was a faint sweet smell to it, and it felt slippery and viscous, thicker than water but not by much.

He heard a commotion behind him and someone calling his

name. He looked back into his chambers to find Bernard in full courtly bow.

"Your Majesty," he said. "It has begun. Her Majesty is in childbirth."

William charged back into his chamber and whooped, pulling a startled Bernard into a jubilant hug.

"The queen's in childbirth!" he shouted. "Ring the bells and let us to chapel to pray for her safe delivery." He swept past those gathered, headed straight for the doors, heart racing with excitement and anxiety, thoughts of his near indiscretion slipping away.

"Come, let us be on our knees, gentlemen."

"Another warm compress," Mary said to no one in particular. Anna's ladies had returned, Margaux smug and unruffled, the rest slightly guilty. The countess handed Mary the next compress. Anna took it gladly, pressing it to her chest, the warmth seeping into her body. The heat on her breasts would speed her contractions, which had slowed after her water broke. Mary was using all her tricks to get the contractions back up to speed, and while she didn't yet look concerned, Anna knew her old nurse would be particularly watchful.

"Drink some more of the tea," Mary said. "Make those sheets straight, Charity. Yvette, see the oils and salve are warmed." The ladies conducted their work with low whispers. A contraction hit Anna hard and she clutched her bedpost.

"Oh my Lord, Mary—" She wanted to fall to her knees.

"That's good, dear, that's good!" Mary wiped back Anna's hair with another wet cloth. "Pain means progress. Give in to it. You know how it's done."

Anna had an overwhelming desire to shout expletives at Mary. What did she know about it? She'd never felt this agony that grasped your whole body, that made you want to crawl outside your skin and huddle in a ball somewhere so far away the pain couldn't reach you. And the damn birds outside. What was there to be chirping so loudly about? As if the sun didn't rise every day.

"Argggh!" It felt like her insides were going to slide out with the child, leaving her an empty carcass.

Mary and Yvette managed to move her to the birthing chair. Mary crouched to check her.

"Still not budging," she said.

"What?" Anna's eyes were crazed. "All this pain and nothing?"

Mary's mouth formed a grim line, her bushy brows pushed down. "We'll get you moving, don't you worry."

The chair made her back ache more, and since walking helped, she began a slow circuit about her chamber. She could see thin slices of the fresh day poking around the tapestries' edges. She longed to be outside. She thought she'd prepared herself, thought she'd pushed her fears aside. But her last time came rushing back the instant her water broke. She also remembered the prostitute in Beaubourg who'd died in her arms. She remembered her mother, she remembered queens before her. Their crowns didn't save them, or their babies, from death. She tried to think on the easy births, the happy births. Were they not the ones she'd seen most often? But she could not expel the terrifying exceptions from her mind.

It was probably around six in the morning. She'd been at this only five hours. She must focus. She tried to breathe and lean into the next contraction as she'd been taught, and it helped a bit, but not enough.

"I want mead," she said.

"But you never drink mead," Charity said.

"I don't care!" Anna said. "I want mead. Now!"

Charity's face paled but she hurried to fulfill her orders.

"Don't take it out on the young'uns," Mary said, again swapping out Anna's breast cloth.

"I'm the queen, and I'm giving birth to the heir," Anna said. "I'll take it out on who I want, when I want."

Mary raised an eyebrow.

"Of all the times in my life," Anna said, "I should be excused my behavior!"

"I'll hate to see you in a few hours, then."

It was the queen's sixteenth hour of labor. William wandered in a manic stupor, unable to concentrate on court proceedings, food, or sleep. He decided to return to his rooms with Daniel, to be close at hand if needed.

As they passed into the corridor that led to his chambers, an earth-rending scream met their ears. William ran to Anna's chambers. The queen's guards stood at attention, blocking entry.

"William!" he heard her scream. "Ah, Wills!"

"Open these doors at once," he said. Not waiting for an answer, he pounded on the great wood barriers. "Anna! I'm here!" He turned back to the guards. "Didn't I order you to open these doors?"

The guards, not knowing what to do, looked in panic at Daniel.

"Majesty, you know you can't go in," Daniel said, trying to guide him away.

"She's calling for me. Can't you hear she's in pain?"

A moan like a wounded elk came through the doors. He pounded again.

"Anna, I'm here!"

"Sire, no man is to enter, even Your Majesty. Especially Your Majesty." Daniel sounded calm as ever. "You'd disrupt the proceedings, possibly be a danger to the queen and the child." He grabbed William's arm and shook it. "Sire, listen to me!"

"She's calling for me." He heard a crash and a yelp. "Blast it all, it sounds like a battlefield in there." Why did no one understand? By God, he was king and would go where he would.

"I hear her," Daniel said. "But alas, she is living out the curse of Eve, Highness. 'Tis supposed to be painful."

"You cannot know what I feel." Memories of his sister Cate's death floated back to him. He had to get in that room. "You've never had someone you love scream for you."

Daniel's face went ashen. He looked at the floor.

"You're quite right, Highness," he said, "I've never known a wife or a family. Apart from yours."

William could kick himself. What an ass he was being.

"Daniel, my dear friend, you know you're family to me."

Daniel nodded, still staring down. "But I can't bear her screams. I must know that she's well, that the baby is well."

"Majesty, if you cannot stand the screams, I suggest we retire to a place where we cannot hear them."

Then the peep-door opened to reveal Mary's pink and sweating face. William pressed himself to the door, trying to look past Mary into the chamber.

"Highness," she said. They were almost nose to nose. "I have a message from milady."

"Out with it," he said, still craning to see in.

"First, she desires your prayer for her and the wee one."

"Prayer?" That was exactly what they'd told him when Cate was dying. "Why does she need prayer? What's wrong?"

"Please, sire, all is well! I was there when the queen herself was born, and half the duchy of Beaubourg to boot," Mary said, too sassy for William's taste at that moment. "I know a healthy birth when I sees it. We were a bit worried at the first, but—"

"Why worried? Why is she screaming for me?" William wasn't about to be brushed off. Anna wouldn't sound so horrid if everything was well.

"That's just the way of women in the birthing, Majesty. If it helps to soothe you, she's yelled for the Virgin, Jesus, and her dear mum as well, God rest her."

"Mary, you know she'd wish to see me."

"Your Majesty, begging your pardon, but I've been charged by you and the Lord in Heaven to watch over her." She scowled. "If you must send me to the gallows for disobedience, I'll gladly go."

"Tush, Mary." William scowled right back. "We shan't send you to your death."

"Then listen and be comforted." She said. "The queen asks prayers for strength, and she begs I relay her love to you. She wishes you happiness this day in the knowledge of the birth and the knowledge of her deep and abiding love."

William hung his head.

"Take heart," Mary said. "She truly be well and almost through her long labor. I do wish Your Majesty could have seen her face when she heard your voice . . ." Anna moaned again. Mary looked over her shoulder, then back at him. "But now, ye must go. I swear you'll be the first outside this chamber to hear the good news."

Anna almost wished she were dead, just to have the whole thing over and done. This must be what it felt like to be drawn and quartered. There wasn't a single stitch of her body not in indescribable agony. Even her hair hurt. But she was progressing. She would soon start to push, Mary said. She must hold on. But where she'd find the strength, she didn't know.

She'd vomited all food, barely holding down the teas and other tinctures Mary gave her. She cursed her lack of sleep the night prior. The contractions were coming on strong, toppling over each other. No position eased her pain, but she was lying on her side, propped by pillows, legs resting on a tuffet off the end of the bed. She had no energy, not even to scream. All she could do was whimper.

She was faintly aware of ladies shuffling about her, yet she felt so isolated. She knew she would die. It was too much.

Another contraction, but different this time, as if all her senses were heightened and honed. She struggled to sit up.

"I have to push, Mary! I have to push!"

Mary's face lit. "All right, everyone to their places! Yvette, you stay next to me. Cariline, hold on to Her Majesty—help her work through the pushing. Charity! More hot water, now!"

The next contraction rolled through her like a great wave, threatening to drag her under. Anna bore down with a strength she thought she'd lost. She was past pain, past thought. All she knew was a powerful physical urge to get her baby out.

Again. Push. Harder, stronger. Release.

"He's crowning! Oh, he's crowning!" Mary popped her head up and beamed. "You're doing wonderfully, dearie!"

"A beautiful head of wavy brown hair," Yvette said.

Anna was awash in euphoria and fresh determination. Wavy brown hair, just like William's.

With four more pushes, her baby was born, squirming and bawling. Mary's eyes were full of tears.

"It's a princess," she said as Yvette cut the cord.

A strange feeling came over Anna. Certainly she'd hoped the baby would be a boy, for William's sake, for the realm's sake, but none of that mattered in the moment. All she wanted was her baby in her arms.

"My baby—give me my baby."

"Let's get her clean first," Yvette said.

"No!" Anna's voice was high and scratched. "I want her now."

Mary gave Anna a knowing look and brought the mewling princess to her, loosely wrapped in a sheet. Anna cradled the baby to her chest. The baby calmed and squinted at her mother, who stroked her cheek and gave her a pinky to squeeze. Anna's heart was bursting. She thought she loved William, but this was wholly different. She was drunk on her daughter.

The baby squeezed Anna's pinky, pulling it toward her cherry mouth and sucking on the tip. She made a perturbed face and spit out the finger. Anna giggled. Then the princess opened her eyes, which were deep, dark blue, like a far-off ocean. Like William's.

She knew William would be at the feast, knew he'd be anxious. But part of her wanted this time, just her and her daughter. She sighed, knowing she could not keep this joy from him any longer.

"Lady Jane, please fetch Bernard," she said, then beamed at Mary. "Let's get the princess ready to meet her papa."

The last thing William wanted to do was sit through another feast while his insides still roiled from the last one. He wasn't the only one ill at ease. Robert seemed downright hostile, scowling at everyone. Daniel fidgeted with his cutlery. Even the gathered nobles seemed on edge, everyone eager for the news.

Bernard appeared before him, offering a formal bow. William beckoned him close, not wanting the whole of court to hear the message before he did.

"The queen is hale, Majesty," he said, voice quivering with contained excitement. William's whole body relaxed. She was safe. "She is delivered of a princess."

"A princess?" William's heart stopped.

"Yes, Majesty, a healthy and by all accounts beautiful princess."
William knew what this meant for the country—it meant
nothing. It meant more strain, more uncertainty. But for him . . .
He rose, overcome, and started toward the throne room. Gasps
followed him. Remembering himself, he stopped, grabbed his
goblet, and hoisted it in the air.

"We have a princess royal! Ring the bells. Send out the criers.
For tonight we rejoice!" His delight was infectious. The crowd
cheered, and William found himself surrounded by a mass of
well-wishers, Robert chief among them. He pushed through
them, begging off. He would not wait one moment longer to
see his daughter.

Anna was bathed and brushed and propped against her pile of
pillows, stroking her daughter's perfect hands. While she knew
that royals never nursed their own babies, it would feel natural
to turn the baby's head to her chest when she made that rooting noise. Anna's breasts, already bound, ached at the thought.
She'd watched with unmasked envy as the wet nurse brought
the princess to her breast for the first time.

But now, nothing need separate them. The baby held a
lock of Anna's hair in her fingers, yanking on it and blowing
spit bubbles. The room was quiet, the ladies talking in excited
whispers, fingering dainty dresses and shoes, marveling over
the tiny velvet caps. The tapestries on the east windows were
finally removed, and Anna had ordered the windows flung
open despite the chill. She could hear the low hum of the Great

Hall and its revelers, a loud laugh here, flutes there. But for the first time in weeks she didn't wish to leave her rooms. All she wanted was right there in her arms. Well, almost all.

She grinned into her baby's face, rubbing nose to nose. The baby made a dovelike sound, and Anna's heart melted anew.

That's when she heard it: a roar of hurrahs erupting from the Great Hall. They knew. He knew. Her smile deepened as the chapel bells pealed. A princess is born. Long may she live.

William extricated himself from the crowd, knowing there was some sort of etiquette to be followed. Daniel had told him as much, and he hadn't paid attention. But no amount of court niceties would keep him from his wife and child. Striding down the hall, he wiped his hands on his trunks and dabbed his face with his kerchief. He stood in front of the two guards he'd nearly assaulted earlier.

"Gentlemen," he said, "please excuse our earlier demands. We should not have put you in such a position."

A smile flickered on the left guard's face. He nodded.

"Her Majesties await," the guards said, opening the door wide.

William had to remind himself to slow his steps. He barely acknowledged the ladies in the outer chamber. Charity, eyes down, blushed as he passed. Coming through the arch to the bedchamber, his breath caught. It was like being hit by a beating sun after a cool swim. He saw Anna, bathed in candlelight, hair cascading down her shoulders, surrounded by a cloud of pillows. And in her arms was the bonniest, tiniest dream of a girl, with a shock of dark brown hair and cheeks as rosy as her mama's. No Madonna and child had ever looked so divine. William didn't think it was possible to love anyone or anything more than he loved them both right then.

In five strides he was beside the bed. In three seconds his boots were kicked off, and he was in bed with his family, Anna's face in his hands.

"My brilliant, amazing, strong wife." He kissed her, then held her head to his chest.

"Don't squish the baby." She beamed at him.

"Oh, there's a baby here?" He pulled back and gazed down at his daughter. Cate's eyes had been brown, almost hazel, but these were blue like his. The baby's mouth twitched.

"Did you see that?" he said. "She smiled at me."

Anna laughed. Oh, it was good to hear her laugh. It had been a long three weeks.

"I don't think babies can smile this early, but I dare not contradict the king."

They both looked at the princess again. She burped.

"Definitely my child," William said. Anna gave him a good-natured swat.

"Isn't she the most splendid thing?"

"That she is." He gave her his finger to squeeze. "Quite a grip!"

"So you're not . . . disappointed?" Anna's voice caught on the last word.

"I'm enchanted with our princess." He drew her to him again, feeling his daughter squirming between them, hands grabbing at his shirt. He kissed Anna once more. "And I know princes will follow, if I have anything to do with it."

Anna laughed. "Hold your royal horses, Majesty."

"Well, they've been chomping at the bit."

"We must wait until I am churched and the baby baptized. And until every part of me doesn't ache."

"Details," he said.

"I've missed you so."

"And I you."

"Though your letters brought much comfort, they were no replacement for your presence." She paused. "Would you like to hold her?"

"Are you sure?"

"Why on earth not?"

"I've never held a baby before. What if I break her?"

Anna rolled her eyes. "You ride out in battle, chase wild boar, lance courtiers with your words, and you're afraid of a baby?" He stuck his tongue out at her. "Very kingly," she said. "Now make your arms into a circle—closer to your body. There. Now, make sure you always support her head and hold her close to your chest."

She laid the baby in his arms, tucking their daughter's head in the crook of his elbow, the baby grunting and wriggling. He was unprepared for her lightness. He was unprepared for his trembling.

"What shall we call you, my sweet princess?"

"Should we call her Mary for the Holy Mother? It's her feast day, after all." Anna brushed her fingers on the top of the baby's head. "Mary Catherine?"

William shook his head. "We shall name her for the women I love most."

"Matilda, then? Catherine Matilda?"

William met his wife's eyes. Those lovely, wise eyes.

"She shall be Princess Catherine Anna."

"Princess Catherine Anna." Tears gathered in Anna's eyes. "We can call her Cate. It's beautiful."

"You're beautiful," William said, kissing her cheek, "and resilient and witty and stubborn and true and everything I want our daughter to be."

Cate whimpered and twisted to his chest, pink hands opening and closing, face rooting around.

"I think she wants to eat," Anna said.

"She certainly won't find any satisfaction where she's looking." William chuckled, and Anna rolled the baby out of his arms. He suddenly felt empty.

Mary hurried off to fetch the wet nurse.

"I wish I could feed her," Anna said, almost to herself.

"You know it's not done." He could see the pain in her eyes. "Besides, the sooner you've no milk, the sooner we can make another."

Anna held Cate close. The newborn started to cry in earnest.

"Shhhh, my girl," Anna said, giving her a pinky to suckle, "we'll fill your tummy and your heart with all good things."

Cate frowned as she sucked her mother's finger, spit it out, and tried again.

"Well, she certainly has your tenacity," William said, petting Cate's head.

"My tenacity is it?" Anna rubbed her face in Cate's belly.

Mary and the wet nurse bustled over, taking the baby. William snuggled in next to Anna, wrapping her in his arms. Mary came back to the foot of the bed.

"Now, Majesty, you best not be thinking you can stay here the night." Mary's hands were on her hips.

"Why ever not, Mistress Mary?"

"You know the rules, Majesty," Mary said. "Besides, the queen needs to rest and recover."

"As do I," William said, making a show of fluffing up the pillows, "for I cannot even remember when last I slept. And it's been a long day."

Mary flung a pillow at his face.

"Mistress Mary, assault on the king carries grave consequences."

Both Mary and Anna laughed.

"Ah, so you *will* have me in chains, Highness?"

"Only if you don't allow me to take my sleep with my wife this night." He tossed the pillow back at her, and she caught it. "I have a very empty and very lonely dungeon that longs for inhabitants."

"If I hear you keeping either one of Her Highnesses awake . . ." Mary wagged a finger at him. He held up his hands in protest.

"I'll be good." He gnawed at Anna's shoulder.

Mary snorted. "Men."

CHAPTER 18

Back to the Beginning

Things were finally returning to some sort of normalcy. The queen was churched, the princess baptized, Robert's wife and Countess Cariline named as godmothers and the Duke of Duven as godfather. Feathers were ruffled, but since a godparent couldn't be related by blood, there was no one else of enough standing to take the post. Robert couldn't be more pleased. Not only had the queen delivered a princess rather than a prince, but also, that princess would surely marry his eldest son someday.

The previous day he'd finally convinced his wife to leave court to be with his boys, allowing Robert to be with Yvette.

Things were still tense between them, but he couldn't determine why. Surely she wasn't still sour over their argument about Margaux? She mentioned not wanting to flirt with Valencia any more, but why should that make her so damned testy?

Robert mulled over the matter as he and Daniel went to fetch the king from the nursery. William spent most of his free time, what little there was, cooing at the new princess, as if the whole country wasn't still about to rip apart. And this new letter from Bartmore would not help matters.

The guards opened the doors to the royal nursery. It looked like a swan had exploded—white bunting and draperies, downy white blankets and feather-topped cradle the size of a small boat, all of it trimmed with gold. The king and queen looked up, dumb grins on their faces, the queen holding the princess, while William tickled her dainty feet. Robert refrained from rolling his eyes.

"Begging your pardons, Majesties," Daniel said, "but we've another letter from the archbishop, and we must craft a response."

William nodded and stood.

"I should like to hear its contents," the queen said, bouncing the baby in her arms.

"I hardly think the nursery is the place for statecraft," Robert said.

"The queen's sure to hear of it anyway," Daniel said under his breath.

"Read on, Cecile," William said, glancing up. A nurse and maid went to the far corners of the room as Daniel unfurled the letter.

"'Dearest and Most High Majesty,'" Daniel read, "'it grieves my heart to hear you believe such foul rumors that hath been spread about me by mine enemies at court, undoubtedly those who wish you and Her Majesty ill.'"

William began to pace.

"I swear to you on the Virgin Mother that they are lies. I did not recall the papal troops from your service, but someone has. Until the truth is discovered, I have decided to take an extended tour here in Rome, to benefit my soul with learning and in turn benefit our people with my invigorate voice. Our new Father, His Holiness, has been a most gracious host and sends you his blessed love. Know that I speak to him of Your Highness's current struggles and beg him for his prayers, which he graciously gives. I am your servant in the Lord.'"

Both king and queen scowled. The princess wriggled.

"He certainly makes much of his influence with the new pope," Daniel said, "but my messengers hear it otherwise. He has only twice been to the papal palace and only once had conference with His Holiness."

"And why would he flee," the queen said, handing the baby to the wet nurse, "if he's innocent?"

Robert swallowed. He doubted that Bartmore was behind all this. It didn't benefit him, as far as Robert could see. But it suited Robert that the king and queen thought Bartmore was guilty. One more screw to turn against the papists.

"Indeed," William said. "Though even if he's innocent, he won't be left blameless for abandoning his post at a time of war."

"Shall I compose a response, Majesty?" Daniel said, looking glum.

"Such lies deserve no response," the queen said.

"We must not forget," Daniel said, "that King Philip of Spain is Pope Gregory's main supporter. We could use Spain's political power, if not its men, in our own wars. We could tell Bartmore we've found a culprit, thus easing the tension there and gaining the pope's favor."

"How could Bartmore gain any man's favor?" the queen said.

"He gained someone's to rise so high," Robert said. "Regardless, there's sense in Cecile's plan, though I doubt His Eminence would believe it."

"Daniel," William said, finally drawing his gaze fully away from the queen, "compose a letter that recalls him to court. Say we were saddened to have the Bishop of Havenside perform the christening rather than him. Make no mention of the troops, but send our regards to His Holiness, etc."

"Surely you don't want him here," Daniel said.

"Of course I don't," William said, approaching the wet nurse, "but I want him to think I do."

"But—" Daniel said.

"That will be all." He made a ludicrous face at the baby. "Good day, Your Graces."

Robert guided Daniel out the door and when it was shut behind them patted his friend's back.

"I don't know what's gotten into him," Robert said.

"I do," Daniel said, "and it doesn't bode well for any of us."

He strode down the hall, leaving Robert with even more to ponder.

William appropriated Cate from the arms of the wet nurse as soon as Robert and Daniel left. He rubbed his nose to hers. Her pink fingers reached out to grab his face as she giggled up milky spit bubbles. He smoothed her hair and gave her his thumb to gnaw on.

"You know," he said, "I'm not convinced that Bartmore's behind that letter."

"Who else could it be?" Anna said.

"He doesn't gain anything by such a tactic. He should want Laureland and all they represent defeated."

Cate twisted reaching for her mama. Reluctantly, he let Anna have her. She skillfully tucked Cate against her shoulder, rubbing the baby's back.

"But he wants to be seen by the pope as a worthy cardinal. He wants to be the cleanser of heresy—he doesn't want you in that role."

William scratched his jaw. Cate continued to mewl, distracting him. He searched for a place to sit in the princess's fairyland. After a moment he gave up and leaned against the hearth.

"Bartmore already saw himself as the chief negotiator with the pope," he said. "Hence he'd have taken credit for the pope's assistance. So why would he call the troops off?"

Cate burped loudly. Anna cocked a brow at William.

"She learned from the best." William walked to his ladies, grinning. "But let us speak of happier things. Christmastide."

Anna's eyes sparkled. "Will you accept my father's invitation? Are we to Beaubourg for the festivities?"

He grinned. "I haven't told the council yet, but yes, I think it important we show the crown unfazed by the war. Besides, it gives us an opportunity to show off the princess."

"You know it will be cramped, Wills. Much less extravagant than at court." She kissed Cate's cheek, handing her to the nurse to have her readied for a nap.

"I've spent a Christmastide sharing the upper room of a pub in southern France with Daniel, Robert, and some live geese." He wrapped his arms around her waist as she laughed. "I'm sure Beaubourg will be a sight for sore eyes."

The next day, Anna found herself waiting outside Daniel's office chambers. He'd summoned her with some urgency, and she could not fathom why. Perhaps he'd heard more from Bartmore. But then why would the king not be there as well? The doors opened to her, and there stood Daniel, warmed spiced wine for her and rich chocolate for himself. He bowed and smiled, but his face looked tense.

"Welcome, Majesty," he said, "I thought you would enjoy some cool weather refreshment."

"Thank you," she said, leaving her ladies in the hall. Daniel's taster poured their drinks, then disappeared into the shadows. Daniel indicated a chair, still smiling.

"And to what do I owe this good cheer?" She took her glass and sat, adjusting her skirts.

"I have a favor to ask," Daniel said, sitting across from her.

"I will do what I can."

"I've tried to talk to the king, and he will hear none of it, so I ask it of you. Out of the love you have for him and for Troixden."

She lowered her mug. "For heaven's sake, Daniel, whatever is this about?"

"I'd like you to convince the king not to bring the court to Beaubourg."

Her heart dropped to her toes. "Why ever would I do that?"

"Majesty, it's not safe. Surely you can see that."

"We'll be surrounded by guards and nobles the entire way, and my father's castle is impenetrable."

Daniel rose and walked to the other side of the desk. "We just fought a war mere miles from Beaubourg. It's only a matter of time—"

"It's a day's ride to the border and farther still to the heart of Laureland. Have you heard word of an attack?"

"Not exactly, but there is movement." Daniel sat again and began to shuffle papers on his uncharacteristically untidy desk. "I do not make my recommendations idly."

"I am the first to be concerned for the safety of the king and the princess." She placed her drink down, barely touched. "I really don't think there's any cause for alarm."

"But any move we make north, no matter the reason, will be taken as another act of aggression. I cannot emphasize enough that the threat, whether you will hear it or not, is real."

"It's an act of celebration, Daniel, bringing the princess to her people! There's a show of strength in it, but surely that's all to the good."

"I'm sorry, Highness, but I cannot agree."

"The king says it will be a strategic advantage if things devolve to a full civil war," Anna said, "that Beaubourg, Ridgeland, and the other northern townships will side with the crown because we show them favor."

Daniel met her eyes, face grim. "The king knows you want to see your home—"

"The king would never allow my personal pleasure to override our safety." Her cheeks grew hot.

Daniel shook his head and snorted. "He would give his life for you to eat oranges year round if you wished them."

Anna stood, hands on her hips, trying to restrain her anger. "Why are you pushing this futile cause to me?"

Daniel rose, his face red. "Because he listens to you! Only to you, always to you! Come hell or high water, I will save him from dangerous influence!"

"This isn't about where the court spends Christmastide at all." She narrowed her eyes. "You fear you've lost the king's ear, is that it?"

"I've lost nothing." He again looked down at his papers. "I know more of his ways than you will ever understand."

"You want to do battle with me over his affection?" Anna gave a short, sharp laugh. "You will not like the outcome."

"And when push comes to shove, are you sure you'll win out?"

"As sure as my heart beats."

She met Daniel's eyes. They looked stunned, filled with grief, with desolation.

"You are probably the smartest person in this court," she said, "but today you have made a grave error. You do not want to make an enemy of me, Your Grace."

He reached out a hand. "Majesty, please. I . . . I intended nothing of the sort. I don't know what came over me."

"Worried I'll tell this tale to the king?" Daniel's face crumpled, and he covered it with his hands. "He has enough enemies at court," she said. "He doesn't need to know his most trusted friend has insulted his wife."

"Thank you, Majesty," he said through his fingers.

"But mark my words, Daniel. If you again question my loyalty to this country or my king, there will be hell to pay."

The simmering anger that had burst forth from Daniel shocked Anna, but more than that, her heart sank to know that a man she had thought she could count on had turned on her. Still, what she'd said to Daniel was true. She would not tell the king. She would hold this card, hoping she wouldn't ever have to play it.

And the court would move north to spend the Christmastide festivities in Beaubourg.

Anna's ladies were helping oversee the packing of the princess's necessities. Her eyes fell on Charity, who was humming to herself, innocent of the knowledge that Anna would leave her behind in Beaubourg.

The prospect of heading north had Margaux in unusually high spirits. She'd never been to Beaubourg and was glad, she said, to not have to go to Mohrlang or Norwick, both of which her brother had suggested. Anna laughed to herself, imagining Margaux among the peasantry and the rather mean quarters her childhood home would provide.

"Besides," Margaux said, fingering a cap, "my son needs the fresh air, and he'll enjoy meeting his relations."

"Relations?" Yvette gave Margaux a penetrating look.

Margaux smiled not so sweetly back. "Certainly. He is cousin to the princess, so the duke would be his relation."

"Not by blood," Yvette said under her breath.

"Regardless," Margaux said, "I'm sure the good people of Beaubourg won't mind the princess's name half as much as the rest of the country."

Anna's breath stopped. "What do you mean, Countess?"

"Has no one told you?" Margaux wore a look of false surprise.

"Margaux, stop it," Yvette said.

"Tell me, Countess." Anna said.

"They say Your Highness purposefully refused to name the princess after Mary, even though she was born on the Blessed Virgin's feast day."

"The king named her to honor his sister," Anna said, "and me."

"Quite right," Mary said, bustling out of nowhere and shooing Margaux aside. "And the king can do as he pleases."

"Perhaps the king would do best to weigh his decisions more carefully." Margaux moved toward the door.

"I have not given you leave, Countess," Anna said. Margaux stood there, nostrils flaring, eyes fixed on Anna's. "In fact, I'm not so sure I desire your company on our northern tour."

"But I simply must go to Beaubourg." Margaux looked horror struck.

"There are plenty of other options," Anna said. "But perhaps you may have a change of attitude before we take leave. You may go and compose yourself, Countess."

Margaux curtsied and left. The rest of Anna's ladies returned to their duties.

"Anna, dearie, you mustn't make an outright enemy of her," Mary said.

"I'm sick to death of her. Trying to hint that she has some special knowledge I don't."

"I'm not saying she's not irksome, but you mustn't rise to the bait." Mary handed her a swatch of silk. "You gained so much clout during the war, don't lose it to this. Especially over her."

Mary was right. Anna had been emotional as of late, crying over trifles, angered by perceived slights. More important, her anger had clouded the issue Margaux raised, that the people thought Princess Cate's name a slight against the church. Anna wasn't surprised that William hadn't told her. He surely knew she would take it too much to heart. She glanced out the window at the gaggle of nurses and ladies in the bright December sunshine, a shade held over the princess. They all needed to get away from court and its trappings. Beaubourg would be a welcome change.

CHAPTER 19

Home Again, Home Again

Saying the quarters in Beaubourg were cramped would be understating the matter. The king and queen had made a much smaller foray to Anna's home at the start of their marriage, so William knew there'd be less space. But he hadn't remembered how much less.

Thankfully he'd done away with separate royal chambers right at the start. He and Anna were together in her father's suite.

"It feels somehow wrong," Anna said, head nestled on William's bare chest in the large feather bed, "to be in my father's room, with you, doing . . ."

"Are we feeling naughty then?" He nibbled her earlobe. "I thought I'd worn you out, but if you insist—"

She rolled her eyes. "It's just . . . I don't know, sacrilegious or something."

William rolled his eyes back at her. "And we have been making merry for quite some time in the beds of both my father and mother. Not to mention my brother's."

"That's different." She sat up, crossing her arms over her breasts. William laughed.

"Look on it this way," he said, untangling her arms. "Your parents' marriage was surely blessed." He sucked on her wrist, running his thumb down her arm. She closed her eyes. "So perhaps it is a good luck." He drew his tongue down to her elbow, feeling her pulse quicken. "And perhaps," he cupped a breast, stroking with his thumb, feeling the silk-soft skin pucker at his touch, "we should make good use of all that . . . magic."

She grabbed his hair, easing herself back on the bed and pulling him on top of her. He drank her in, one hand tangled in her hair, the other traveling over the peaks and valleys of her skin. Her eyes raked his body, her cheeks flush. She wrapped her hands around his neck, forcing his lips to hers. He gave her a half grin and glided his hand down to her hips and around her thighs.

"Magic is fleeting, Majesty," she said, teasing. "But love is as relentless as death."

Then his mouth was on hers, and he was lost in her once again.

Anna was intent on celebrating St. Stephen's Day as they always had at Castle Beaubourg, by throwing the doors open to as many villagers as could come. This year they would have to erect tents and torches in the stable yard to fit everyone. Children were also allowed, and she couldn't wait to show off the princess.

Margaux fussed over her son Frederick, who refused to keep his velvet cap in place. His red hair had turned to curled locks of gold like his mother's. Even Anna had to admit he was a striking lad.

The ladies went down to the festivities, Anna and the princess receiving much fanfare. William kissed Anna's hand and took Cate into his arms as the gathered nobles applauded. The royal family made their way to the Great Hall, Anna and William in the center, her father at William's other side, then Robert, Daniel, Halforn, and other court gentry following by rank. Margaux, being of highest rank among Anna's ladies, sat to her right, fidgeting as each Beaubourgian guest was presented.

"Countess," Anna said, "you show your displeasure too perceptibly." She looked sidelong at Margaux and realized she did not look bored. She looked nervous.

"I am not displeased, Majesty," she said. "Merely impatient to get to the feast so my dear Frederick can do as he is wont to do."

"Regardless," Anna said, smiling to the tavern owner Mrs. Cleaves, who had brought a supply of William's favorite brew, "I have not known you to be anything but decorous. In public."

"I do not have the gift of falsifying my feelings as some do, Highness."

"Then motherhood has changed you?" Anna watched the oncoming stream of people, and her heart stopped. There stood Bryan, blue eyes twinkling, arm in a sling. William rose at the sight of him.

"Sir Bryan!" William walked down and clasped Bryan's uninjured arm. "You are welcome, lad. How's your arm?"

"Still sore, Majesty, but I hope it may be back to rights soon."

"Good, good." William escorted him to the bottom of the dais.

William had told her of Bryan's daring rescue and their escape together, but to have him so affable with a man he'd wanted dead? This night was proving most strange.

"Majesty," Bryan said with a formal bow. Rising, he gave Anna the sweet smile she remembered.

"Sir Bryan." Anna couldn't help smiling back. "I have not yet had the opportunity to thank you for bringing our king back to us in one whole and happy piece. I and the realm owe you much, sir."

"It was my duty and my honor." Bryan bowed again. Rising, he flicked his eyes to Margaux. Color rose to his cheeks. She had that effect on most men.

"Majesties, I almost forgot." He retreated a few steps and took the hand of a young woman Anna had never seen. She had auburn hair and a wide, kind face but could not be called pretty, exactly. "I wish to introduce you to Lady Magdalene of Kilburn."

Lady Magdalene curtsied to the floor, which was not far for her to go.

"Milady," William said, "you are welcome. And to what do we owe the honor?" He took Anna's hand, his calloused thumb brushing her knuckles.

"Our fathers have decided . . . ," Bryan said, "Well, it is our hope that we . . ."

"I seem to remember a similar audience with you, Sir Bryan," William laughed. "Though this one I am sure will end in a more pleasant manner."

"Yes, Majesty." Bryan visibly relaxed. "It's our families' wish that you consider consenting to a betrothal between us."

Anna sighed. She could not be more in love with William, and she hadn't loved Bryan with half the intensity he'd felt for her. Still, seeing her girlhood beau with his future wife gave her a twinge.

Margaux cleared her throat. Anna gave her a pointed look, ready to shut down any snide comment. But she saw no malice on the countess's face. Instead, Margaux was hastily putting away her handkerchief, her eyes red rimmed, looking anywhere but at Bryan. Had she been crying? It couldn't be. Anna snuck a look at Frederick, who yelped, his bright blond curls framing his face, wriggling to free himself from his nurse's arms. Then she looked back at Bryan, who was avoiding so much as a glance at Margaux, or the boy.

Holy Mother of God, it couldn't be.

Anna pulled Yvette aside at her evening toilette and drew her into a closet, hidden by paneling and curtains off the upper hall, next to where the unmarried ladies were housed.

"Majesty," Yvette said, "why all this intrigue?"

"Tell me and tell me true," Anna said. "Is Frederick Sir Bryan's child?"

Yvette frowned.

"Did you not see how they reacted to each other?" Anna said. "Did you not notice how she kept scooting Frederick past Bryan, how his face turned ashen when recognition set in?"

Yvette shook her head. "Majesty, I was much occupied with . . . other matters." She flushed.

"So you know none of this? Robert knows none of this?" Well, Yvette would certainly tell him. But Anna couldn't help herself. She had to know.

"It finally all makes sense." Yvette nodded, eyes wide. "She'd taken to visiting the poor and imprisoned she said. She was always messed when she returned."

Anna shook her head. "How did I not know of this?" But then she remembered that early morning and Margaux filling a basket. . .

"She only went on her days off. I knew she was up to something. I had her followed, but she always disappeared. I gave it up, as there were more important things . . ."

"And what might those be?"

Yvette looked at her, eyes hooded. "Majesty, it is said that court is like sausage—quite delectable, but one does not wish to know how it is squeezed into its neat casing."

Anna made a note to come back to that particular tidbit. "Well then, what about Frederick?"

"You must be right. I'm astounded I didn't see it myself." She helped Anna straighten her attire. "And will you tell the king?"

"I suppose I must. We have no secrets." Even at this she felt her stomach churn, for it wasn't true anymore. "And you will tell Robert."

"Yes. But what good it will do either of them to know, I haven't a clue."

Anna led Yvette out of the closet and back into the open hall. As she closed the door behind her, she swore she saw Daniel flit behind the corner.

Anna sat in William's lap by the fire. He stroked her hair as she told him her suspicions.

"I guess Robert was right then." William chuckled.

"He knew?"

"No, no," William waved the idea away. "At one point, briefly, he considered having Margaux and Bryan marry. But he knew I'd have none of it."

"They would've loathed each other," Anna said.

"Apparently not." He laughed. "Poor Eustace. The bastard has his own bastard."

"But isn't there something . . . I don't know, *official* we're supposed to do?"

"The truth will out soon enough. Court gossip is more punishment than I could ever dole out." He kissed her shoulder. His amusement with all of this surprised her.

"But the child . . ."

"Will be raised with more privilege than his true station deserves, and with a lineage in looks that will serve him quite well."

"And even knowing this, you will approve the betrothal?"

"Bryan does not strike me as a serial adulterer. He strikes me as a man imprisoned till death, with access to a willing and beguiling conquest."

"When you put it like that . . ." She frowned. She didn't like to think of her friend in those terms. William nudged her off his lap and rose, stretching his arms above his head.

"Come to bed, my queen," he said, "for I grow weary of speaking of other people's children. I'd rather beget more of my own."

The tight quarters meant a shared nursery for Cate and Frederick. Which meant that when Anna went to see Cate the next morning, she would also have to see Margaux.

Initially, Margaux had likely gone to Bryan out of spite, probably hoping to upset Anna or gain information. Yet Margaux's red eyes the previous night, the whiteness of her face . . . What surely started out as manipulation must have become something more, at least for her.

Anna heard Frederick's giggles as she approached the nursery. The door was slightly ajar, and what she saw stilled her.

Margaux spun round, head thrown back in laughter, hugging Frederick to her chest as he squealed in delight. She bent her head to nibble at his earlobe, which sent him into peals of laughter.

"No more, Freddy," Margaux said, broad smile on her perfect lips, "Mummy will fall down." She kissed his golden head and hugged him close. "My sweet, sweet boy."

"Uhn uhn!" Frederick said, pointing his pudgy arm toward Cate's room.

"You want to see your baby cousin?" Margaux laughed again. "All right, pumpkin, here we go." She started to gallop across the floor.

Anna entered the room, stopping Margaux. The countess's face went smooth and cold, and she curtseyed as best she could with a child in her arms.

"Why, milord Frederick," Anna said, approaching the pair, "I hear you wish an audience with your cousin." Frederick cooed at her. "Come with me, and we shall see her." Anna nodded. "Countess, you look well this morning."

"Majesty." She followed Anna to the princess's room, cheeks pink.

Cate's nurse was rocking her cradle and singing softly. She dropped into a curtsy as Anna moved to her daughter's side. Cate was wide awake, blue eyes soaking in the world, hands grasping at the air.

"Oh, my darling." Anna lifted Cate to her chest, breathing in her clean, linen scent. She kissed those rose cheeks, stroked the unruly hair, and something in her heart loosed its grip and flew away.

"Catey, we have visitors today." Anna smiled at Margaux. Frederick was wriggling out of Margaux's arms, trying to get as close to Cate as possible. "You may approach, Countess."

Margaux came closer, trying to hold down Frederick's arms.

"Oooo," he said, eyes wide at the sight of the princess. Cate's arms waved in the air toward him, and Frederick grabbed at one.

"No," Margaux said, holding his arms down. "You may not touch the princess."

"As long as you are gentle, milord," she said, then gave Cate her pinky to hold and brought the princess's hand toward Frederick. "Gently."

Frederick reached out, awestruck. He patted her hand with his palm. Cate released Anna's fingers and grabbed Frederick's. He giggled and bounced her hand up and down.

"Would you look at that, Countess?" Anna said, smiling. "Perhaps they shall be friends . . . as all their parents once were."

Margaux met Anna's eyes, face drained of color, and swallowed. Anna gave her a nod as if to say, *yes, I know your secret, and you are absolved.*

"Nothing would please me more, Majesty." Margaux kissed her son's head, and Anna thought she saw wetness in the corners of her eyes.

Despite Daniel's arguments against it, William knew that going north was the right decision, just by watching his wife. Wrapped in white fox fur, her face shone in the sun's stead as they walked beside the creek, Anna pointing out all her favorite childhood haunts to the princess in her arms. William envisioned a girl of eight tromping through the cattails, ruining her skirts . . .

"And this is my wishing willow." Anna came under the tree's leafless drapery. William rested his hand on the rough bark and felt the groove of carving beneath his fingers. Seeing the outline of a heart, he looked away. That was a childhood memory of hers he'd rather not resurrect.

Cate's nurse took the princess from Anna, covering the baby's hands in fur muffs. Anna snaked her arm under his coats and around his waist.

"Thank you." She beamed into his face. "This trip has done me good."

He rested his chin on her head. "I can see that, my dear."

Looking across the stream, he saw a five riders galloping toward the royal party. They flew a white flag, but the standard next to it, a rearing stag beneath a thistle, was not one he recognized. He tensed, shifting Anna behind him.

"William, what—" She stopped and followed his gaze.

"Guards!" But they were already forming a defensive line. He sent a page on horseback for reinforcements. "Get the princess back to the castle. Now." Anna beckoned for a guard to accompany Cate and her nurse.

"And you too, my dear," William said. The castle gates were a mere hundred yards away. She would be safe before the riders reached them.

"I will not run from my own people," Anna said.

"'Tis not fear, 'tis caution."

"They fly the white flag."

He grabbed her by the arms. "We waste time. Away, Anna!" But he knew that look in her eyes. She would not leave. "Then for heaven's sake, get behind me."

His own mounted guard arrived and flanked him and the queen.

The man at the center of the riders was a hulk, but rode slightly hunched. Their pace slowed, and William's eyes narrowed as they neared. It couldn't be. But it looked like . . . Another horseman arrived from the castle and dismounted behind the king.

"Majesties." William turned to see Robert, cloakless but armed with broadsword, dagger, and hatchet.

"You come prepared, friend," William said clasping his shoulder. "Whatever happens, you must protect the queen." Robert flicked his eyes to Anna and nodded.

"I think it's Westerville," William said. Robert's jaw tightened. William moved Anna closer to the thick tree trunk, placing Robert next to her. Then he faced the riders, who had stopped on the other side of the twenty-foot-wide creek.

"Hail, Majesty!" Westerville called. "We come in peace and in full disclosure."

"That would be a first," William said. Westerville dismounted with the help of all four of his men. A cane embellished with gold and jewels was produced, and he used it to hobble forward a few feet. William relaxed. There would be no combat. Westerville waved his free hand in the air.

"I bring you news, Highness."

"And why would I trust any news you bring? Indeed, you should be arrested for treason."

"Ah, but I know you, Majesty. You are of too noble a mind to arrest one under the white flag." He gave an oily smile. Looking over William's shoulder, he saw the queen and made a clumsy bow. "Majesty, the rumors are true," he said, "for you are more fair than even I had imagined. No wonder your countrymen and your king fight to the death for you."

"You will not speak to Her Majesty," William said, advancing toward the creek bed. "At all."

"I come not to gaze upon beauty but to tell you to watch your back. Ha! More I should watch mine around you!" The man actually laughed.

"You ride under the white flag, then threaten me?"

"Not a threat, my liege. Information about those who surround you at court. Information worth its weight in gold."

"Your problem from the very start, Westerville, has been your underestimation of my reach."

"It is you, Majesty, begging your pardon, who underestimates the ambition of those who follow you." He flicked his eyes to Robert.

"Do you not know when you've been dismissed?" Robert said, stepping in front of the queen. "Take your lies and ply them elsewhere."

"Why, Norwick—do you fear what they reveal?"

William strode to Robert, grabbed his cousin's dagger, and returned to the creek edge. He gripped the hilt, breathing deep to calm his rage as he leveled his gaze at Westerville.

"Your days of threatening me, my family, my men, and my country are over." The man's smile faded. "If you have not left these grounds by the time my party makes the castle walls, I will ride out myself to finish what I started in Laureland." William turned on his heel, strode to Anna, and grabbed her elbow, guards falling in behind.

"Is that the man who held you captive?" She glanced behind her shoulder. "You can't let him go free."

"Even if he doesn't play by the rules, I will," he said. Her lips tightened, and she frowned at the frozen grass as they walked.

"Majesty," Robert said, falling into stride with William and the queen, "perhaps we should have him captured and questioned."

"I know what he speaks of," William said. "I do not need to hear him twist it to his own ends."

"Bartmore?" Robert spit to the side. "But how would Westerville know about that letter?"

"He speaks not of Bartmore. He speaks of heretics in our midst."

William held the dagger out, returning it to Robert. Robert grabbed the hilt, but William pulled the dagger toward himself, bringing Robert in so close Anna couldn't hear. The last thing she needed was more ammunition against the duke.

"He speaks of you, my friend," William whispered. Robert's eyes widened. William let the dagger go, and they fell back into step together.

"We will not let his insinuations ruin the festivities." William placed his arm around Anna's shoulders. "But we must all of us watch our words and our steps. It is a precarious time."

They reached the castle's gate. William looked back toward the willow. The riders faded into the tree line beneath the overcast sky.

That's right, bastard. Run.

When Anna returned to the castle, she went straight to the nursery. She knew Cate would be safe and sound, but she needed to see to believe. Sure enough, the princess was sleeping, snuggled under her down blankets, her mouth slightly open.

Anna left to make ready for that evening's feast, but as she passed the ladies' chamber she heard terse whispers. Opening the door, she saw Yvette, arms crossed, glaring at Margaux.

"Ladies," Anna said. Both women gave a start, then curtsied. "And what are we whispering about?"

"Nothing you do not already know, Majesty." Yvette looked at Margaux, who scowled.

"I was just leaving, Highness," Margaux said, grabbing her cloak.

"Enjoy your time, Countess," Yvette said, "for it is surely your last."

Anna had the distinct sense that if she weren't there, Margaux would have spat at Yvette. Instead, she curtsied again and hurried out of the room.

"And what was that all about?" Anna said.

"See for yourself," Yvette said, indicating the window.

Anna walked over to the familiar view. She placed her hands on the desk—how many hours had she spent there, studying, daydreaming, longing?—and looked down into the stable yard, where soft puffs of snow had started to fall against the darkening sky. After a short while, Margaux appeared, clutching her cloak around her, scurrying to the stable. She stopped at the door, looked around, then went in.

"She's to ride?"

"I suppose you could call it that."

Sure enough, along came another figure, a man similarly cloaked. He too paused at the stable door, and as he looked around, Anna caught the glint of blond hair beneath his hood. Her stomach flipped. It was one thing to know he was bedding her nemesis, but another to see it for certain. And in the stable? At least they could be less . . . clichéd. She grimaced and looked away.

"He's about to be betrothed."

"To a woman he does not love," Yvette said. "Majesty, what you and the king share is a rarity. Not everyone is so fortunate."

"Yet I did not love him on our wedding day either. Bryan should give his poor future wife a chance, before . . ." She flicked her hand toward the window.

"Men will be men, and Margaux will be Margaux." Yvette took up a glass of wine. "Would you care for any, Majesty?"

Anna shook her head. "Actually, I'm glad we're alone. As the king and I were on the grounds, we were approached by some riders. One of whom was the man who held the king captive in Laureland."

Yvette set down her cup. "What happened? What did he say?"

"Among other things, he said there was a heretic in our midst and that the king ought to watch his back."

All the color drained from Yvette's face. "What did the king say?" Her voice cracked.

"He waved it off, but I know he'll ponder it." Anna stepped closer to Yvette and lowered her voice. "Do you think this Westerville knows of Lady Jane?"

Yvette startled but recovered herself. "There's no way he could know."

"All the same, I know the king will get to the bottom of this.

He will dig like a terrier after a rat. And I will not be able to keep Lady Jane's secret for long."

"I promise you, Majesty, it's not Lady Jane this man speaks of. It cannot be." She took Anna's hands and gave them an encouraging squeeze. "He would have bigger fish to fry than a lady-in-waiting."

Anna groaned. "What has my damnable soft heart gotten us into?"

"Whatever it got us into, that same soft heart will get us out of it. Worry not, my queen."

Anna gave Yvette a lackluster smile. But as she quitted the room to find her husband, she could not convince her nerves.

CHAPTER 20

Twelfth Night

William had never smelled a stable so sweet. Even Palace Havenside's had the constant odor of manure and sweat amid the fragrance of fresh hay and oiled leather. But the Duke of Beaubourg's stable was near fresh as the king's chambers, and as warm. These were pampered horses.

It was three days until Twelfth Night, and William had just returned from a ride with Robert and the duke, sizing up a potential addition to his own stables. The dappled gray was fleet of foot and rode like still water, even across the fresh snow. William picked an apple out of the waiting barrel and held it out to his mount, feeling the tickle of whiskers and velvet lips as the horse ate its reward.

"He's certainly a prize, Your Grace," William said, patting the horse's neck. The duke's reputation for acquiring impeccable beasts was well earned.

"I sought him especially for you, Majesty," Beaubourg said, smiling in his easy way.

"And what of my mount, Your Grace?" Robert said. "Is he for sale as well?"

"I would part with him only for someone as discerning as Your Grace," Beaubourg said with a bow. "Shall he board in Norwick or at the palace?"

Their talk was interrupted by the approach of a contingent of men, Daniel at the head.

"Excuse me, Majesty," Daniel said, bowing, "but this news cannot wait."

William and Robert exchanged a wary glance. "Proceed, Your Grace," William said.

"Bartmore returns. He has sent a squire here to inform us. But that is not all." Daniel looked around the stable filled with grooms and frowned. "Perhaps we should retire to the castle?"

"Do not hesitate now, Your Grace," William said. He clapped, dismissing the servants. Anna's father made to go as well.

"Beaubourg, you may stay," William said. "For certainly this shall out to council soon enough." Daniel nodded. "So, Daniel, what more?"

"We have ferreted out the culprit, the man who called off the pope's troops. It was Valencia."

"Valencia?" William put his hands on his hips, mind churning.

"One of his secretaries confessed under, shall we say, intense examination," Daniel said.

"So a confession under duress is all we have to go on?" William said.

"He also turned over a multitude of Valencia's papers. Most of them were written by scribes, but a few were in Valencia's own hand. My men have just returned with those. The handwriting matches the damning letter exactly."

"And where is he now?" William said. "Has he made it to Spain for the season, or does he still travel?"

"I am seeking that information at present, Majesty."

"What would I do without you?" William patted Daniel's shoulder.

"There were many hands a part of this work." Daniel looked down, but William could see his smile.

"I don't doubt it," William said, "but the triumph is all yours." He frowned. "And yet, an errant churchman be easier to contain than the whole of Spain. While I'm glad to have the truth, it brings a heavier load."

"Philip must be behind this," Robert said, the thrill of the fight dancing in his eyes. "Valencia's too much of a dullard to concoct this of his own volition."

William sighed. A country his size could never win against Spain.

"But why would Philip want to see us fall?"

"Indeed," Daniel said. "And with his cousin Maximilian as Holy Roman Emperor, defender of the faith, it makes even less sense."

"Obviously it's strategic," Robert said. "He wants to intervene, to be the hero."

William stopped. Why had he not seen it before? All of Valencia's insinuations against the queen, his veiled threats to report back to Philip, his befriending of Bartmore. . .Those damnable Habsburgs!

"He doesn't want to be a hero." William looked at his friends. "Philip wants Troixden."

"What?" Robert screwed up his face.

"England," William said. "Philip needs another route to get at England. And he intends to make it Troixden."

As reluctant as Robert had been to go to dreary Beaubourg for Christmastide, it was far enough from Norwick that his wife couldn't join him. And while seeing his nephew Frederick and even princess Cate—Lord, she was the spitting image of her namesake—did cause him to miss his sons, he was happy to have his own room and his own mistress.

"I knew Valencia was up to no good," he said, scratching his chest as he sprawled on the too small bed. "And if I do say so myself, it was quite fortuitous of me to have you follow him."

Yvette gave him a tight smile as she righted a goblet. He wondered, not for the first time, why she always had to tidy the room after their coupling.

"And you say he never gave you much notice?"

"He was quite free with his words around me," she said. "He

thought I only knew a bit of Spanish. I made more . . . connection . . . with his secretary."

"Ah, my clever girl." He rolled on his stomach, resting his head on his hands. She was looking more curvy lately, more filled in. He liked it.

"I know you did not enjoy the task, but look what it has gained us."

"Nothing!" Yvette slammed down a wine bottle, and Robert sat up, startled. "It gains us nothing, can't you see?"

"Why, darling, whatever is the matter? 'Tis not like you to be so testy."

"Can't you see it's all been for naught?" She stood, hands at her sides, face almost desperate. "The king will never leave the pope with Spain at his door! He risks not only the lives of a rabble in the north but the very realm's existence."

Robert rose and went to her, smoothing down her arms.

"My dear, you get ahead of yourself. Once Valencia's treachery is revealed, Philip will not be able to move against us, or he'll risk the pope's disfavor."

"And if Troixden declares for the Protestants?" She threw up her arms. "The Spanish will crush us."

"Not if we have the German states and England behind us." He kissed her forehead, trying to calm her. "Besides, the emperor has not been the ruthless defender of the faith the pope had hoped he would be."

Yvette broke from Robert's arms to pick up her cloak, crumpled on the floor in front of the fire.

"The fight isn't over," Robert said. "It's barely begun."

She shrugged the red silk cloak over her shoulders. "No,

Robert." She wiped an unshed tear from her eye. "The fight has been lost before it even began. And so much more with it."

"What are you talking about?" She brushed past him. "Why are you leaving?" She hurried to the door, not looking back. "Yvette!"

Damn! What was she not telling him? And what made her tremble so?

Anna couldn't sleep. She felt as though she were on a run-away carriage with nothing to stop her from going off a cliff. How William could fall asleep so quickly and soundly after hearing such news she couldn't fathom. Their coupling had been fast, furious in its intensity. Perhaps he'd spent all his demons with her.

She sat up gingerly so as not to wake him. He snored slightly, arms akimbo. She wanted to nestle next to him, but it would be cruel to wake him.

She crept out of bed, donned her robe and slippers, and slipped out the door. The hall was quiet save the crackle of wall torches. Sometimes her father paced the castle, sleepless as well. She would look to see if he was by the hearth in the Great Hall, as was his habit on such nights. She had barely had a moment with him since their arrival and missed his easy way, joyful smile and tender council.

Tiptoeing toward the grand staircase, she heard weeping from the privy at the corner of the castle. It was generally only used during the day, as most of the chambers had their own, a modern luxury her mother had insisted on. Anna went closer to the door. It was definitely a woman crying, but trying to stifle her tears.

It must be Margaux. As much as Anna wanted to loathe her, she could not help pitying her. It appeared she had found something resembling love—or certainly deep attraction—and knowing the affair must soon end . . . Well, any loss of love was something to mourn.

She paused, weighing whether she should go in or not.

She pushed the door open. At the sound of hinges, the weeping stopped. But it was not Margaux who sat shriveled on the floor. It was Yvette, a candelabra by her side, blood surrounding her on the stone floor.

"Oh, God." She wrenched her face away. "Please, Highness, leave me."

Anna stood in shock. She'd never seen, never imagined, Yvette in such a state. She knelt beside her, careful not to step in the blood. The air smelled acrid, like iron and sweat. Yvette twitched, curling away from Anna and into the wall.

"Lady Yvette, my dear woman." Anna reached out to smooth her brow. "What's happened? Are you ill?"

"I can't tell you. You mustn't ask." She sniffed.

Anna looked at the dark puddles and noticed something glinting in the candlelight. It was the long, thin copper hook from Mary's midwifery kit.

Her hand leapt to her mouth.

"Hail Mary full of grace," Anna said, unable to stop the prayer that came to her lips, "the lord is with thee. Blessed art thou among women, and blessed is the fruit of thy womb, Jesus . . ."

Yvette convulsed in quiet sobs. Anna draped an arm across her shoulders.

"Milady," Anna said, scooting closer to her, "what has brought you to this, this . . ."

"Abomination?" Yvette choked out.

"Tragedy." She pulled Yvette's head to her chest. Anna could see she was cupping something tightly in her hands. She closed her eyes. "Robert is not so cruel as to send you away if you had his child."

Yvette pulled away from Anna's embrace, shaking her head.

"It wasn't his."

"But I thought . . ."

"He told me to follow Valencia. To make his men trust me. To find him out." Yvette gave a mirthless laugh. "Well, he's sure found out, is he not?"

"You knew he wrote the letter?"

"I knew he was planning something, but I thought it was only an attempt at a cardinalship." She shifted, bringing her closed hands back to her lap.

"Does Robert know . . .?" She couldn't bring herself to say it.

Yvette again shook her head. "He must never know." She looked at Anna with desperate eyes. "He can never, ever know. It would break him—it would break me. Majesty, I beg you, and I'm not one to beg. I know you have no love for my Robert, but if I have ever done you a kindness, have ever helped you in your own love, I beg of you never to speak a word of this."

"You know I cannot lie to the king."

"I am not asking you to lie. Merely not to speak. Think of it the same as Lady Jane." She thrust her closed hands toward

Anna. "For the sake of my child."

"Oh, Lord Jesus . . ." She closed her hands around Yvette's. Tears ran down her cheeks. "Save us."

Their foreheads met, making a protective arc over the still and silent babe in Yvette's hands, murmuring prayers, crying together until there were no more tears to shed.

William sat at the end of the Great Hall table, looking to each grim face of his makeshift council.

"Valencia is in Rome," Daniel said, "and we've instructed he be kept there until we can get word to Philip through our own ambassador."

"And Bartmore's progress?" The Duke of Halforn said, leaning in.

"His ship is set to make landfall in Havenside tomorrow."

"Whether that be a Twelfth Night gift or nightmare is yet to be determined," William said. His head ached. Looking across the table he spied Robert frowning down at the wood. *Oh, my friend, that you were in my place . . .*

"Philip will publicly denounce Valencia, probably have him killed." William flexed his hand. "But that doesn't mean Philip wasn't behind it. Only time will tell."

"Which means it's all the more important that we prove our loyalty to the pope," Halforn said. "Which probably means war again with Laureland."

"Not necessarily," William said. "While Laureland has no desire to be ruled by me, they have even less desire to be ruled by Spain. They are shrewd enough to know that they and all their kin would burn under Philip's rule."

"But if they feel they have the support of the German states, and perhaps even the Netherlands . . ." Beaubourg said, his thick brows furrowed.

William shook his head. "Damn, this is a great mess."

"We can do nothing at the moment, my liege," Robert said. "We must wait to see where the pieces fall."

William guffawed. "And even Norwick advising caution? It's a Christmas miracle."

"There are simply too many unknowns," Robert said. "But we do hold the advantage."

"And that is?"

"They don't know we've found them out yet."

William squeezed Robert's shoulder. "With that good cheer, shall we put away diplomacy for the next forty-eight hours and pretend we've not a care in the world?" William flashed a brilliant smile, but it didn't reach his eyes.

Twelfth Night dawned with a clear blue sky, snow glinting. William had made sure the fire in the hearth was high and the queen's tea hot as he waited for her to wake. She looked so peaceful, down quilts tucked around her, hair splayed about her head. She was opening and closing her mouth as if talking to someone. But even amid this lovely scene, William's heart was heavy. How would he save his country when half of Europe was against him, either way he turned?

He looked out to the tall pine trees, green branches laden with white. They wouldn't care who ruled here, as long as they could stand and grow. Maybe his people were the same. What was it Anna had once said to him? Kings come and go, but Beaubourg remains.

She stirred. He went to her side, curling a lock of hair behind her ear.

"Good morrow, my queen." Her watched her arch her back and stretch her arms.

"What time is it?"

"Time makes no difference today," he said, handing her hot tea with honey. She took a grateful sip.

"As a matter of fact," she said pushing herself up, her auburn hair cascading down her shoulders, "there are a few things I must see to today." She gave him a mischievous smile.

"Be that so?" He grinned. "Well, I certainly hope whatever those things are can wait." He removed the mug from her hands and placed it on the side table. "For the moment, there are a few things I must see to." He trailed his tongue up her neck and kissed her beneath her earlobe. "Like your pulse." She moaned.

"Hmmm," he said, moving his lips down her chest, "I think I need closer observation." He swept a hand up her spine, lowering her back down on the bed, then pulled down her shift and let his lips find her heart.

"There," he said, nestling his ear against her chest, hearing the rhythmic thumping, its pace quickening as his hands slid down her body.

"I could have told you my heart still beats," she said, "but I like your way better."

"Yes, well," he said between kisses to her cheeks and chin, "you are not the only keeper of the healing arts."

She pushed him over and rolled on top of him.

"If this is how you practice," she said, giving him her thumb to suck, "then I gladly give up the title."

He grinned, popping out her thumb. "Well then, milady, shall we do a full examination?"

Her kiss was her only reply.

Despite all the doom and gloom of the previous days, Anna couldn't help her high spirits, and indeed welcomed them. She needed a bright spot in all of this bleakness, and William did too. That is why she had planned this surprise for him.

She had finished speaking with the cook and kitchen servants about the arrangements, and everything was going as planned. Even Robert was in on it, albeit begrudgingly. Though she rather thought this was a type of intrigue he secretly enjoyed.

She came to his chamber door and entered. The room was strangely tidy, and Robert's face was drawn, a deep frown replacing his jocular demeanor.

"Majesty, just who I wanted to see."

"That's a first," Anna said.

He snorted. "I wonder, Majesty, if you have seen Lady Yvette as of late." He raised his brows. Anna's heart leapt to her throat. "I have not seen her since yesterday afternoon, and we were scheduled to go over arrangements for tonight's celebrations."

"She should be with the rest of the ladies," Anna said, avoiding his piercing black eyes.

"That's just it. None of them have seen her either. I suspected my sister at least would have kept an eye . . ." He wandered toward his window and frowned down at the snow.

"I must say it warms my heart to see you so concerned."

He studied her. "Am I so evil in your mind that you think I care not a whit for those whom I hold dear?"

"My apologies, Your Grace," Anna was taken aback by his earnestness, "for I only meant to tease."

He nodded, then strode to the desk, picking up a parchment. "So this is the list for this evening?"

"Yes. You've everything you need? My father and our household are as always at your service."

She could not help her pity for him then, his trying so hard to be in control, not knowing the awful lengths to which Yvette had gone to keep herself in his good graces. She wanted to believe he would not have sent her away, wanted to believe he too would have wept with her on that privy floor.

"Of course, Majesty." He looked up, brows raised. "If that is all, I have much to attend to."

She came to the desk and touched the top of his hand. "Robert." His stare vibrated through her whole being. No wonder Yvette was drawn to him. "Lady Yvette is surely resting or refreshing herself and has lost track of time. 'Tis a holiday, after all."

Robert nodded again, then gave a slight bow. "Highness."

"Your Grace."

It didn't take her long to discover Yvette's whereabouts.

Coming around by the kitchens, she saw her and Mary standing in the herb garden, stalks of brown plants folded over in the snow. Mary wiped away a tear. Anna saw a spot where the snow was browned with dirt and patted back down.

In two quick strides Anna had Yvette in her arms. "Oh, my lady," Anna said.

"I am better," Yvette said. Anna released her. Her face was strained, as Robert's had been, but there were no trace of tears.

"You've told Mary, I see."

"Caught her sneaking in my kit," Mary said. "She tried to come up with some excuse but I saw right through it." She gave Yvette a kindly smile.

"I am sorry to draw you into this, Mistress Mary," Yvette said.

"Oh tush, milady. You be not the first woman who's sought me out for such." Mary picked up her skirts, leading the way back to the castle through the kitchens. "And as with the rest of 'em, you have my sympathies and my silence."

"I am grateful."

Anna threaded her arm through Yvette's and whispered, "Robert is looking for you. He's . . . well, he's worried about you."

"Did you tell him anything?" Yvette's eyes widened.

"Of course not." She lifted her face toward the castle. "As Mary said, you have my sympathy, my silence—and my heart-break."

Anna was up to something. It obviously had to do with the Twelfth Night festivities, but try as he might—seduction, tickling, following her about—William couldn't find out what it was.

As was their tradition, Anna and William were alone in their festival finery, enjoying mulled wine together in her father's chamber, awaiting the start of the feast. She positively glowed. If he could hold this moment and make it last a lifetime, he could be content.

"What is it, Wills?"

"Well . . ." he reached in his pocket and pulled out a velvet box. "If you're not going to tell me what my present is, I shall have to give you yours."

Her smile grew. He grinned back and placed the box in her hands.

"You know that coming here for the month was more than present enough," she said. "But now that you've laid something small and pretty in my hands, I can't resist."

She opened the lid to reveal a gold ring, band encrusted with oval sapphires. The top of the ring was a large diamond, encircled by more sapphires. She pinched the ring out of its pillowed box.

"Oh Wills, it's stunning." She shook her head. "The stones, they match your eyes." She looked up and laughed. "I have your heart, and here are your eyes."

"Close, but not quite." He took the ring from her hand, digging his nail under the diamond. "It opens, you see?" He flipped the diamond up on its gold mount, revealing a locket with a miniature portrait inside.

She brought her hand to her mouth, gasping.

"It's Cate! Oh, she's beautiful."

"And someday," he said, straining to keep his voice from trembling, "be it a very, very long time from now, she can put a portrait of you facing hers and wear it to remember her mama."

"Oh, Wills, you dear, dear man!" She leapt up and embraced him, kissing him all over his face. "Here, put it on my finger, will you?"

He obliged, sliding it down her right ring finger and kissing her knuckles.

"And there it shall remain," she said, taking both his hands. "And now, my king, for your present." She bid him rise. "While it may not be something tangible, I still hope you will keep it in your heart."

"My Anna," he laughed, "whatever have you done this time?"

Her brows danced, and she drew him to the chamber doors. "Just you wait, husband."

She threw open the doors and led him to overlook the Great Hall. All of court stood below, dressed in cloaks and muffs and warm clothes. When they saw him they cheered.

"Long live the king! Long live the queen!"

"What on earth?" he said.

"It's such a lovely evening, I thought we would eat out of doors."

"A picnic? At night? In the snow?"

She bit the corner of her mouth. "Sort of."

She pulled him down the hall and took his arm as they descended the stairs, a page ready with their fur cloaks. The crowds parted as they made their way toward the main door.

Outside awaited an open-air, gold sledge with two horses bedecked in bells and furred livery. The sledge was piled high with furs and blankets, and a tray held steaming drinks in two tankards, pomegranates, oranges, cheese, and still warm bread.

"Your chariot awaits, my liege," Anna said with a formal bow.

He shook his head at her and laughed. Climbing into the sledge, he helped her in beside him, nestling her under his arm and wrapping them both in a fur. A chamberman sat across from them, pouring the hot mulled wine. The rest of court alighted to their own sledges, some preferring to walk, hands warmed with their own mugs. The air was thick with anticipation and good cheer.

His chamberman let loose the reins, and the horses began a slow, steady walk.

"We aren't going far," Anna said, snuggling her head into his shoulder.

"At this pace, I certainly hope not." He kissed her hair and puffed out his breath, watching the cloud it made float off into the darkness.

The lively train meandered down a trail through the tall evergreens, and ahead, William saw light. As they neared, he could hear music, fiddles and pipes and drums.

They came to a large clearing. Lanterns hung from all the trees, their branches festooned with berries, flowers, and candles. Long tables placed along the edges were piled high with delicacies, and two boars were roasting on spits above an open fire.

A stage had been built with lanterns as footlights. A velvet curtain was hung behind, with garlands draped on top. The horses halted, putting king and queen in the center of it all.

Anna sat forward, throwing her arms wide.

"Merry Christmas, Majesty," she said.

William took her face in his hands, closing his eyes to the world, savoring the moment, savoring her warm lips. He drew back and gazed upon his queen. With the stars sparkling in her eyes, the moon glowing down on her, it was as if she were a fairy materialized from the snow, a lovely sprite to grant him all his wishes. And for tonight, just this one last night, he would pretend it was true.

Acknowledgements

I first and foremost want to thank you, reader. The world of Troixden comes alive only because you are here to read it. Otherwise, it would have just bumbled around in my head, my long-suffering husband hearing random plot points of my imaginings. Of course, he still hears random plot points, but now they have more purpose.

I am continually indebted to the talent, wit, kindness and professionalism of everyone at The Editorial Department, specifically my editors Renni Browne, Shannon Roberts, Amanda Bauch. Morgana Gallaway and Kelly Leslie do stunning work, publicist Beth Jusino makes me look better than even my mother could, and Jane Ryder keeps me sane and smiling.

To my insightful, delightful and cheerleading beta readers: Cari Armbruster, Stephanie Larson, Amy Owens, Maureen McQuerry, Chanpreet Singh, Susan Turner, and Kevin Monohan, your words have spurred me on in the best of ways.

To my family, especially my kiddos and that long-suffering husband, you make me happier than any single person deserves.

Can't get enough of Troixden? Not to worry! The third and final installment of The Realm Series, *Crown & Thorns* is headed to your hands soon.

King William has more to worry about than the religious tension in his own lands. His country has unwittingly been made a pawn in the vast European fight for land, power and religious freedom, and many think his cousin, the Duke of Norwick would make a more decisive king. Especially since Queen Annelore has still not conceived a son and heir. And as the threat of invasion and civil war grow stronger, she will have to make a decision that could very well break her heart. When friends become enemies, and enemies wield incredible power, will the kingdom of Troixden—and Will and Anna's marriage—survive? Find out in *Crown & Thorns*.

For more information on this and any of J. L. Spohr's titles, please visit her website at WWW.JLSPOHR.COM.

About the Author

J. L. SPOHR has studied the trials and tribulations of royals since Princess Diana took that long walk to the altar. Author of mainstream fiction, her debut historical novel, *Heirs & Spares*, received rave reviews and rankings. She brings an informed perspective to the 16th century, having focused on the Reformation extensively for her Master's. She is an ordained minister and lives with her brood in Seattle, WA.

Head to WWW.JLSPOHR.COM to sign up for her weekly blog posts, exclusive contests & more. She can also be found at **facebook. com/jlspohr**, Twitter @jlspohr & goodreads.com/jlspohr.

CPSIA information can be obtained at www.ICGtesting.com
Printed in the USA
LVOW07s0845221215

467370LV00044B/1126/P